MW00624805

PRAISE FOR W. GLENN DUNCAN'S RAFFERTY P.I.

"At first sniff, it may smell a like Spenser with a cowboy hat, but take a good whiff: W. Glenn Duncan's Dallas, Texas private eye Rafferty was actually a blast of fresh air in what was becoming a glut of sensitive, soul-searching, overly politically-correct cookie cutter P.I.s … of course, it helps that Dallas ain't Boston." | *Kevin Burton Smith*

"Rafferty tends to play dirty, boasting at one point that he 'hasn't fought fair in twenty years.' No brainiac, his chief MO seems to be to stir things up, and then see what happens. And he tends to be pretty stubborn, as well. 'I often ignore what people tell me to do,' he says. Like, no kidding. And that's part of the fun." | *ThrillingDetective.com*

"Thing about Rafferty is the fun with the noir aspect. Only a deft hand at word magic could accomplish the mix so smoothly." | *5 star Amazon review.*

"Duncan captured the essence of the definitive smart-ass P.I. in his character Rafferty. Take part Sam Spade with a little Mike Hammer, mix in some Spenser and you have an awesome character." | *Cliff Fausset*

"The Rafferty books are terrific!" | *Paul Bishop*

"I love that Rafferty is straightforward about who he is and what he's good at. The dialogue is witty and the action moves well. As a woman, I like his girlfriend, who isn't whiny about his work or odd hours, and that he talks to her about his work. So often in this genre, the girlfriend/wife are just for sex or to give the hero a soft side." | *Minnie - 5 Star Amazon review*

"I don't know much about W. Glenn Duncan except that he wrote a dandy private eye series set in Dallas, Texas ... and I think of them as throwbacks to the kind of P.I. books ... in the '50s, except influenced as much by Robert B. Parker as by Spillane." | *Bill Crider*

"Rafferty: Fatal Sisters won a 1991 Shamus for Best Paperback Original. All in all, an entertaining, and very highly recommended series." | *ThrillingDetective.com*

"At first blush, the framework for Rafferty appears to be yet another Spenser clone (Cowboy, Rafferty's semi-sociopathic partner channeling Hawk; Hilda, Rafferty's significant other who is a less irritating version of Susan Silverman; an equal number of wisecracks, fists, and bullets), but it's quickly apparent in the first few pages of the series, Rafferty and company are in a class of their own." | *Paul Bishop*

WRONG PLACE, WRONG TIME

A RAFFERTY P.I. MYSTERY

W. GLENN DUNCAN

d squared
publishing.

ALSO BY W. GLENN DUNCAN

Rafferty P.I. Series

Rafferty's Rules

Last Seen Alive

Poor Dead Cricket

Cannon's Mouth

Fatal Sisters

Wrong Place, Wrong Time

Copyright © W. Glenn Duncan 1989

The moral right of the author has been asserted.

All rights reserved.

No parts of this publication may be reproduced, stored in a retrieval system, or transmitted in any form or by any means, electronic, mechanical, photocopying, recording, or otherwise, without the prior written permission of the copyright owner.

This book is sold subject to the condition that it shall not, by way of trade or otherwise, be lent, resold, hired out, or otherwise circulated without the publisher's prior consent in any form of binding or cover other than that in which it is published and without a similar condition including this condition being imposed on the subsequent purchaser. Under no circumstances may any part of this book be photocopied for resale.

This is a work of fiction. Any similarity between the characters and situations within its pages and places or persons, living or dead, is unintentional and co-incidental.

First published in the United States in 1989 by Ballantine Books, a division of Random House, Inc., New York, and simultaneously in Canada by Random House of Canada Limited, Toronto.

This edition published in 2017 by d squared publishing.

Ebook ISBN: 978-0-6480370-6-4

P'back ISBN: 978-0-6480370-7-1

For enquiries regarding this book, please email: enquiry@raffertypi.com

Cover Design by Jessica Bell

This one is for Dad and Jeanne

PROLOGUE

May 19th

Dear Mike:

Way back when in medical school, did you ever think you'd be letting yourself in for this kind of workload? Me neither.

Greta's left for the day, like any self-respecting office worker, so you'll have to put up with my typing.

I saw your young patient this afternoon, Mike. You've got your work cut out for you, pal. I say "you," because I was thrown out on my ear. Mom arrived with the start of visiting hours. She was not pleased to see me. She says her little darling has no need of "some screwball shrink with a big nose." Mom is a shortsighted bitch, in case you hadn't already noticed.

(You only wanted a horseback opinion from an old buddy, right? Even so, you better burn this letter. I find myself becoming most unpsychiatric.)

At any rate, to work. Remember now, this is all based on

one short, interrupted visit with the subject. And, of course, those fragments of family history that prompted you to call me.

Und now ve vill zimply ... (Old, feeble shrink joke. Sorry about that.)

Seriously now.

I found the subject alert, self-confident, and quite composed, considering he's only eleven years old and is hospitalized minus an appendix, thanks to you. Those characteristics mitigate somewhat against my conclusion, but I'm eighty-five percent sure I'm correct.

It's the history that troubles me, Mike. Individually, those incidents can be explained away as reasonably normal juvenile high jinks. Lots of kids have set fire to the garage. But three times in four years?

Plus, there's the nocturnal enuresis well into the seventh year—any bed-wetting past age five means trouble, in my book—and the preoccupation with fashioning hangman's nooses and playing "chicken" with passing cars. That sort of thing, when repeated, seems to me to be a form of suicide "gesturing."

Plus, historically, childhood hyperactivity is a clue. Okay, it was phasic, but even so.

The real red flag, though, is the history of specific animal cruelty. The way you've described it, he slowly killed that dog over a period of almost two years, with widely separated attacks during an otherwise loving "family pet" relationship. (Makes you wonder how blind parents can be, doesn't it?)

So what do we have here? Sociopathic tendencies, certainly, but this is even more exotic, I think.

For one thing, the classic sociopath is a loser; characterized by restlessness and instability, definitely not task-oriented. Yet this boy gets good grades in school, he's highly numerate, and he seems goal-motivated. (He wanted to know how much money I made. Not enough for the hours and heartache, I should have told him.)

Anyway, I think you're dealing with a case of EDCS here. (That's "episodic dyscontrol syndrome" to you semi-literate cutters.) There is evidence emerging of an EDCS sub-classification that seems to fit this case. The characteristics are: (1) episodic incidents, (2) attacks on specific individuals or *animals*, and (3) no alteration in the state of consciousness during the incident. Guess who?

Obviously, you, or whoever Mom will let near the boy will need confirmation. And that may not be easy. Look for nonspecific EEG abnormalities. That might require several attempts and, perhaps, sleep studies. Try nasopharyngeal leads. Hint: glucose tolerance tests sometimes provoke dyscontrol. However it is found, a significant dysrhythmia will indicate EDCS.

Treatment? A good question. The pharmacology is very iffy. Some people say anticonvulsants work. Try carbamazepine. Or phenytoin. I've heard lithium works some of the time, but other times it only aggravates the condition.

Prognosis? Another good question. If not treated successfully, expect the kid to become an adult with either an alcohol abuse problem or acute alcohol sensitivity; a real two-beer screamer. He'll probably collect a pile of reckless-driving tickets and may eventually commit suicide. Any marriages or major relationships will either be short and tempestuous or one-way: *his* way.

He won't be able to—whoa! Too much conjecture here. I

only saw the kid for thirty minutes, after all. Do the EEGs, then you'll know more.

Mike, please keep me informed about this kid. He's a sicko, but he's a fascinating one.

Oops, that's it. When I start using terms like "sicko," it's time to quit for the day. I think I'll go home now and see if Jill and the kids still recognize me.

Mike, do you ever wonder if it's all worthwhile?

Remember our old party act? "Roll Me Over" on the Sigma Chi piano? Hey, if you ever want to step off this medical treadmill and try show business, call me.

Regards,

Carl

CHAPTER 1

And then there was the time we went looking for Luis Ortega in a west Dallas pool hall. Afterward, I swore I would never, ever, no matter what, work with a bounty hunter again.

It started out as such a peaceful day. I was sitting—loafing, actually—in my office, browsing through a gun-shop catalog. The only question in my mind was whether I should treat myself to a set of new grips for the .45. Those fancy, nonslip grips were nice, sure, but why spend the money when a guy could just as easily put a couple of rubber bands around ...

"Rafferty?" a voice behind me said.

I put down the catalog and turned around, trying to remember which was my client-reassurance smile and which was the one Hilda called my "grimacing chimpanzee" imitation.

He was a big guy, meaty in the good-ole-boy style you see all over Dallas, and he leaned against my door frame like he was shoring it up for an impending earthquake.

"Name's Wells," he said. "Toby Wells. Reckon you could help me this afternoon?" He pronounced it "hep."

Wells had a broad, cheerful face that went with his booming voice and down-home drawl. He also had a fringed leather jacket that went with his western-style shirt and boots. All in all, he looked like Johnny Cash with a different head.

"Don't tell me," I said. "Let me guess. The fiddle player sprained his arm, and you want me to fill in."

Wells grinned. "You a wiseass, all right. Me, Ah'm a bounty hunter. Got to collect a runner, and the neighborhood ain't what you'd call salubrious."

"Well, that explains it, then. A clean-cut bounty hunter like you can't go wandering around places that aren't salubrious, can he?"

He grinned again. "That's a nine-dollar word for 'healthy.' *It Pays to Increase Your Word Power*, right?"

"Right. So tell me about this runner you want."

Wells pulled a sheaf of papers out of his fancy jacket. "Luis Ortega, his name is. I got all the paperwork right here. He jumped bail in Houston last week. I spotted him this morning in west Dallas, in front of a pool hall his brother-in-law owns."

I said, "The neighborhood can't be too unhealthy if you already found him."

"Driving past is one thing. Dragging Luis out is another."

"Yeah," I said, "but it'll be easier with two of us dragging. Two hundred sound fair enough?"

"Sure," he said, and dropped a pair of hundred-dollar bills on my desktop. I folded the bills, tucked them into my jeans pocket, and tried to act like they weren't the first hundreds I'd seen for a while.

"Tell me," I said. "What does this Ortega do when he's not on the run?"

"Holds up gas stations, mostly, but this time they got him for pistol-whipping a liquor-store clerk."

I dug my shoulder holster and .38 out of the desk drawer and took my blue nylon windbreaker from the wall hook. "Okay," I said. "Let's do it."

Wells looked at me with a small smile. "You sure you got everything you'll need?"

I shrugged. "Got a gun, old clothes, and sneakers. I can shoot, fight, or run. I'm ready for anything."

Wells said, "You ain't seen Ortega's neighborhood yet."

We left my office and wandered out past the other one- and two-room businesses in my building. The place used to be a radio station way back when. Very trendy for its day, probably, but the layout always reminded me of a factory-reject rabbit warren.

At the top of the stairs down to the street, Wells and I bumped into Honeybutt. Well, he bumped into her; I side-stepped and pretended I didn't see her.

Honeybutt worked for the insurance broker who rented the old radio station newsroom. The wall between her office and mine—I had the old control room—was mostly plate glass. There were drapes on her side, but Honeybutt almost never drew them. So we winked at each other, and I admired her backside when she filed things in the bottom drawers. And presumably she admired some portion or another of my manly physique from time to time.

Honeybutt and I had the same relationship as any of a

thousand pairs of strangers on a given day. We flirted silently, mildly, and safely, knowing—hell, depending!—on the fact that it would never grow into anything more.

Which is why I didn't like the way Honeybutt looked at me when she rebounded off Toby Wells.

She was a world-class ignorer; I knew that. She was probably even a little better than I. But this time she didn't play the game. She lurched away from Wells, grinning and rolling her eyes at his gaudy jacket, then she noticed me. She stopped short and watched me closely. Perhaps speculatively?

What the hell was *that* about?

Wells hadn't even slowed down. He must have skipped *Word Power* the month they covered "chivalry."

Honeybutt and I stood there for a moment, looking at each other. She seemed cool and appraising; I was a gangly, stupid kid again. *Ohmygawd! Now what do I do?*

Finally, I turned and went after Wells, feeling equal parts coward, clod and confused.

Wells was down on the street, unlocking a green F100 pickup with a small Fiberglas camper top over the tray. "We'll take my wheels," he said, "so's we got a place to keep our little buddy once we git him."

So we took his wheels and we trundled off to west Dallas while the cassette player whined at us with Willie Nelson's voice.

CHAPTER 2

Toby Wells was right; Ortega's neighborhood was definitely not salubrious. The pool hall was three doors from a street corner, sandwiched between a pawnshop and a bar with a Spanish name. Two hookers lounged in front of the bar. Their faces lit up when they saw the truck, then they dropped the masks and ambled in tight circles when Wells drove past without slowing.

Three blocks farther on, Wells stopped the truck in front of an abandoned building. There was a wino slumped in the doorway. He goggled at us briefly, then tucked his bottle under his arm and went back to sleep.

Wells drummed his fingers on the steering wheel. "That sucker's gonna rabbit soon as he sees either one of us," he said. "What say you drop me in the alley behind the pool hall? Then you go in the front, big and bold as you please. Ortega will come out the back, quick-smart. Then it's just 'Hey, boy, stick 'em up.' I march him back in through the pool hall, and we get the hell out the front before he and his pals know what happened."

"Okay," I said.

Wells grinned. "Now," he said, "one more thing. Word is Ortega's not real excited about another visit to the slammer."

"Do tell."

"Yeah, well, he might have organized him some help. Now I ain't never seen a greaser could fight for sour apples, but if they was to be a whole bunch of them jumped us all at once, well—*anyway*, I brought these."

These were two Remington 12-gauge pump shotguns Wells pulled from under the seat. He handed me one. It was fully loaded, safety on, and slippery with oil. I wiped the grip and pump with my handkerchief. "You have shares in an oil venture somewhere, Wells?"

"Sorry about that. You ready?"

"Sure."

Wells got out; I slid over behind the wheel. Wells carried his shotgun while he walked around the truck and got back in on the passenger side. The old wino in the doorway was awake at the time. He lurched to his feet and shuffle-ran down the block in the direction from which we had come.

I got out of the truck and called to him: "Hold it, pops."

He froze in mid-shuffle, but didn't turn around, even when I walked up to him.

He had a face like crumpled gray tissue paper.

"Didn't see nothin'," he mumbled. "Don't know nothin'."

"Right," I said. "Where's the nearest liquor store?"

He turned around and pointed past the truck. "Coupla blocks that way."

I handed him two dollars and nodded in the direction of the liquor store. He took off at his version of a dead run.

When I got back into the truck, Wells smirked. "Friend

of yours?"

"I'd rather slip him a couple of bucks than have him earn his Ripple telling people we're here and hunting."

"Good point," he said. "Let's roll."

The F100 rolled well. It was nicer to drive than my Mustang, which seemed reasonable. After all, it was at least ten years newer.

I dropped Wells in the alley. He stood beside a filthy brick wall opposite the rear door to the pool hall. He cradled his shotgun in his left arm and used his right hand to give me a thumbs-up sign.

I double-parked in front of the pool hall, a move that intrigued the sidewalk loungers. Three potential car thieves on the corner perked up their pointy ears and nudged each other. One of the hookers stepped off the curb with an expression on her face that could have been ersatz lust, legitimate indigestion, or anything in between.

It didn't seem to be the neighborhood or the mission for finesse, so I came out of the truck cab with the shotgun at high port and jacked a shell into the chamber.

Suddenly, the sidewalk was empty. No hookers, no car thieves.

Inside, the pool hall looked like a bad stage set. The air was blue with smoke. The place smelled like the police incinerator on Wednesdays, when they burn the confiscated grass. There were six tables, four of them in use by quiet brown and black men who carefully ignored me. There was a hint of movement at the far end of a narrow corridor in the back, then nothing.

At a counter to the right of my doorway, a fat Hispanic glowered at me. His right hand was below the counter level.

When I looked at him and shook my head, he slowly brought his empty hand up and put it on the counter.

"Luis Ortega," I said. "Tell him his long-lost cousin is back in town."

Except for a short "humpf" from one of the pool players, no one made a sound.

"Okay," I said. "Try this one. I bet twenty bucks Luis Ortega will come outside with me. Any takers?"

Very slowly, the fat counterman pointed at a tattered cardboard notice on the wall. It said: NO GAMBLING.

A skinny black man in a pimp hat stroked a cue. A ball rumbled into a pocket. "Well, sheeyitt!" said the other man at the table.

A fat fly buzzed past my ear, circled the shotgun muzzle twice, and departed for parts unknown.

The same pool player sank another ball; the other guy said "sheeyitt" again.

I told the counterman: "Tell Luis I'll wait for him in the truck." He picked his nose, examined his fingernail, then looked at me with the same expression.

I checked behind me, then backed outside. A half-dozen people ducked back into doorways and the sidewalk was empty yet again.

Then a shotgun boomed in the alley behind the pool hall and the day started downhill in a big way.

I got into the truck, started it, and waited for Wells to come through the pool hall with or without Ortega. At that point, I was betting on without.

When nothing happened, I popped the pickup into gear and took the first right, then braked at the mouth of the alley. Twenty yards down the alley, near the pool hall exit, a man's body was slumped against the wall. Most of his face was missing.

At the far end of the alley, Wells threw his shotgun into the passenger seat of a waiting red Pontiac, then jumped in after it. The Pontiac lurched out of sight in a swirl of tire smoke.

Rafferty's Rule Nineteen: When you can't tell the bad guys from the good guys, it's time to get the hell out.

So I got the hell out, but not quite soon enough.

A solid black Electra came sliding around the corner as I left a sizable chunk of Wells's tires on the pavement. I beat the Electra to the first corner by five or six feet, no more.

There were several men in the car chasing me. I couldn't tell exactly how many. At least five, though, including the driver and the front-seat passenger with the machete.

Behind the Electra there was an old Ford with another two or three angry men. Maybe four. The rearview mirror was pretty jiggly; I couldn't tell for sure.

It probably didn't matter much how many men there were in the Ford; the Electra was closest to catching me and they didn't look like good sports about sharing.

The only bright spot was the F100. It was wide to begin with, and it was light enough in the rear end that I could hang the tail way out on the corners. The Electra couldn't get past me. And the Ford couldn't get past the Electra.

It was exciting, in a way, but I kept thinking about fox hunting. From the fox's viewpoint.

Then the right front tire blew out.

The wheel jerked viciously in my hand; a spoke slammed back against my right thumb. It hurt so much that I stupidly glanced at my hand to see if the thumb was still there. Then the Electra rammed me from behind. The F100 bucketed up and over the curb, missed a fire hydrant by an inch or so, and shuddered back onto the road.

The Ford was already there, waiting. It rocked sideways into the F100; I bounced back up onto the curb. I had a fleeting glimpse of an old woman in black being dragged into the open door of a small grocery, then I was back on the street, fighting off the Ford by trying to side-bash him before he hit me. Behind us the Electra made random lunges at my rear.

It wasn't a very even contest. For one thing, they each had four tires and I had only three. For another, there was this huge Hispanic who was leaning out of the Ford. He had a Zapata mustache, long arms, and a baseball bat. He kept bashing the bejesus out of the F100's windows and roof.

I was getting slower and slower, being dragged back by the flat tire and repeated collisions with the Ford, the Electra, various curbs, and the occasional parked car. The F100's motor sounded willing enough, but I couldn't seem to get any of that power to work for me. We—the entire insane caravan—were down to about twenty miles per hour, roaring and scraping and smashing across one of the few major thoroughfares in that part of town, when I spotted the patrol car.

It was a Dallas Police Department Dodge, it was blue and white, it was only half a block away, and it was beautiful.

I turned toward it, expecting the Ford and the Electra to peel off when they spotted the two cops ticketing a motorcycle rider. They didn't. On the wider street now, the Electra moved up on my right and tried to coordinate with the Ford's rhythmic crashes.

We—the Ford and I—became entangled. We locked wheel arches, bumpers, something. The Ford's designated hitter used the opportunity to lay the wood to my windshield. Things got pretty dim for a while there, then a grapefruit-sized chunk fell out and I could see again.

We separated—with a long, screechy noise—then I swooped back to the left, muscled the Ford out of the way, and crossed the opposing traffic lane, aiming for the parked cop car. The cops saw us coming—how could they not?—and jumped for the curb.

It was sort of a formation crash: I hit the police Dodge in the side, the Ford hit the rear wheel, and the Electra nailed the front wheel.

I kicked out the rest of the broken windshield, crawled out onto the F100's hood and kept going, right on over the top of the patrol car. I took the shotgun with me, partly because it was evidence, but mostly because I didn't want to leave it where the angry friends of Luis Ortega could get their hands on it.

Then there was a little bit of confusion. I remember the guys boiling out of the Ford and the Electra; there were nine of them, by actual count. I remember them howling abuse at me, but not being quite game enough to come over the patrol car.

I remember having the time, finally, to be angry at Toby Wells or whatever his name really was.

I remember the two cops pointing their sidearms in my face while the skinny one jerked the shotgun out of my hand.

And I remember the funny looks they gave me when I said, "Boy, am I glad to see you guys."

CHAPTER 3

"Let me make sure I understand this," Lieutenant Ed Durkee said. "This stranger walked into your office and said he was a bounty hunter. He seemed like a nice guy, so you waltzed over to west Dallas and helped him whack out a twenty-three-year-old pool cleaner." Ed rubbed his basset-hound face wearily. "That about it?"

"Ortega was a pool cleaner?" I said.

"A pool cleaner. Not a bail jumper."

Sergeant Ricco was there in Durkee's office, too. He said, "You know, Rafferty, a pool cleaner. Guy with a great tan, carries brushes with long handles. He scrubs that green shit off the walls of a swimming pool. A pool cleaner." Ricco leaned back against the wall, but he did it carefully, to maintain the crease in his trousers. As always, Ricco was dressed for a Damon Runyon theme party.

Ed Durkee glared at me. "Did this Wells character show you any ID?"

I shook my head. "Why would he?"

"He pay you?" From his tone, Durkee only seemed interested enough to hope I'd been stiffed for the fee.

"Two hundred."

Ricco snorted. "Goddamn, Rafferty works cheap, Ed. Everybody else charges at least a grand for a hit. And he even drives his own getaway car. You suppose he validates, too?"

I said, "Droll, Ricco. Very droll. You guys let me know when you're finished with this game, then maybe we can play a quick round of My Friend the Policeman Solves a Case."

Durkee looked at Ricco; they both shrugged. Ed pawed through the papers on his desk and opened a file. "Okay," he said. "Well, at least the victim's name really was Luis Ortega. That's something, I guess."

"And he was only a pool cleaner?"

Ed looked at me even more dismally than usual. "You think I'm making that up, for God's sake? He worked for an outfit called Aqua-Tidy."

"Okay, okay," I said. "I'll buy all of that, even a name like Aqua-Tidy. But can he please be a mad rapist on parole or something?"

Ed shook his head. "No way. Ortega was clean with us. No record, no warrants, no wants."

"Uh, about Wells..."

Ricco came off the wall to get his two cents' worth in. "That one don't fly, Rafferty. We got nothing on a bounty hunter named Toby Wells. How good did those bail-bond papers look?"

Oops.

"Tell you the truth, guys, I didn't exactly look at the papers he had. He looked at them, read a bit to me, then put them back in his..." Why go on? It was too embarrassing.

"So he could have been anybody," Ricco said. "Just some hot dog who walked in off the street." His standard sneer became a trifle more pronounced.

"Well, hell, what was I supposed to do? Exchange secret handshakes? Check for initials inside his Bounty Hunter Magic Decoder ring? You know those bounty-hunter types. This guy just seemed right for the part. What can I say?"

Ed and Ricco looked at me like they had several ideas, none of which I might agree to.

"Okay, then," I said, "the truck. Wells had that F100 I was driving and—"

"Stolen yesterday," Ricco said. "From a used-car lot on Colorado Boulevard." He grinned savagely and added, "They're trying to total up the damage bill now. I think they might want to talk to you."

"The Wells guy had a helper in the—"

"Besides you?" Ricco said, and wheezed at his own razor-sharp repartee.

"—in the Pontiac. I couldn't see much because of that corner where the alley … uh, but …" I wished I hadn't brought it up. It even sounded feeble to me.

Ricco, on the other hand, loved it. He cupped his right hand in front of his mouth and became a B-movie police dispatcher. "All Points Bulletin," he droned. "Stop all Pontiacs on sight. Any model, any color, anywhere. Shoot to kill. Occupants may be …"

Ed and I just waited until he ran down. Then I said, "How about prints on the shotgun Wells gave me?"

"Lots of prints," Durkee said. "One set where that uniformed officer took the gun away from you and a whole bunch more, all from the same person. Which means you.

Which means it was wiped clean before it was given to you."
Ed waved a big hand vaguely. "We're going to match the
prints, of course, but that's what we'll find. Wait and see."

"Yeah." I didn't tell them I'd wiped the gun myself because
it was so oily. I didn't have the nerve to admit I was that
dumb. "Okay, then, how about the bail-bond companies? All
those bounty hunters work for bail-bond companies. And
this guy was pretty distinctive."

"You ever noticed how many bail-bond outfits there are?"
Ricco said. "And you did say Ortega was supposed to have
jumped bail in Houston, right?"

Ed rummaged through his desk drawer searching for
something, gave up, and looked at me blandly. "Morton and
Hancock have been phoning Dallas bondsmen for a solid
hour," he said. "A sergeant at Houston PD who owes us a
favor has been doing the same thing down there. So far
nobody has turned up anything. Plus, Houston hasn't
charged—or bailed—anyone named Luis Ortega for fourteen
months. Plus, Ortega's boss says he's been showing up for
work every day for the past year and something. Plus ... Aw,
plus I don't know what else. Point is, Rafferty, does all this
tell you anything?"

"Yeah," I said. "It tells me the dude was not a righteous
bounty hunter, no matter what his name was."

"Right," Ed said.

"And because young Luis Ortega—who won't be getting
any older—was clean as the pure driven snow, we do not
have lead one to indicate why he got whacked. Or why Wells
sucked me in on it."

"Right," Ricco said.

"And the only good news is that because my shotgun

hadn't been fired, and because you know and trust this smiling honest face, I'm not gonna be charged with anything."

"Right," Ed said, but considerably slower.

"But," I said, "the bad news is that I screwed this one up horribly. Fat, dumb, and happy, I let that country boy con me. And you guys aren't gonna let me forget it."

"Right!" they both said.

CHAPTER 4

"Hilda, babe, that's the sort of thing I do. I'm a thug, remember?"

There I was, lounging in my office chair, feet up on my desk, a cold beer in one hand, and a telephone line to Hilda Gardner in the other. It's amazing how rich and full life can be once you get organized.

Hilda said, "I know you're a thug, my love. In fact, that's my line. So, you messed up pretty bad, eh?"

"Atta girl. Be nurturing and supportive." I took another long sip of beer. "But you're right, Hil. I did not do well. My screwup didn't make any difference to the Ortega kid; Wells would have nailed him whether I was there or not. One way or another." I swigged more beer. "But Wells probably wouldn't have gotten away if I hadn't been there. This thought does not please me."

"I can tell. Excuse me a moment." Hilda spoke softly to someone at the shop with her. I drank beer. After about twenty seconds she came back. "Rafferty, I have to go. We have an offer on that colonial sideboard I've been holding for months. Time to wheel and deal, big guy."

"I shall murmur incantations to the gods of antiques, thus ensuring your success. Tiffany. Fabergé. Sotheby's."

"You wouldn't be getting the tiniest bit drunk, would you?"

"Of course not. Chippendale. Sheraton. Limoges."

"You nut," she said. "Tonight? My place or yours?"

"Don't play hard to get with me, cookie. Your place. I'll bring food. And this magnificent body, of course. Doulton. Wedgwood. Ah …" I couldn't think of any other names.

Hilda laughed and hung up.

I finished my beer and got another bottle from the office refrigerator. I was drinking Shiner Bock beer at the time. Since I'd quit smoking, I found myself drinking more beer—figure that one out—and I was going through all the different brands I could find, a case at a time. Man's never-ending quest for knowledge.

I worked out how many Shiners I'd had and decided to stop after that one. There was rush-hour traffic to fight, and I hadn't eaten for a long time. And that was breakfast. I had missed lunch altogeth—

The knock on the glass window surprised me. It was Honeybutt. She smiled—a little tentatively, I thought—and did a broad "May I come around and see you in your office?" pantomime.

"Goddamn it," I said to myself. Then I pointed at the clock, which said four-fifty-five, and shouted, "Not now! Tomorrow."

Honeybutt nodded with an exaggerated movement, held up eight fingers, and arched her eyebrows.

I shook my head and held up nine fingers.

She nodded, waved good-bye, and walked out of her office. She really did have a great backside.

I finished my bottle of Shiner and left about ten minutes later. As I closed the office door, the last thing I could see was the window, and through it, Honeybutt's office. And I thought about all the times we had winked and flirted and leered at each other.

She was coming to see me at nine o'clock tomorrow morning.

Now, why would she want to ruin such a good thing?

CHAPTER 5

Hilda Gardner's hair was backlit by the glow from the hallway outside her bedroom. But it wasn't much of a glow, and because her hair was so very black anyway, I could see her only as a shimmering gray nimbus surrounding the tiny glints of her eyes.

That was the seeing part; the feeling part was much better. Hilda was lying on her stomach, propped up on her elbows, her body jammed tightly against—trust me, the feeling part was better.

"Hey, big fella," Hilda said, "why don't we both spend the next couple of days right here? We can cuddle, sleep, occasionally make a picnic lunch." Her voice had a throaty burr to it.

"Tempting," I said. "Mighty tempting. But what about the big deal you said you had to finish tomorrow morning?"

"Oh, damn. I forgot about that."

"And I should go in, too, babe. I have to preside over the end of an era. Though it's a pitiful thing to contemplate."

Hilda put her head on my chest and nuzzled against me. "Whatever are you babbling about?" she said.

I almost forgot what I was babbling about. I swear, if they ever start an Olympic event in nuzzling …

"Oh. Right," I said. I told her about my nine o'clock appointment with Honeybutt.

"You'd better not call her Honeybutt to her face, you sexist turkey. So what's the problem?"

"Well, there's not a problem, really. It's just that after tomorrow, we'll sort of know each other; we won't have that 'two strangers across the aisle on an airliner' feeling. I won't feel right about winking at her, admiring her backside when she files things, stuff like that."

"Got a good tushy, does she?"

"Nice, I must admit. Very nice even, though not as good as yours."

"How reassuring. Rafferty, can you believe this conversation?"

"Well," I said, "I suppose I shouldn't dwell on my own little problem. Imagine how Honeybutt must feel. Tomorrow morning she'll be face-to-face with her favorite sex symbol."

Hilda let that one drift away in the gloom. After a long silence she said, "Were you scared today?"

"Scared? I was terrified. Honeybutt was pounding on the door, you were off somewhere selling old furniture, and there I was, trapped in my office with only three beers left in the fridge. And I haven't even decided which brand to try next, so—ummph!"

"Don't be silly or I'll do that again. You know what I mean, Ugly. Were you scared when the men in those cars were chasing you?"

"That's just not the way it works, honey. You get scared before or after; you don't get scared during."

"Why not?"

I shrugged; the waterbed jiggled in response. "I don't know. There's not enough time to be scared, for one thing. But that's odd, now that I think about it, because usually time slows way down. It seems like you have forever to do whatever you have to do. Maybe it's all the adrenaline sloshing around. Anyway, you feel sort of detached; objective and cool. 'Oh, yeah,' your body says, 'I gotta shoot now and run over here and dodge that and ...'"

I rubbed Hilda's back; she made an appreciative sound and nuzzled me again. I made an appreciative sound then.

Hilda stopped nuzzling and said, "A lot of people, maybe most people, wouldn't feel that detachment. They'd freeze. They'd be scared 'during,' as you so coyly put it."

"Maybe, but those people can do things I can't. They understand double-entry bookkeeping or they know how to fix TV sets or drive trains or make furniture. We all have different skills. Like you say, I'm a thug. Pretty goddamn good one, too."

"Are you in trouble with the police because of today?"

"No," I said. "They're satisfied that I wasn't involved. Well, I was involved, but not ... you know what I mean. Durkee and Ricco will give me a hard time for the next twelve or thirteen years, but I was dumb enough to deserve that, so ..."

After a long, quiet moment Hilda said, "Are you going to be able to walk away from it?"

When I didn't answer her for a while, she said, "You can't, can you?"

I said, "Well, I thought I might poke around a little. Between other cases, of course."

"Hah! I know you, Rafferty. You're going to hunt down that fake bounty hunter."

"Oh, I think 'hunt down' is a trifle strong."

Hilda sighed and moved restlessly. Her skin was cooler now, and we didn't fit quite so perfectly together, side by side. "It won't do that poor man any good, you know. He's already dead. And it was *not* your fault."

"I know that, babe."

With a sudden fierce movement she thrust herself up and pushed her face close to mine. "Tell me this," she said. I could feel her breath on my chin. "Is it because of what he did, how he killed that man, or is it because he made you look foolish?"

It took me a long time to come up with the only answer I could honestly give her.

"I don't know, Hil. I wish I did know, but I don't."

CHAPTER 6

Eight-forty-five the following morning. I unlocked the office door and went in, feeling vaguely uneasy about the coming face-to-face meeting with Honeybutt.

On the other side of the big plate-glass window, she was already hard at work, head-down over a desk covered with forms and reports. She must have sensed my presence at the window; she looked up at me, smiled hello, then returned to her work.

I cleaned up the office some. I threw away yesterday's paper, and I dusted my desk and the client chair. I felt a fleeting temptation to straighten the untidy stacks of old city directories and telephone books, but the feeling passed quickly enough. Checked the office fridge; not much beer left. Oh, well, it was probably too early to offer Honeybutt a drink, anyway.

I took the coffee mugs down to the men's room, washed them, and remembered to bring back a fresh paper towel for the coffee tray. I loaded the percolator and turned it on.

Eight-fifty-five. I sat down and watched Honeybutt work. I found myself sighing and hoping she wouldn't turn out to be an airhead with a screechy voice and too much perfume. Alan Alda and New Age men be damned; it wasn't easy to end a nice, stable, sexist relationship like the one Honeybutt and I had.

Promptly at nine Honeybutt looked at the clock, then at me, and mouthed, "Okay now?"

I nodded. She got up and headed for her office door. Before she reached it, though, inspiration struck. I knocked on the window.

Honeybutt stopped and turned back with a quizzical look on her face.

Hamming it up as much as I could, I went into an exaggerated bodybuilder's pose. She looked at me strangely, then the corners of her mouth twitched. I flexed every muscle I could think of and imitated some of those routines the oily guys in little bitty underwear did on television.

Honeybutt smiled first, then she grinned, and finally she launched into an outrageous mock leer. She did a brief war dance and stuck her little fingers in her mouth in that gesture that means "I'm whistling" but no one can really do.

Maybe Honeybutt could whistle that way, though, because her boss came to the doorway of his office enclosure and looked out. He was a thin, balding man with a long face. He had several pens in his shirt pocket and a sheaf of papers in his hand. He looked at each of us in turn, shook his head as if confused, and closed his door.

Honeybutt watched him go, then gave me a broad, saucy wink and turned sideways to me. She put her hands on her hips and bent forward from the waist. While I clapped and leered and pawed at the ground, she arched her back and wiggled her bottom. And she was grinning as broadly as I was.

Honeybutt was wearing a high-neck, frilly white blouse and a beige pair of those baggy-legged slacks invented by a misogynist, so the overall effect wasn't especially sexy. Which didn't matter at all.

Finally I waved a "come on over" gesture, she stopped posing, called out something to her boss, and went out her office door.

Twenty seconds later, she came bursting in, slightly flushed with a big, open smile. "That was great," she said. "The perfect way to, what, shift gears?" She stuck out her hand. "Beth Woodland," she said. "Hi."

"Rafferty," I said, and we shook hands. "Coffee?"

"Oh, yes, thanks."

We went through the coffee-pouring routine—cream? sugar? a mug okay?—and came out the far end seated across from each other, sipping tentatively, and still smiling.

"So," she said, "you're really a detective."

"Really am. Wanna see my blackjack collection?"

"No, that'll be all right."

Honeybutt—Beth Woodland, dammit! I'd have to watch that—*Beth* had not changed physically when she came from her office into mine. She had the same shortish brown hair, the same heart-shaped face, and the same nice figure I'd admired bending over filing cabinets for years. But she wasn't quite the same, not really. It was hard to explain.

"Tell me something," Beth said. "About a year ago, there

were three men in here. One of them was angry, I think, and he pointed at you. Then you got up and ..." She looked at me closely. "Did you really break his finger?"

"Yes."

"Why?" She held her coffee mug with both hands, up close to her lips, and she took small sips as we talked.

"He threatened the woman I love. I broke his finger to show him how seriously I take threats about Hilda."

"Would he have really hurt her? If you hadn't done that?"

"I don't know. From what I learned later, probably not, but I couldn't take the chance."

A small sip, then, "So you'd do it again."

"In a New York minute," I said.

"I'm sorry, a ... what?"

"A New York minute. Smallest known unit of time. Busy, busy, rush, rush."

"Oh," she said, and smiled. "You know, I'm not as uncomfortable as I thought I'd be. It's funny, though. After four-and-a-half years on each side of that window, but not ... Ron —that's my husband—Ron said maybe I should ask someone else if I felt that way, but I'm glad I didn't."

"Well, uh, Beth," I said, "what can I do for you?"

"Oh, right. I'm sorry. The problem is Thorney, my great-uncle."

I was still trying to work out what a great-uncle was when Beth said, "He's my grandmother's brother. Her older brother, in fact. Thorney's eighty years old. He'll be eighty in a few months, anyway."

"Okay, now I know his age and his name is Thorney—"

Beth cut in. "Sorry! Ron says I always start in the middle

31

somewhere. His full name is Walter J. Thorneycroft." She smiled fondly. "But don't ever call him Walter. He hates it."

"Got that. And what exactly is Thorney's problem?"

"Oh. Yes, of course. A couple of nights ago, Thorney took his rifle out onto the porch and shot at the neighborhood kids."

CHAPTER 7

Beth Woodland sighed and said, "At least Thorney didn't hit any of those kids. He says he missed deliberately. He's such a ... a *capable* old fossil he might be telling the truth."

"Maybe he is," I said. "You don't always shoot to kill."

"But if he can still shoot that accurately, it means he could hit one of them anytime he wanted."

"Missing is always easier than hitting, no matter how good you are. But I see what you mean." I gathered up our coffee cups and poured another round. "Anybody call the cops?" I said.

"Oh, yes," she said bitterly. "Thorney's wonderful neighbors didn't waste a second calling the police."

"I take it he wasn't charged."

"No. Thorney told them he'd only fired down into the ground to scare the kids. And maybe he did." She smiled fondly. "He can be a charmer when he wants to. Anyway, they lectured him for a while and let it go at that. But the older policeman said he'd charge Thorney if it happened again."

I handed Beth her fresh coffee. "Here you go, Ho—Beth!" I scuttled behind the desk with my own cup. "I guess you know he could have been charged with anything from discharging a firearm within the city limits to attempted murder, depending on how near the miss was."

That cheerful observation clamped her eyebrows down. "I know. Ron said almost the same thing."

"Where did this happen?"

"At Thorney's house. He has an old place a few blocks off Fitzhugh."

"I'm not surprised about neighbors calling the cops, then. In the wilds of Highland Park they use lawyers, not guns, on each other."

"Thorney's place is just outside Highland Park, but you're right. Look, Thorney's not rich or anything. He bought that house years and years ago with money he made opal-mining in Australia."

I grinned at her. "Old Thorney really got around, didn't he?"

Beth shook her head. It was an amazed shake, not a negative shake. "You have no idea," she said. "Anyway, the house is smaller and not as well kept as the rest of the block, but it's no dump. It's just that Thorney lives alone and he's old and, well, the other people practically encourage their kids to pick on him."

"That's why he took a shot at them?"

She nodded rapidly. "Right. Oh, I hope you didn't think he just—No, the old guy put up with a lot before he fought back, bless his heart. Even so, he shouldn't have shot at them, of course." She took a quick swig of her coffee and put it down. "There's this gang of kids, they're, oh, probably thirteen or fourteen years old. They're decent-enough kids, I suppose, most of them. But there is one, a boy named Gortner. He's a little older, apparently, and he's the troublemaker. His father is some political bigwig, and the kid thinks he can get away with anything."

"What have they been doing to bug Thorney?"

"Well, most of it is pretty juvenile. Or it was at first, anyway. Soaping windows, throwing toilet paper around, annoying phone calls, that sort of thing. But now they've started breaking things and throwing paint. Thorney got upset and ..." She shrugged helplessly.

"What did he shoot at them with?" I said.

"An old rifle he's had for years. A Krag? Is that the name of a rifle?"

"I'll be damned. Old is the operative word, all right."

Beth nodded. "Krag is probably right, then. Ron and I took it away from him. It's at home, in the closet."

"You know," I said, "he probably did fire into the ground. Lotta houses and people out there; if he didn't aim for dirt, he'd have hit *something*."

"Oh, good. I think. Anyway, will you help him?"

"Sure, if I can."

Beth Woodland beamed. "Tremendous. That would be great."

I put on my stern, client-admonishing look. Despite what Hilda says about that expression, I find it effective. "Beth. Listen carefully. I cannot arrest those kids. I may not be able to keep them from bothering Thorney in the future. But, if worse comes to worst and Thorney pops off another round or whatever, you'll have my reports as evidence of harassment. Thorney's lawyer could plead provocation. Okay?"

She nodded solemnly.

"And," I said, "who knows? Maybe when the kids see me putzing around the edges of this thing, it will cool them down a little."

"Thank you. And what do you charge?"

Uh-oh. That added an interesting element. I didn't think this would take more than a few hours; charging her like she was a stranger just didn't seem right. But then again, not charging her might be ...

Hell with it. Rafferty's Rule Thirty-One: When in doubt, dodge. "I'll have to get a feel for what's involved. I'll let you know."

Beth looked at me oddly but didn't say anything.

"So," I said, "I'll drop by and see Thorney this afternoon or evening. I have another little project scheduled for today, and ..."

"Make it this evening," she said. "I'll meet you there. I'd better introduce you. And I still have to think of a way to sell the idea to Thorney."

She gave me the address and we agreed on a time. She was leaving; was halfway out the door, in fact, when she turned back.

"I'm sorry," Beth said, "but I have to ask this. Not knowing is killing me. A while ago, you started to call me something, then you caught yourself and stopped." She looked me right in the eye; a little smile flashed on and off her mouth. "Tell the truth now. Before today, before we just met, had you made up a name for me?"

"A name? What kind of thing is that to—"

"Because—oh, God, this is embarrassing—I had a name for you. Then. Before now, I mean."

"Oh."

We looked at each other for several seconds, then she said, "I'll tell you yours if you'll tell me mine."

"Well..."

"Please?" she said.

"Honeybutt," I said.

She giggled. "Hotstud McGoodbuns," she said, and turned and strode briskly away. As she rounded the corner down the hall, I heard Beth whoop with laughter.

Looking through the big window, I saw her enter her office. She seemed to be chuckling. She went straight to her desk and jauntily sat down. She picked up a letter or something, then caught me looking at her. She waggled her fingers, smiled, and turned her attention to the letter.

Even though she was reading the letter very, very intently, her shoulders kept jiggling up and down. Just a little bit, but they were definitely jiggling.

I, on the other hand, had mentally moved on to other business. Places to go, people to see, things to do. I looked up the address for Aqua-Tidy Pool Service, switched off the coffeepot and left. Briskly. Seriously.

Hotstud McGoodbuns?

Goddamn.

CHAPTER 8

I thought I had written down the wrong address. I had expected to find Aqua-Tidy Pool Service on a noisy thoroughfare crowded with used-car lots and furniture discounters.

This, very much on the other hand, was suburbia. Circa 1950, with lawns and trees and sidewalks, all that old-fashioned stuff they tend to leave out now, but definitely suburbia.

I was probably lost. Still, it seemed to be a nice neighborhood for it.

The street number I'd copied from the phone book was a small two-story frame house with a porch that ran all the way across the front. There were no business signs on the house or in the yard. There was a garage, though, a big garage, with what appeared to be several drums stored in it. Chemicals, Sherlock? Perhaps.

I pulled in to the curb, stopped, and got out of the car. As I walked away from the Mustang, a brief, ominous hiss came from under the hood. It sounded like something expensive might happen soon. Maybe this was not a good time to be working on simultaneous, financially bereft, cases.

The house was painted a very pale yellow color, like a white watercolor but the brush hadn't been quite clean. That sounds strange, but it looked nice. The planked floor of the front porch had a reasonably fresh coat of that old-timey battleship gray paint. Nostalgia City.

I knocked, still wondering exactly what I expected to accomplish here. Even if this was, in fact, the long-lost corporate headquarters of Aqua-Ti—

"Hey, man, whachoo want?" It was a deep voice, so downtown angry soul brother it was almost satirical. It came from a scowling black face awkwardly poked through an open window a half-dozen steps down the long porch.

I started along the porch toward him. "Good morning." How's that for a catchy ad-lib?

He shook his head angrily. "You stay righ theah, whitey!"

I stopped. "I'm looking for a company called Aqua-Tidy. This is the right address, but ..."

"Ah knowed it. Damn! Wha kinda humbug roust you gonna lay on ..." He scowled again—or still—but differently now. "You from the council?" he said. "You don't dress like you from the council."

"I have no idea what council employees wear on house calls," I said, "but I believe my ensemble makes its own bold and personal fashion statement." I was wearing old jeans, older desert boots, and a polo shirt. I couldn't remember which little animal that particular shirt had on it; a warthog, possibly, or something equally silly.

"Wait a minute," the black man said, and he gingerly

39

pulled his head inside the window. He seemed to have a certain amount of difficulty in doing that.

A full two minutes went by before he opened the front door.

He was in a wheelchair. He wore beige canvas trousers which did not disguise his emaciated legs or the stiff, awkward way they were folded to one side of the wheelchair. His face was smooth and calm now, about eight notches down the anger scale from his recent window performance. His upper body was slender, but strong-looking, and he, too, wore a polo shirt.

I pointed at his left chest, looked at my own, and said, "Aw, hell, you win. You've got a beaver. Beaver beats warthog; warthog beats penguin—"

"Come on in," he said. "Don't know who the hell you are, but none of those turkeys from the council have a sense of humor, so you must be somebody else." He spun the chair around and wheeled himself down a hallway toward the back of the house. I followed him.

"Rafferty," I said. "I'm a private cop and this has nothing to do with you personally."

"Larry Davis," he said. "It better not."

There was a staircase leading upward off the hallway, an old wide one with carpeted steps and a bannister darkened with age. I wondered if, and how, Larry Davis ever used his upstairs rooms.

We rolled and walked on down the hallway, past an office with a pair of three-drawer file cabinets and a desk but no chair. At the end of the hall we entered the kitchen.

Davis went straight to a refrigerator, pulled out two cans of Pearl Light, and handed me one. "Sit down," he said, and motioned to a table with three chairs. "Usually I drink 3.2 beer," he said. "I can't handle much of the full-strength stuff." He waved at his legs. "Not enough body mass. I get drunk too easy."

I sat at the table; he rolled into the chairless space. I drank some Pearl, then said, "Will we be joined for drinks by your twin brother, Super Black the Ferocious?"

He grinned hugely. "Like that? I use that routine when the council comes to hassle me about running a business in a residential area. Confuses the hell out of 'em. The liberals eat up that angry-black-stallion number and the rednecks get tight-assed when I tell them how if dey fucks ovah me, mah black brothers gonna come pourin' outta the ghetto."

"Ghet-*to*!" I said. "Nice touch."

Larry Davis sipped his Pearl contentedly and shook his head. "It works for me," he said, "but you just don't have the complexion to make it play."

"True. What can you tell me about Luis Ortega?"

He nodded to himself. "Thought that might be it." He shrugged. "Way I hear it, Luis got himself offed in a pool hall somewhere. Down in the ghetto, maybe."

"Not quite," I said, and wondered which way to play this. I decided to take a chance on losing my private-eye merit badge; I told him the truth.

He waited quietly while I explained how I'd been there, told him about Toby Wells, and admitted I was poking around for myself, not a client.

He frowned slightly. "You got cop trouble because of all that?"

"Not headed-for-the-slammer trouble; it's not that bad," I

said, "but Wells made me look pretty goddamn stupid. I want to find him."

"I expect you do," Larry Davis said. "Don't know how I can help, though."

"I figure to backtrack through Luis Ortega. About the only sure thing in this whole mess is that it was a planned hit. Wells even used Ortega's correct name when he conned me. So—"

"So this Wells dude must have a reason, right?"

"I hope so," I said. "A nice emotional one, with any luck. If Ortega knocked up his daughter or stole his car or made him lose his job, anything like that, I'll turn over Wells as I work backward through Ortega."

"You called it a hit. What if this bounty hunter was a pro? He wouldn't have been close to Luis until he actually offed him."

I nodded. "And if it was a pro hit, the guy will be back in Detroit or Miami now. Even so, I might find whoever hired him. I don't have many choices here, Larry. Ortega is the only string I can pull and hope it all unravels." I shrugged at him. "It's the way I work."

Davis sat, apparently thinking, for a while, then roused himself and said, "First, I have to tell you what I told the real cops." He smiled to soften the phrase "real cops," as if he thought I might be offended. It didn't bother me; I'd been a real cop once.

"This pool-cleaning gig isn't much of a business," he said. "Oh, I do all right, but *Fortune* hasn't been around to see if good old Aqua-Tidy should be in this year's five-hundred." He held out his arms expansively. "What you see is what you get. I got three of those little bitty Jap vans, a garage full of chlorine and stuff, and this house. Which is really my home. Which drives the local council crazy and makes me invent all kinds of weird defense tactics.

"Peoplewise, I got one salesman and two full-time pool cleaners. The third truck and weekends I cover with a roster of a dozen guys who work part-time; some pretty regular, some only occasionally. Luis Ortega was a part-timer; he worked three or four afternoons a week."

He took a quick sip of Pearl and put the can down immediately. "Plus, I got an accountant who comes in once a week to do the books and a cleaning lady who comes in once a week to do the floors. And a kid who cuts the grass whenever I can find him, which isn't often enough. And that's the Aqua-Tidy story, as they say in the company propaganda videos. It ain't much, but it keeps me off the streets and out of the food-stamps line. For a black cripple, that ain't doing too bad, thank you very much."

He slapped his hands down on the arms of his wheelchair. "The whole point is, I don't know much about my people's private lives. That's none of my business, for one thing, but mostly—as I just explained—we all do our work separately. Hell, they're out cleaning or selling, and I'm in here answering the phone, sending out bills, making heavy-duty management decisions like do I change my Yellow Pages ad this year? So when would we get together and become good buddies? Luis Ortega was an average guy. He worked hard enough to keep his job, not hard enough that I worried about losing him. He showed up on time, mostly, and he got along with people as far as I could tell."

He looked me in the eye and said, "And that's what I told the real cops, too."

"Uh-huh."

"However," he said, "I believe I forgot to mention to them that Luis has—had—been renting one of my upstairs rooms. Probably some of his stuff is still up there."

I said, "I can see how a thing like that could slip your mind."

"Actually," Davis said, "it didn't slip my mind. I was waiting for them to beat it out of me. But they didn't."

"Imagine that."

"Yeah," he said. "And they called me sir." He shook his head sadly. "It's enough to make a man lose his faith in social stereotypes."

CHAPTER 9

"I suppose," Larry Davis said, "you want to go up there and rummage around in Luis's room."

I snapped my fingers. "That's it! I knew the book from Famous Detective School had mentioned this. I just couldn't quite remember—"

"Ho, ho, ho," he said. "Look, I was gonna go up myself. My old chair's up there, but it's a bitch of a job to drag myself up those miserable steps. So I'll tell you what. You go do your Sam Spade thing, but you gotta do two things for me, okay?"

"Probably. What?"

"First, see what you can find out about Luis's relatives; see if there's anyone I can phone or write, so they can get his stuff." He frowned. "Assuming he left anything up there. Anyway, you'll find that out. Second, make sure he didn't leave anything too embarrassing, eh? I don't want to have his people go up there, find any inflatable women, drugs, black-magic bullshit, whatever. I mean, what good would it do; the guy's dead, right?"

"You got it," I said. "How long did Luis Ortega live here?"

"Couple of months, maybe a little longer. I can check my deposit slips if you need to know exactly."

It was my turn to shrug. "I don't know yet. Where did he live before he moved in here?"

"Good question. He's been working—uh, he worked for me for three years, off and on. I mailed his first W-2 to whatever address he put on the form, I forget now what it was. It doesn't matter; the W-2 came back. Luis tried to laugh that off. After that I just handed him his W-2s with his paycheck."

"What a wonderful word, paycheck. As it happens, I remember the part about tracing checks very well. Would you mind ...?"

"I'll get one of his canceled checks for you," Davis said.

"Good." I drained my beer and went upstairs.

At the top of the stairs I stopped beside the worn old wheelchair there and looked back down. I had climbed the flight of stairs in, oh, less than ten seconds, surely. I tried to imagine crawling up, with my legs dragging uselessly behind me. I felt vaguely lazy and embarrassed because I could walk.

There were four rooms off the upstairs hallway. Two were empty; one was half-filled with old furniture. There were spiderwebs and dust balls in the rooms. Larry's cleaning lady needed a swift kick in the scrub brush.

At the end of the hall was a small bathroom—clean enough, without being television-commercial sparkly—and across from the bathroom, Luis Ortega's room.

There was a single bed, a rumpled easy chair covered in floral fabric, a small table with an el-cheapo television set on it, a pine dresser, two shelves, and a closet.

I tried to tell myself that the room was filled with juicy clues. I didn't believe me, but I went to work anyway.

It took me an hour to toss the room properly. It wasn't the most fruitful hour I'd ever spent, but it wasn't the most useless, either.

The general impression was one of impermanence. Ortega had a full complement of clothes, but he was light on other things. This was a place for sleeping or killing time; it wasn't a permanent residence. The feel of the room was wrong for that.

In addition to vague impressions, I found two addresses for Ortega. One was on a layaway receipt for fifty dollars from a Grand Prairie menswear store. The date on it was five months ago. I found it at the bottom of a wastebasket with a batch of other junk that seemed to be debris from that typically male ritual: the periodic wallet cleanout.

The other address was more iffy. It came from the back of a snapshot tucked in the mirror frame over the dresser. The picture showed a beaming Hispanic family posed in front of a small, white stucco house. Mom & Pop, three girls, and a boy. The boy was in his late teens and there was a five-year-old date penciled above the address on the back of the photo. So the boy might be Luis. Might be. And the address would help if the more recent address on the receipt turned out to be a loser. Maybe. Still, in my business, very often maybe was as good as it got.

I left the room carrying the photo, the receipt, and the wastebasket. The wastebasket was for the half-dozen issues of soft-porn men's magazines, the little Baggie of grass, and three pairs of panties I'd found tacked to the inside of his closet door.

All in all, I was disappointed. I hadn't learned much about

Luis Ortega, especially anything to tell me why anyone wanted to cancel his breathing permit.

Larry Davis must have heard me coming down the stairs; he called out as I reached the bottom step. Supersleuth that I am, I tracked him down in his office on the first try.

He handed me three canceled paychecks made out to Luis Ortega. "Dead end, looks like," he said.

Each check had been endorsed by Ortega. Below those endorsements was a red FOR DEPOSIT ONLY stamp with an account number, then CASH-QUIK.

Davis said, "You're the hotshot private eye and all that, but I don't like your chances of tracing Ortega back through a street corner check-cashing service. You ever see one of those places on a Friday afternoon?"

I wrote down the details anyway, and showed him the addresses I'd found. He wrote them down.

"Want lunch?" he asked. "I doctored up a frozen pizza with extra onions and all, put it in about thirty minutes ago. Plenty of beer left, too."

"Pizza and beer?" I said. "No red beans and rice, no corn bread? No greens? Davis, my man, you are missing an integral part of the black experience."

"I've experienced it. You want some pizza or not?"

"Sure."

So we ate pizza, drank beer, and leafed through Ortega's magazine centerfolds. There was some brief discussion about relative merit, but not much. Larry Davis and I both preferred women with IQs above room temperature.

After lunch, I threw the magazines away, along with the grass, the panties, the pizza crusts, and the empty beer cans.

CHAPTER 10

"Goddamn if I understand this," the old man grumbled. "What's coming next, missy? You gonna try to put me in a home somewhere?"

Beth Woodland patted his hand. "Now don't be silly, Thorney. Of course not."

We were sitting in the living room of Walter Thorney-croft's house. It was a nice house, built in the twenties or early thirties probably, with heavy dark timber throughout the interior. As Beth had said, it was slightly smaller than most of those nearby, but it was no dump. If old Thorney ever decided to cash it in, he'd get a check with lots of zeros on it.

Much of the property in and around the Park Cities was like that. A lawyer I occasionally snooped for had pointed out a house a little like Thorney's. It was less than six blocks away, and it was backed hard up against the new DART track. One-point-two million. Numbers like that—for a house!—were beyond me.

Thorney pointed at me angrily. "What is he, a male nurse

or something? He gonna put me on the crapper every couple of hours?"

Thorney was a good-looking old guy. Not handsome, but still rugged. He had somehow avoided getting either fat and wobbly or cadaverously thin. I decided I wanted to be like Thorney when I grew up. Grew old. Older. Whatever.

Thorney still had plenty of hair, too. It was cut short but shaggy and worn uncombed like a white skullcap. His right ear was slightly cauliflowered; probably an interesting story there. Thorney had icy blue eyes, with crinkles at the edges. I decided he'd stared into big chunks of sunlight. And he had worked with his hands, not just occasionally but long and often. His hands were huge, big-knuckled and sausage-fingered. All in all, Walter Thorneycroft looked like the kind of guy I'd like to know better.

If only he hadn't been such a whiny son of a bitch.

Thorney was still pointing at me. "He supposed to wipe my bottom like I was some broken-down old fool who can't look after himself?"

"Thorney …" Ron Woodland said patiently. Beth's husband was a blond guy in a sport coat. He did something in the education department, he seemed totally unper-turbable, and he'd been saying, "Thorney …" for the past several minutes.

"And I don't need a bodyguard, either," the old man rumbled. "Not to protect me from those snot-nosed little pukes."

While Beth and Ron Woodland tried to calm the old man down, I got up and wandered around the room. It wasn't an especially large living room, but Thorney had a batch of terrific junk in it.

He had a framed map of Australia hung on one wall. Between the map and the glass there were five or six old snapshots with crinkly edges and black-and-white images; old-fashioned box Brownie photos. One was a picture of what seemed to be a mining town in a desert; another showed a fairly large gaff-rigged sailing boat. In another snapshot two men stood on a city sidewalk. They had their arms thrown over each other's shoulders and they grinned self-consciously at the camera. In the background there was a car loaded down with a contraption I'd never seen before.

"What's this funny-looking car?" I said. Behind me the muttering and grumbling stopped abruptly.

"What's it to you?" Thorney snapped.

"If you don't know, don't worry—"

"What car? What about it?"

"It's in the background here," I said. "It's old and lumpy, probably British, but what's that big bag for? And the thing bolted onto the rear bumper? Some sort of steam gizmo?"

"Naw. That's a charcoal burner. Aussies couldn't get much gasoline during the war and right after. Rationing. Some smart cookie came up with those burner things. They made something; coal gas maybe, I don't know for sure. Whatever it was, a motor would run on it. Filthy, stinking gadgets, but they worked."

"I'll be damned."

I studied the boat photo next and wondered how big she was and how far you could sail in her and whether she was still afloat. Not for the first time, I wondered if I'd been born about fifty years too late.

Thorney kept bitching at Beth and Ron. "Why'd he want

to know that? What's he gonna do, ask me every stupid question he can think up?"

Beth said something soothing. Ron made his "Thorney ..." drone again. I kept working my way around the room being nosy.

On a shelf near one corner I found a wooden box about a foot square and six inches high. It had tarnished brass corner protectors and a scuffed leather carry strap. I peeked into the box.

A sextant. Old, probably. Well-worn, at least, because the markings on the arc were dim and hard to make out. That was the third time I'd seen a real sextant close up. Again I promised myself I would learn how to use one someday.

"That's it," Thorney roared. "Bad enough you all got to come around here, taking up my time. Now he's pawing through my stuff. Get away from there, you."

I gently closed the box and turned toward him. "I'll pay you two hundred dollars if you'll teach me how to use a sextant," I said.

"Go on, get out of here, all of you." The old man was seated on a cracked leather couch beside Beth. She tried to calm him down. He waved his arms around, to keep her from touching him, apparently. She kept trying; he kept flailing his arms. Twice he almost clipped her in the face with one of those big hands.

I stepped over and grabbed his right wrist. "Settle down! Or you'll hit her by mistake."

Beth shrank back to her end of the couch. Ron stopped saying "Thorney ..." and started saying "Rafferty ..."

"Lemme go, you big hunk of ..." Thorney said. He struggled. Got to give him credit, the old man was powerful for his age.

I motioned to Honeybu—why did I keep reverting to that name?—I motioned to *Beth* and she left the couch. When she was out of Thorney's range, I let him go. He snatched his arm up close to his chest and rubbed his wrist with the other hand.

I sat down beside him. "Now listen to me, you snarly old fart. These people care for you. They've wasted the last half hour trying to convince you to enjoy what's going to happen. Me, I don't care whether you enjoy it or not. So I'm not asking you, I'm telling you. I will be around here off and on for a few days. I'll be assembling a file that might—repeat, *might*—help you in case you pull another screwball stunt like shooting at those kids. That's what I'm going to do whether you like it or not, whether you help me or not. If you will help me and if we get lucky, maybe I can get those kids off your back."

I gave him a chance to say something. He didn't take it, didn't even bitch at me. Hot damn, I was winning him over.

"I'm working for her," I said. I made a belated gesture toward Beth; the delay was almost Nixonesque. Gotta work on that. "However. Strange as it may seem to you, I do not get off on browbeating people twice my age. So I'm gonna give you your only chance to get rid of me."

Thorney looked up at that. Beth frowned. Ron looked interested. Not excited or anything, just interested.

"You beat me at something," I said to Thorney, "and I'll go away."

Thorney frowned suspiciously. Beth started to say something, but Ron shook his head quickly.

"Anything at all," I said, "as long as it's reasonable. For example, no arm-wrestling or foot-racing; I'm younger and stronger. And no flipping coins; that's just blind luck. You have to actually beat me at something."

Thorney turned to Beth and said, "Where did you find this crazy bastard?"

Beth shrugged and smiled tentatively. "He, uh, works in the same building I do. And, um, I ..." She mumbled to a halt, shrugged again, and looked at me. You could practically see a big question mark on her forehead.

"Come on, Thorney," I said. "Put up or shut up. I don't have all night." I noticed Ron Woodland smiling to himself.

The old man chewed his lip and eyed me narrowly. "I got an old set of throwing knives from—"

"No way!" Beth said.

"Not at each other," I said to Beth. "At a target or—"

"Got a target painted on a chunk of pine," Thorney said in a confident tone. "We could—"

"I don't care," Beth said. "No knife-throwing. None. Forget it, both of you!"

Thorney offered to thumb-wrestle. He opened his eyes wide and smiled when he suggested it. I looked at his giant hands and thought about how easily my right thumb dislocated. I let Beth talk us out of thumb-wrestling.

For a variety of reasons, she also vetoed contests based on bourbon drinking, tobacco spitting, age at loss of virginity, and who could field-strip a Colt automatic the fastest.

"Well, hell, Beth, what do you suggest?" I said. "Slapjack? Trivial Pursuit?"

Thorney said, completely deadpan, "We could go out to the bars; see who's best at picking up broads."

"Thorney!" Beth looked miserable. "Oh, I don't know ... Hey, poker! That's all rough and tough and macho, right? One hand of poker, okay?"

Thorney looked at me. "That's about all she's gonna go for," he said.

Cards were not what I'd had in mind. A single, winner-take-all poker hand was pure luck, not skill. But I already wished I hadn't started this stupid contest business in the first place, so ...

"Okay, let's do it," I said.

Thorney hopped up and scuttled around the room with surprising agility. He pulled open drawers and pawed at shelves. "Cards, cards, lemme see now, where did I put—" He darted into the next room.

Beth went after him. At the doorway she turned back, winked, and made a circular "okay" sign with her right hand. She followed Thorney then, and they clattered around looking for the cards.

"What was that all about?" I said to Ron Woodland. He shrugged. Mr Excitable.

"Come into the dining room, Rafferty. Thorney's found the cards." Beth came rushing back into the room. She was speaking too loudly. "This ought to be very interesting. Poker. Wow." Her delivery was as phony as a telephone sales pitch, mostly because she was busy waving things at me with one hand and making shushing motions with her other hand.

She held up two cards, both aces. "Come on now," she said loudly. "Thorney's ready to play." She handed me the two aces and silently mouthed, "Win!"

And I had thought Beth was such a nice girl.

CHAPTER 11

No doubt about it, this racket did things to your faith in human nature. Beth Woodland, a woman I'd known for years —well, sort of—wanted me to cheat at cards. To beat her dear old great-uncle Thorney.

Of course, that seemed like a pretty good idea to me, too.

Beth gave me the two aces, I palmed them as well as I could, and we went into the dining room. Thorney sat at an ornate dining table, scowling and shuffling cards. I sat down opposite him. In the process I dropped the aces into my lap. Rafferty, the riverboat gambler. All I needed was a beaver hat and a waxed mustache. Good grief.

Beth stood near a large sideboard, chewing her lip. Ron ambled into the room; she threw him a quick smile.

"Howdy, stranger," I said to Thorney. "Aren't we supposed to have our guns on the table? And long black cigars in our mouths so we can scowl at each other through the smoke?"

He said, "You wanna make jokes or play cards?" Grouchy tone, intimidating look; the old goat was trying to psyche me out.

"Name it," I said, "and you better stop pestering the school-marm, too."

"Not funny," he said. "Five-card stud. There's only the one bet, no need for openers." He shuffled once more, reassembled the deck, and plunked it down in the center of the table. I cut it, then watched while Thorney dealt. I had the sudden thought that Clint Eastwood could have played this scene much better than I was handling it.

My cards weren't the worst stud hand ever, but they weren't all that good, either. At least, they weren't good enough for a sometime poker player like me to be confident. King of spades, jack of clubs, ten and eight of diamonds, five of hearts.

Across the table, Thorney didn't look too happy with his cards, either. Hah! I figured that sly old man could have four aces and he'd still look like that.

All in all, it didn't seem like a good idea to leave things to chance.

I did some card-snapping and hand-curling and ferocious squinting—all that show-biz stuff—while I lowered my hands below the tabletop, dropped the five and eight, and replaced them with the aces Beth had slipped me.

I kept up the scowling and snapping and such to get the cards back up again, then slapped them facedown on the table and said, "Hey, this is a sudden-death stud hand. What are we fooling around for?"

Thorney put his cards facedown, too, and tapped them with one finger. The general effect was like thumping them with a salami. "Together," he said. He flipped over and spread out his cards. So did I.

I had a damned good stud hand now, thanks to Beth: pair of aces, king, jack, ten.

Thorney had a great stud hand: three aces, ten, seven.

Whoops.

Beth goggled, reddened, then pointed and rushed at Thorney. "You … you cheated, you …" She reached down into his lap, came up with two cards, and threw them onto the table. A ten and an eight, both hearts.

How about that? He had sandbagged aces, too.

"Thorney, I'm ashamed of you," Beth said. She had her fists on her hips, and she looked like an angry kindergarten teacher. Ron Woodland chortled softly. That was probably as close as he came to unbridled hysteria.

Thorney glared at all of us, unrepentant.

"Well, goddamn," I said, "there goes another great idea right down the tube." I picked the discarded five and eight out of my lap and threw them on the table.

Beth blushed and turned away.

I took my illegal discards and rearranged my hand to the way it had been dealt. Then I did the same thing with Thorney's cards.

I was back to king, jack, ten, eight, five. Thorney had ace, ten, ten, eight, seven. Both hands were a useless mixture of suits.

"Your pair of tens is too good for me," I said. "You won yourself a little peace and quiet, Thorney."

Ron Woodland shrugged; Beth said, "Wait a minute, Rafferty …"

Thorney still hadn't said anything. He peered at me closely.

"We had a deal," I said to Beth. "Cheating was stupid—for both of us—but when you back out that part of it, Thorney won. I'll go."

Thorney said, "Just hang on one goddamn second there. I'll tell you when I'm ready to collect my winnings." He looked at Beth, Ron, and me in turn, then shook his head. "Dumbest thing I ever heard of, but …"

The old man rose slowly, with his huge knuckles rammed against the tabletop. He glared down at me. "You think you could keep a civil tongue in your mouth? If I was to let you hang around here?"

"I doubt it very much."

He nodded. "I expect that's right. What about that celestial navigation thing? You really want to learn or were you just trying to butter me up?"

"Being able to locate yourself on earth by measuring angles in the sky seems almost magical to me. I repeat: I will pay you to teach me how to use a sextant. Name a price."

"Naw," he said. "The only thing I need is time and you can't pay me that. I'll teach you." He straightened and held out his right hand.

I stood up and took it. We shook. My god, he was strong.

He squeezed even harder. "Reckon you can stand it, being around a—what was that you called me?—a 'snarly old fart'?"

I squeezed back. It was a good thing he wasn't twenty years younger. "No problem," I said. "We'll hang out together, suck up the Geritol, maybe beat up on snot-nosed little pukes."

We gave up on handshaking before we hurt each other, and we all had a drink. Actually, Thorney and I had two.

Later, as the Woodlands and I were leaving, Thorney showed us how to find the constellation Orion and its navigational stars, Rigel and Betelgeuse. And Sirius, off to the side.

Fantastic!

CHAPTER 12

"Hotstud McGoodbuns?" Hilda said. "She called you Hotstud McGoodbuns?" Then she rolled over and buried her face in her pillow. She was probably trying to make me think she was laughing.

"You sure know how to take the fun out of early-morning pillow talk, babe." I got up, went to the window, and looked outside. Seemed to be a nice day shaping up. Inside, however …

"Hotstud Mc—" Hilda chortled as she came up briefly to breathe. She said something else, too, but the pillow muffled it. Probably just as well. I went to the kitchen for coffee.

Despite Hilda's attitude, I carried a cup back to the bedroom for her. "You don't deserve this," I said, "but I'm willing to turn the other cheek. Uh, let me rephrase that …"

She turned red and barely managed to put the cup down without spilling it. Back to the face-in-the-pillow giggles. Sometimes the woman has absolutely no self-control.

Ten minutes later I was in the shower, halfway through a stirring rendition of "They Built the Ship Titanic," when

Hilda came into the bathroom. She knocked on the glass shower wall. "Leave it running, please," she said. I backed up against the glass and wiggled. She made a noise like a cat gargling and left in a hurry.

One for my side. About time, too.

Breakfast was a delicate affair. Hilda and I carefully avoided words like *bottom* and *but* and so on. I'd never realized there were so many words like that. Or how many of them began with *b*.

By nine-thirty I was headed across town, hot on the trail of Luis Ortega. And, I hoped, the elusive Toby Wells.

The address from Ortega's layaway receipt was a small apartment building painted an unfortunate shade of green. The paint had flaked away from the concrete block structure in several places. The timber trim didn't even remember when it was painted last; it had weathered to an even gray. As apartment buildings go, it was not what you'd call uptown. On the other hand, it was considerably more uptown than the sprawling housing projects in other parts of west Dallas.

Ortega had supposedly lived in apartment C, but the name on that mailbox was M. Hermosa. Undeterred, I went searching.

There were two floors, with two apartments on each floor. C and D were upstairs.

The two apartment doors faced each other across a combined breezeway and stairwell. When I knocked on the C door, the D door opened first. A man—short, muscular, twenty-sixish—planted himself in his doorway and watched me.

The C door opened. A Hispanic woman in her early

twenties smiled at the man in his doorway, then said to me, "Yes? May I help you?"

Her face tapered from a wide forehead to a narrow chin. She had small features but large eyes. She was handsome, not pretty, and she was one of those people who exudes restraint and maturity.

"My name is Rafferty," I said. "I'm a private investigator. I'm looking for information about a man named Luis Ortega. This was his address once."

She said pleasantly, "There is no Luis Ortega here now."

"I know that," I said. I stood slightly sideways to her so I could watch the man across the breezeway. He hadn't moved or said a word.

The young woman kept smiling. Her face was composed, but I had the impression she was working at it. "Didn't you look at the mailboxes?" she said. "The name on the mailbox is not Ortega."

"Dogged determination in the face of all obstacles," I said. "It's sort of a personal creed with me."

"I'm sorry," she said. "I don't understand."

"How long have you lived here?" I said. "Maybe I'm wasting your time."

She looked from me to the man, then back to me. "A year. A little more, perhaps. Why?"

"Luis Ortega is dead. I'm looking for the man who killed him. I need your help." Off to my right, the short man shuffled his feet once and sighed.

The woman dropped her head and nodded. "I know Luis is dead," she said.

The short man said, "Maria, don't—"

"It's all right, John." Then, to me: "Come in. I don't think I

63

can help you, but …" She stepped aside and I went into the apartment. The short man came, too. He whispered something to her, she whispered back in a soothing tone.

She introduced herself as Maria Hermosa. The short man was "John, from next door." She left us in the small living room while she made coffee and scurried around in the kitchen. I sat; John from next door sat, too, and he glared at me.

Despite the state of the building exterior, Maria Hermosa's apartment was immaculate. The paint was fresh, the furniture, what there was of it, was spotless. There were icons on a table and religious pictures on the walls, mostly the kind of pictures with big thorns and blood and halos like flat gold plates.

Marie hustled in. She had a tray loaded with coffee fixings and a plate of tiny pecan cookies. John glared even harder. He probably didn't want to share those cookies with me.

Maria began to hostess the hell out of our impromptu conference. She distributed cups, filled them, offered cream and sugar, and spoons and napkins and cookies, fiddled with this and adjusted that. When she started to rearrange the cookie plate for the third time, I said, "What is it about Luis Ortega that frightens you?"

She shook her head. "No. You are wrong. I am not frightened. I am ashamed."

"Aw, Maria," John from next door groaned. "You don't have to—"

She silenced him with a gentle wave of her hand. He slumped in his chair and gave the ceiling a nasty look.

Maria Hermosa folded her hands in her lap and looked at

me. "Luis Ortega used to live here. With me." She swallowed. "He was my husband." Another swallow, deeper this time. "Common law."

"Maria, don't do this to yourself." John sounded like a man in pain.

"No," Maria said to him gently. "It's all right. It helps me, truly." She turned to me and went on. "We were not married in the church. Luis would not. He said it was old-fashioned and we should grow up. Be more like the Anglos, Luis said." Maria's serene expression turned wistful. "Luis said the love words, too, and he gave me things, little gifts. Not expensive things, but small things, things of the heart. I was a very stupid woman. I listened to my heart, not to my head, and I let Luis bring me here. So we called ourselves married. Like the Anglos who are not old-fashioned."

Maria looked around the room for a few seconds. "At first it was wonderful. Each morning, Luis would walk with me to the bus stop. I was so proud! Luis would wait with me and wave as the bus drove off. The other women on the bus would tease me about how my man walked around with his head in the sky because of his great love for me.

"While I worked at the credit union, Luis would work, too, at cleaning the swimming pools. He said. He told me how hard he worked and how he put his pay in the bank, in the special account for us. And he said that was why we must use my pay for rent and groceries and the expenses of living. So his pay would make the special account grow fat."

Maria bit her lip for a half second, then said, "That was what Luis told me, but it was not true. None of it. Two, sometimes three, days each week, Luis would not go to clean the swimming pools. He would go to places where the *coyotes* go, to bars and pool halls and to places to watch women without shame do things I do not like to think about. There was no special account at the bank, either. Luis would drink and gamble and waste his pay, then he would come back here in the afternoon to tell me his lies."

I asked, "Why do you think Luis was killed?"

She shook her head. "I do not know. In such places, the men fight. Sometimes they cut each other with knives. But that is not how Luis died, I think."

"How did you find out about Luis?"

Maria's eyes closed for a beat. "One day my girlfriend, Margarita, came to me crying. She had a new job—she is a maid—at a very fine house out near the lake. And on the third day, when a man came to clean the pool, it was Luis. He did not see Margarita, but she saw him and she saw how Luis and the woman of the house acted toward each other.

"She did not tell me then," Maria said. "She waited until Luis had been there three times to clean the swimming pool and she saw, with her own eyes, how Luis and that *puta* behaved; like the animals in the field and brought me this great shame."

It was obvious that the admission hurt her, but Maria held her chin high. That stupid bastard Luis didn't know what he'd given up.

"Maria," I said, "are you absolutely sure—"

"I am sure," she said. "When Margarita came to me, I said there must be a mistake, Luis would not do this thing to me. But Margarita's brother took me one day in his Ford after I lied to the credit union and said I was sick and must go home. You see what sort of woman I have become? Anyway, we followed Luis, and I saw for myself the places he went."

She shrugged. "We could not follow him at work. I did not see him at the swimming pool of the rich *puta*. But I know it was true. That afternoon when Luis came back and saw his things outside the door, he, too, said, 'Oh no, there is a mistake.' I told him to kneel down and hold the cross and swear to me he had not done such a thing. He could not. Even Luis could not tell such a lie with the cross in his hands."

She rose to her feet with great natural grace and dignity. I had a sudden flash of her as a Mayan princess, serene in gold and jade, on a stone throne in a jungle temple.

I handed her the photo I had found in Luis's room at Aqua-Tidy. "Who are these people?"

"This is Luis. When he was younger, of course. And his family. They moved to California a year ago. To Los Angeles." She said Los Angeles with the Spanish pronunciation.

"I thought they might know of any enemies Luis had."

She looked down at me and said, "If you wish to find the man who killed Luis, I think you should visit the husbands of the *putas* in the big houses with the swimming pools."

She might be right, I thought. And the gambling angle might have legs, too. Especially if Toby Wells was a contract hitter.

"This is a matter of great shame for me," Maria Hermosa said. "My friend at the counseling center says I must accept it and look ahead now. Telling you of my foolishness with Luis is a way to do that, I think. But now you must go before I embarrass myself more by crying before you like a silly girl."

I let John from next door hustle me out. He came, too, and when Maria closed the apartment door behind us, John whirled and grunted, "That son of a bitch!" He punched the concrete block wall with his right hand. Then he slumped against the wall, drew in an agonized breath, and began to suck on his bloody knuckles.

"Fella could get hurt that way," I said.

He stopped sucking long enough to say, "You find the guy who killed that motherfucker Ortega, you shake his hand for me."

"From what Maria says, Luis was a real bastard, all right."

John waved his lacerated hand and grimaced. "Hah," he said. "You want to know about a bastard? I'll tell you about a bastard. She's four-and-a-half months pregnant with Ortega's kid."

Then his eyes misted over with something more powerful than the pain from his battered hand. "And she won't let me take care of her," he said. He trudged into his apartment and closed the door.

I went down to the street, opened the Mustang's doors, and waited for the bake-oven heat to dissipate. While I waited, I carefully considered my next move.

Drinking lunch seemed to have a lot going for it.

CHAPTER 13

"Sure, a jealous husband might have had Ortega whacked," I said around a mouthful of rare roast beef. "Hell, to judge from the way Maria talked—and from the underwear trophy wall I saw in Ortega's room—there might be whole herds of hubbies out there." I shook my head. "There are better angles, though."

"Name two," Hilda Gardner said. She took a bite of quiche, put down her fork, and touched her lips with her napkin. Great lips.

"Oh, gambling, for openers, with the mystery bounty hunter as muscle for whomever Ortega owed. That assumes more action than I'd expect from the snake-pit joints where he supposedly hung out, but it's possible."

I sipped my beer; Corona this time. I'd never believed those rumors, anyway, and I had drunk Corona all the way through their troubles. I was even considering it for the next Rafferty beer of the week. Which made me wonder: Would they give a discount for brand loyalty?

"You were saying?" Hilda prompted. She slipped another forkful of quiche into her mouth. Great teeth, too.

"Oh, right, well, I wonder about relatives. Hil, you should see this Hermosa girl. Ortega dumped on her pretty badly; she's hurt by it, but she's working it out, plugging right along. She has so much class you wouldn't believe it. But there could be a brother or father or uncle out there with revenge on his mind. A hot-blood intent on upholding the family honor. It happens."

"I'm sure it does," Hilda said, "and you seem to know every arcane honor code you men have ever devised. But I thought that sort of thing was personal. If this Maria had a brother or whatever, wouldn't he go after Ortega himself? Hiring someone else doesn't sound like Latin machismo to me."

"Yeah, I know," I said. "That's the problem with that theory."

Hilda frowned. "That bounty hunter, Wells. He couldn't have been Hispanic, could he? Disguised, maybe?"

"No. Besides, a disguise and the con he ran on me doesn't fit the Latin firebrand image, either." I picked up my roast beef sandwich—Rare and Juicy on a Crusty French Loaf, the menu had said, a Continental Luncheon Treat Par Excellence —and took another bite. It was crusty, all right; crusty like having a grenade go off in your mouth. Crumbs drifted down on each side of my plate.

Hilda said, "What about Maria's neighbor, uh, John what-sis-name? He sounds very protective."

"You've got that right. He would have loved to rip out Ortega's heart and spit in the hole. Trouble is, your argument about not hiring it done applies to him, too."

Hilda grimaced. "You don't have to be quite so graphic," she said. She poked around in her spinach salad. She was probably trying to find something edible in there. "Are you going to tell your police friends about him."

"I don't know. I think Maria needs him, even if she doesn't realize it yet. And he definitely needs her. I'd hate to interfere with that by setting him up for a roust." I bit into my sandwich again. Another explosion of crumbs.

"Hey," I said to Hilda, "why does this always happen. Whenever we eat in a classy place, your side of the table stays super-neat; my side looks like I've been pushing the food up through the tablecloth."

Hilda smiled like Jane Pauley. That was a bad sign. It usually meant there was a zinger headed my way. She said, "Perhaps you should order different food. There are dishes that are light, elegant, cohesive. And—wonder of wonders!—many of them are actually good for you."

"No. Hold it. You're not going to get me on to that wimpy stuff you eat. Not out in public, anyway." I leaned over the table toward her and said in my most serious tone, "It's not that I object if people want to eat those things in the privacy of their own homes. Not at all. But when they make a public display of their—"

Another Jane Pauley smile from Hilda. This one was even broader. "Your tie is dangling into the juice that leaked out of your caveman sandwich."

Dammit, she was right.

I lifted the tie clear and mopped at it with my napkin. The process didn't do the tie much good, but it gave the linen napkin a nice mottled look. Tough. It hadn't been my idea to wear a tie in the first place.

"Stupid house rules in this joint," I said. "How about I beat up the maître d'?"

"Oh, no, you don't," Hilda said. Then she frowned thoughtfully. "Check back with me on that if they're out of Black Forest cake again."

After lunch, Hilda and I walked around for a while. She window-shopped; I enjoyed being with her. At one point I rolled my soggy tie into a ball, took one step, up and zap! Plunked that tie into a curbside trash can without ever touching the side.

Hilda put her arm around me. "Sign up with the Mavericks," she said. "They'd never pass up a jump shot like that."

"Only my retiring nature and innate modesty restrain me."

Hilda laughed and squeezed. I squeezed her back and watched the wind ruffle her hair.

There could be no better way to spend a sunny afternoon.

But there were worse ways, and I found one of them an hour later, when I drove out to Thorney's house.

CHAPTER 14

Thorney sat in a cane armchair on his front porch. He watched a heavy blond man tease a pane of new glass into a front window frame. The man wore a uniform shirt with the name of a glass company on the back.

Thorney had a sizable goose-egg on the right side of his forehead, a bandage on the center of the goose-egg, and a sour look on his face.

The look didn't improve when he heard me step onto his porch. "'Bout time you showed up," he grunted. "Remember all that crap about how you were gonna stop this?"

The glass man turned, too. According to a patch on his left chest, his name was Ronald. He had the glass pane in place now, and he began to push metal wedges into the frame to hold it there.

Every window up and down the porch except one had been broken. At least they all had little glass company stickers on them now. There was a cardboard box containing glass fragments, and bits of old, dried putty scattered across the porch. After the window Ronald was working on, there was only one more to do: a small, pebbled glass panel in the front door.

The pebbled glass had a circular hole in the center of a star-shaped pattern of cracks. It was a big hole, .50 caliber size or damned close to it. Near the broken panel, in the wooden part of the door, there was a round, smooth crater. The crater was a good quarter-inch deep, maybe a little more.

Ronald saw me studying the crater, shook his head in a "how 'bout that?" gesture, and kneaded a ball of glazier's putty in his hands.

I said, "Thorney, what the hell did this?"

There was a drawstring bag on the table beside the old man's chair. He picked up the bag and shook it. Whatever was inside made a clunky metallic rattle.

"Nineteen of 'em," he said. "May still be some more around here, too." He dipped into the bag and came up with three ball bearings. They looked small at first, but that was only because Thorney's hands were so big. The bearings were larger than marbles; they were chromed, solid spheres. They had a certain science-fiction-movie menace about them.

I picked one off Thorney's palm and hefted it. Moving at a decent speed, it was heavy enough to kill if it hit you in the right spot.

"Did they throw 'em or use slingshots?" I asked.

"Slingshots. Piss-weak little bastards couldn't throw hard enough to do this." He waved vaguely at his forehead.

Behind him, Ronald the glass man pursed his lips and frowned.

Thorney said, "And before you start mother-henning me,

the doc's already seen it. I'm not hurt. The little puke didn't hit me square-on."

I bounced the ball bearing in my hand. "When I saw that window, the first thing I thought of was a .50 caliber slug."

"Not far off," Thorney said. "I put my micrometer on one of 'em; .472 inches."

"Do Beth and Ron know about this?"

Thorney shook his head doggedly. "Not yet. Maybe I'll give them a call tonight. If I feel like it." He looked up and dared me to make something of it.

"Okay," I said. I handed the ball bearing back to him. It made a solid thunk when he dropped it into the bag with the others. Ronald the glass man finished puttying the window and started work on the front door. I leaned against a porch column near Thorney's chair and crossed my arms and feet. "Tell me about it," I said.

Thorney squirmed and absently touched the lump on his head that he said didn't hurt. He winced and pulled his hand away. "It was this morning," he said. "All of a sudden there was this banging noise, like somebody pounding with a hammer. Then I heard a window break, and then a couple more right after. I came out here, saw the rotten little pukes over there, hunkered down by the hedge.

"There were three of them, maybe four, I'm not exactly sure. They got me with one of those bearings right off. Made my eyes water pretty bad." He made a smacking noise with his mouth and seemed unable to fix his glance on any one thing.

I thought Thorney was having a blackout or something, then I realized he was embarrassed because he hadn't stopped them or caught them or done whatever he thought he should have done.

He jerked his head up to face me and said, "By the time I could see again, they'd run off. Chickenshits!"

I said, "I'm glad you didn't chase them. Did you see the dent in that door frame? With a solid hit, one of those things would kill you just as dead as a small handgun."

"I know, I know," he said, waving one arm at me. "That's not the point. What I want to know is, what are you gonna do about it?"

"You recognize the kids?"

He nodded. "Couple of 'em. One was that Gortner brat from a couple blocks over, the one I told Beth about. And one was a pal of Gortner's. I've seen him before. Not sure about the other one or two. Anyway, I figure they were on their way to school and decided to break something. For fun, probably. Sorry little rat-fuckers."

Ronald froze for an instant when Thorney said "rat-fuck-er," then continued his work. I hoped Ronald never did any window repairs for Hilda. The two of them might form a committee to advise Thorney and me on our language. And wouldn't that be a pain in the ass?

I said to Thorney, "If those kids went to school, they have to come back. Do they walk past here on the way?"

"Not right in front," Thorney said. "Up the other street, at the corner there. They'll be going by about three, three-fifteen."

It was early, so I waited on Thorney's porch. We watched Ronald the glass man do his thing. He finished, eventually, and presented the bill with a flourish. Thorney paid him and he left whistling something vaguely gospelish.

Thorney grunted. "Guy probably hands out slingshots just to keep his business going."

"You're a bitter old fart, Thorney," I said.

"You're goddamn well right about that," he said.

After that, I still had time to kill, so Thorney and I had a beer. He got out his sextant and showed me how to check the mirrors for proper adjustment.

Then it was three o'clock and time for me to go roust the kids. It was like too much of my work; it was something that needed to be done, but I wasn't looking forward to it very much.

CHAPTER 15

When schoolkids began to pass the corner, I stopped the first one who fit Thorney's description—"big for his age with curly red hair"—and said, "Are you Gortner?"

The boy shook his head and pointed back down the block. "He's coming now."

"Thanks."

Gortner was with another kid; they both wore baggy pleated pants and light-colored shirts that were too big for them. They—and most of the other kids passing—were dressed so alike, they might have been wearing uniforms. They wouldn't have seen it that way, of course. We didn't either when I was their age.

Gortner and his pal also had what I considered goofy haircuts and, between them, an easy three hundred dollars worth of fancy shoes and watches. And they carried book bags.

In my school days, we'd have pushed a wheelbarrow—hell, we'd have *carried* a wheelbarrow—before we used a book bag. These kids didn't have that tunnel vision. They each had one of those soft synthetic shapeless bags that people use to lug clothes or sports gear or books. As Gortner sauntered past me, I reached and snagged his bag out of his hands.

He stopped, amazed. "Hey, wha ... you can't do that!" he said. His partner stopped, too. He held his bag behind him.

"Don't be silly," I said. "Of course I can do that. I just did. You want to guess what happens next?"

Other kids hurried past. They watched and put their heads together and looked excited, but they kept moving. No-one said a word to Gortner and his buddy. And no one stuck up for them. Very interesting.

"Okay, man, all right now. Gimme the bag back, okay?" Gortner bounced and blustered and shifted from one foot to the other. He was trying so hard to be cool.

I said, "What happens next is this. The three of us are going for a little stroll so that an old man can have a look at you two. Think of it as your first lineup." I smiled at them. "You will doubtless have many more, if I decide to let you grow up."

The Gortner boy seemed to be a year or two older than his friend, but he was still only a kid, still carrying his baby fat and acne. Maybe lines like "if I decide to let you grow up" were a touch overdone. On the other hand, maybe not; I wanted him off-balance. And he was.

Gortner bobbed his head rapidly and rocked it from side to side as he talked, like kids do when they're caught off guard. "No way, man. I don't know who you are, but you're in trouble, man. You can't make—"

Gortner's buddy butted in. "Are you a co—uh, a police officer? Sir." This kid was thin-featured and dark-haired. He had more acne and less bullshit than Gortner. More brains, too, apparently.

"I'm a private cop," I said, "but it doesn't matter whether I'm the sheriff of Tombstone or a cab driver. You have only two choices. One, you come with me. Two, I go to the cops and your folks and tell them about this morning's ambush and what you have in here"—I swung Gortner's book bag in a lazy circle—"besides your algebra homework."

I was only guessing the slingshot was there, but that seemed a pretty safe bet.

It was. Gortner bounced and bobbed off on to a new tack. "Yeah, what the fuck, Eddie, let's go see what this guy is talking about."

Eddie wasn't too happy about that, maybe because Eddie still had his book bag. "Uh, Jerry, I don't think—"

Jerry Gortner whirled on him. "Come *on*, man! You're coming too, Eddie. Or you'll be sorry!"

Eddie mumbled and stared at his feet, but it seemed obvious he would be joining us.

I smiled at them again. "Aren't team spirit and loyalty wonderful things?" I waved them ahead of me. They shuffled and they dogged it but they slowly moved toward Thorney's house.

Jerry Gortner looked back at me furtively a couple of times, then squared his shoulders, and tried to sound self-confident. "I bet he's one of those perverts you hear about, Eddie."

Eddie mumbled something disgusted-sounding.

"Yeah," Jerry said even more loudly. "Betcha he's gonna take us somewhere and try to do something awful. Probably gonna take out his wanger and want us to play with it. Filthy

old pervert." He looked at Eddie. "We could run, Eddie."
Eddie shook his head.

Jerry went on, "If my dad heard from us, from *both* of us,
what this guy did and … and how he, uh …" Eddie kept
shaking his head. Jerry persisted. "How he grabbed us, Eddie,
I mean *grabbed* us, right, then nobody would believe what he
said about—"

"That's them!" Thorney roared from his porch.

Both boys stopped short. I poked them between the
shoulder blades, and they reluctantly shuffled up Thorney's
sidewalk.

The old man had moved the cane chair so that it sat
squarely at the top of the four steps up onto the porch. He sat
there now with his huge hands splayed on the arms of the
chair, his face set like old rock. He glowered at them. The old
guy did a terrific glower.

Jerry Gortner and his friend stopped at the bottom of the
steps. It didn't seem likely they'd go any farther.

I took out my notebook, flipped to a fresh page, checked
the time, and pointedly wrote it down. "Now, Mr Thorneycroft, can you identify either of these suspects as the person
who assaulted you this morning?" It was all bullshit, of
course, but I figured Jerry and Eddie probably flunked Civic
Studies and wouldn't know the difference.

Thorney picked up on it right away. He peered at each of
them in turn and said formally, "I do so identify these boys as
the ones who—"

"Hey, wait a minute," the Gortner kid said. "This old man
is … is senile. He's crazy, everybody knows that. He doesn't
know what he saw or anything." He frowned for a second,

then delivered his ace in the hole. "He's got old-timer's disease," he said smugly.

Eddie rolled his eyes and softly hissed, "Alzheimer's."

Jerry looked confused for a moment, then pointed to Eddie. "Yeah, that's right. He's got … uh, what Eddie said."

"Charming pair, aren't they?" I said to Thorney. I squatted down to open Gortner's bag. He spluttered and reached out to stop me.

Gortner was a social retard, but he got the idea fast enough when I looked up at him. His hand stopped six inches short of the bag; he slowly straightened and stood there, head down, looking at his shoes.

Down in the bottom of the bag, under the textbooks and loose-leaf folders and other school junk, there was a slingshot. And it was one helluva slingshot, too.

It was black metal and carbon fiber with round, surgical rubber tubing that led to the leather pouch for the projectile. The handle had a grip with finger notches, and then the handle continued down the back to form a padded bar designed to rest on the top of your forearm. Presumably the surgical tubing was too powerful to be countered with only the strength in your wrist.

I'd seen these things advertised as hunting weapons, but I'd ever examined one up close. The workmanship was good and the components seemed rugged. I picked it up—I put it on, would be a better description—grabbed the empty pouch, and drew it back; the slingshot version of dry-firing a handgun.

There was an impressive amount of energy stored in those stretched rubber tubes. Thorney was very lucky he'd caught only a glancing blow.

I let the stretched tubing relax and handed the slingshot to Thorney. I pawed through Gortner's bag again.

"Now what are you looking for?" he said sullenly.

"Little-bitty buddy, if I find any ball bearings in here, you're going into a cell so far back they'll have to pipe in the daylight."

Gortner broke then. He gave an agonized howl, turned, and ran. He wasn't too coordinated and he ran clumsily, but he covered ground at a respectable rate. He ducked around the end of Thorney's hedge, we heard his feet slapping concrete for another ten seconds or so, then he was completely gone.

Eddie didn't run. He watched his pal Jerry Gortner abandon him, and he stood there with a resigned look on his face. Then he made a noise that was half sigh and half sob. He knelt and took a similar slingshot out of his book bag. He handed it to me without a word.

I stopped searching Gortner's bag; there weren't any ball bearings in there, anyway.

"Let's see some ID, Eddie."

Wearily, he dug a wallet out of his pocket and showed me a school pass. His last name was Wisermann. I wrote his name, the school, and the home address he told me in my notebook, then handed him Gortner's bag.

"Listen to me very carefully," I said, "and tell Gortner this, word for word."

Eddie Wisermann nodded dumbly.

"I'm going to give you two clowns a break," I said. "One break. This time only." Eddie looked up with a mixture of wonder and awe and surprise on his face. People who win state lotteries have expressions like that.

"I expect you and Gortner to pass the word to the other jerkoffs, but I'm holding you two responsible for the assault on Mr Thorneycroft today. And that is absolutely the end of it! I know who you are, I know where to find you, and if this trouble doesn't stop, I'm coming after you."

Coming after you? What was I saying? To a pimply-faced adolescent, for Christ's sake.

"You got that, Wisermann?" I growled.

Cheap shot, Rafferty. A very cheap shot.

Wisermann nodded so rapidly I thought he might hurt his neck.

"Get outta here," I said with a disgusted tone. John Wayne, from any of a dozen movies. At least I didn't say "pilgrim."

Wisermann took off with more grace than Gortner, even though he carried both bags and they whumped the hell out of his kidneys

I felt vaguely schizo. They could have badly hurt Thorney in the slingshot attack. And they did cost him a bundle for new windows. But they were still only kids and ... aw, the hell with it.

I said to Thorney, "Maybe tomorrow I'll take a flamethrower down to the grade school and really have some fun."

He was made of sterner stuff. He harrumphed. "I thought you were pretty easy on 'em."

"How about next time I shoot them on sight? So you can dance on the bodies. What the hell is the matter with you?"

He went sullen on me. He flicked one hand toward the slingshots lying on the porch beside his chair. "Bastard kids could kill somebody with those things," he said. "And you want give 'em another sugar titty, I suppose."

"Thorney, come on. You know, and I know, that no-one's going to do anything about it. You'd better face that. We can't prove it was them."

"When I give my word—"

"It would be your word against theirs, with no independent witnesses. They might get a lecture, but that's it. This way, maybe we scared them enough to make them lay off."

"Cops used to know how to handle kids like that," Thorney said. "A good clip on the ear, that's what they need."

"Cops can't do that anymore, remember? And neither can we or we'll be ass-deep in juvenile cops and ACLU lawyers." I shook my head. "Thorney, let's give it a day or two and see if it worked, all right?"

"A load of birdshot in the backside used to work pretty well, too." He looked at the slingshots thoughtfully. "Do you suppose we could rig those to shoot—"

"No, I don't." I remembered Thorney's routine with the rifle that had gotten me involved in this mess in the first place. I took out my pocket knife and cut the rubber tubing off both slingshots.

I said, "None of the clichés fit you, do they, Thorney? Sunset years, golden age, peaceful retirement. Does any of that ring a bell?"

Thorney snorted. "Maybe later on. When I get old."

CHAPTER 16

The next day was Friday. As Fridays go, it wasn't much.

Admittedly that Friday started out nicely; Hilda had spent Thursday night at my place. On such occasions we usually don't make it a point to get up too early. That's why I decided to check for messages before I went to the office. And maybe I did have a fleeting thought about taking the day off, if Hilda could do the same. So what?

There was a message for me, though. *Phone Don Sweetham soonest.* Damn!

Don Sweetham was Sweetham Finance, a small loan company occupying an obscure strata somewhere in the lower middle of the financial industry. It was a step up from the down-market places with their three-hundred-dollar loan limits, but it was a big step down from Republic Bank. Correction, make that: several flights of big steps down from Republic.

Sweetham Finance Company made cash loans to a typically unsophisticated clientele. How unsophisticated? Well, most of Don's customers would have guessed that Standard

& Poor's was a street intersection in Houston. Let's face it, Don worked the rough end of the market. Which meant he occasionally needed someone like me.

In the past I had done periodic escort work for Don; cash doesn't walk itself to and from the bank. I don't mind baby-sitting cash.

I once did a month-long bodyguard gig, after a disgruntled customer threatened to remove Don's heart and hold it front of Don's face so he could see the icicles on it. I don't mind baby-sitting Don, either.

And occasionally—only rarely, thank god—Don asked me to do a repo. I hate repo work.

Most of Don's repossession work was done by a scrabbler called Ten Foot the Pole. I don't think Ten Foot was actually Polish, but his name had several *w*'s and *y*'s and a *z* in it, and he was tall enough to stare down a college basketball center so the poor guy never had a chance.

"I know you don't like repos, Rafferty," Don said when I phoned him, "but you gotta help me out. Ten Foot's got the flu or the clap, I don't know what he's got, but he sounds like he's dying, believe me."

"Yeah, well ..." I couldn't help thinking that I could use the money. You think of things like that when you're independently poor.

"Rafferty, Rafferty, this is a class job I'm offering. A Porsche, for crying out loud. Most guys would pay me to let them snatch back a Porsche, right?"

"Since when do you make that size loan, Don? I thought you were more into eight hundred bucks on a rusty Citation."

"Be nice," Don said. "Okay, it's not what you'd call my

normal loan. But the guy was hurting for cash; had to have it that afternoon. Besides, it's only two thou and do you know how much a year-old 928 is worth? No, you don't. Not you. Anyway my problem is, this guy is late—on his third payment, can you believe that?—and now I find out there's another lender in line. Look, I got the papers, this repo is as legal as getting married in church, and I gotta have that Porsche locked up in my yard right now, if not sooner. So when I found out Ten Foot was sick, I thought—"

"Don, I'll do it." I'd caught Don's routine before; the next stage was outraged indignation, closely followed by sorrowful disillusionment. It was easier to give in now and chalk it up to customer relations. "I'll pick up the papers and the gadget in a half hour."

And so Friday began in earnest. I went straight from home to Sweetham Finance, and from there directly to the deadbeat's business address.

And a very classy address it was, too; one of those architectural erections full of companies where they're smugly confident that the cleaning staff are the only ones who have their cars repossessed. Which shows how much they know.

I found the Porsche I wanted tucked in a parking bay two levels deep in the underground parking garage. The Porsche was beautiful; it was bright red and it seemed to be doing eighty-five just sitting there.

The parking-garage attendant came around to chase me away. I gave him a big smile, a peek at the repossession order, and twenty bucks to not call upstairs. He went back to his office cage.

I stuck the business end of Don's key gizmo into the

Porsche's door lock and listened while it worked its magic. Incredible. How could it do that?

There should have been a burglar alarm fitted to the Porsche somewhere, but I didn't see any winking lights inside. Maybe I'd be lucky; maybe it wasn't turned on. That's one of the things I hate about modern repo jobs. They can be so damned noisy.

Hot damn; the door came open without setting off World War III. I got in and worked on the ignition. Eventually, I got the motor fired up and drove the Porsche around to the attendant's cage. He thought I was going to pay the parking fee, the silly bastard, but instead I handed him the personal junk from the back. There was no reason why the guy should give up his fancy hat, driving gloves, and copy of *Forbes* just because he couldn't make the payments on the car.

Then I found out the attendant had stiffed me for the twenty. Two young hotshots burst out of the elevator and ran toward the car. They looked like an ad for the Gordon Gecko School of Business Dress Sense: baggy pants, embroidered suspenders, hair slicked back. One of them threw himself headlong onto the Porsche's hood. He started crying and screaming. "My car is my life" seemed to sum it up.

The other guy wanted to argue about the legality of the repo. He calmed down after I showed him the paperwork. "Poor Ernie," he said. "First the Austin account, now this."

"Hell of a shame," I said. "Would you like to help me, uh …"

We cajoled and tugged poor Ernie off the Porsche, and I tried to leave. But then the cops arrived. Ernie's barracks-lawyer buddy had phoned them from upstairs.

So then I had to walk the uniform guys through the

whole song and dance, and that got Ernie going again. This time, he threw himself down in front of the Porsche.

The cops moved him for me but they started out by asking, not dragging, so it was another ten minutes before I finally got away from there.

And then the goddamned Porsche had a flat tire halfway to Don Sweetham's office. I had to change it under the watchful eye of a traffic cop—after which she sauntered over to take me through the entire repo paperwork again—and while all that was going on, I kept expecting the emotional borrower to show up one more time.

To repeat myself, I hate repo jobs.

Eventually, after taking the Porsche to Don and cabbing back to the Mustang, I drove to my office on Jackson Street, seeking solace and peace.

'Twas not to be.

The instant I sat down in my office chair, Beth Woodland looked up from her desk in the insurance office, leaped to her feet, and set a new world land-speed record for appearing in my doorway.

"Why didn't you stop them?" she said angrily.

"I'm trying," I said. "The borax hasn't worked too well, but I picked up some new stuff at the hardware store and I—"

"What are you *talking* about?" Her voice got a little shriekish in the middle there.

"The ants under my kitchen sink," I said, "but that's not fair. I apologize. You're talking about Thorney and so will I." I shrugged and immediately felt foolish. When someone is worried about a loved one, you shouldn't shrug. "What can I say, Beth? Even if I'd been there with him, he probably would have still run out and gotten that clout on the head. You can't slow the old fart down without nailing his shoes to the floor. Did he phone you?"

Beth shook her head and dropped into the client chair. "No. I stopped at his house on my way to work. He wouldn't tell me much about it, except that he thinks you're pretty good."

"Jeez, Beth, you should have seen me. I knocked out the eight-year-old with a right cross and—sorry, I have a bad case of the Rafferty blues."

I got up, offered Beth coffee or beer, and thought about which one I wanted. She didn't want anything; I took the fourth last Shiner bottle out of the refrigerator and made a mental note to decide on the next brand of beer to buy. Then I told her what had happened to Thorney.

She listened intently. Afterward she said, "You're probably right, but ... Wouldn't it be better if someone was there with him all the time? I'd feel better."

I said, "If that's what you want, it can be arranged. There are a dozen rent-a-cop outfits in town. But they don't come cheap. You'd better be ready for that."

She nodded and tapped her lower lip with her forefinger. "I'm probably overreacting. If it's only kids ..."

I finished my Shiner. "It is only kids. I hope I've scared them off. Note, however, my use of the word *hope*. Note also how carefully I avoid terms like *predict* and *guarantee*."

I shrugged again. "Frankly, Beth, the best thing you could do is convince Thorney to use a little common sense. Being angry about having his windows broken is logical enough; rushing out into a barrage of these things is not." I took one of the ball bearings out of my pocket. I had taken it to browbeat the Gortner and Wisermann kids the day before, then forgotten I had it.

Beth looked at it closely. "That's what they were throwing or slinging, or whatever you call it? They could have *killed* him!"

"I know," I said as patiently as I could. "See why I want you to hose the old guy down?"

She stayed for a while longer, indecisive about what to do or not do for Thorney. Finally, she decided not to decide and she left. I drank another beer. As an appetizer. While I decided where to lunch today.

I settled on a barbecue place not far away and left the office a little after one. As I stepped out onto the street, a man leaning on a black Continental levered himself upright and stepped over to me. He was big, about my size, and he had done enough boxing to break his nose and thicken his ears and brows.

"You Rafferty?" he said in a wheezy voice. He'd been punched in the throat a few times, too.

"Actually, I'm his appointments secretary," I said. "Who shall I say is inquiring?"

He blinked a couple of times, then dropped the oldest cliché in the business on me.

"Get inna car," he wheezed. "Da boss wants to see ya."

CHAPTER 17

"Da boss wants to see me?" I parroted. "Who writes your material, for Christ's sake?"

The big guy didn't say anything; he just reached out for my left upper arm. I knocked his hand away with a forearm block. He sighed happily, curled into a boxing stance, and began to feed easy, testing jabs at me with his left fist. I blocked some and slipped others. Trouble was, he wasn't really trying yet.

He was—or had been—a pro. He had the moves, the stance, the air of easy competence. He wasn't perfect, though. He carried his chin too high and his shoulder a touch low; no wonder he had that wheezy voice.

He kept floating those lazy jabs at me; I swatted them aside and waited for the explosive right that would come sooner or later. At the same time I wished I had something to hit him with; I didn't want to box with him. I wouldn't jog for money with Carl Lewis, either.

The right hand finally came, blasting out through the smoke screen of jabs like a runaway bus. I slipped the punch, but I felt the wind when it went by. He was a little slow to get his arm back, so I went in close and gave him three quick shots in the ribs. *Zot, zot, zot,* with a little bit extra behind each one because I was tired of this crummy day, and because I thought he could beat me if the fight lasted long enough.

I bounced away quickly—he looked like he might be a hugger—and checked to see how much the body punches had hurt him.

He wasn't hurt. He grinned at me and shuffled forward, still throwing those annoying little jabs.

Uh-oh.

I was not without resources, of course. I could work on that poorly guarded throat, try for a kick to a knee or his crotch, or I could run. All three options seemed equally attractive.

Then a man got out of the backseat of the Continental and hurried toward us. "Dave," he called, "Dave! Cut it out, hey? What's gotten into you?" He slapped the boxer's shoulder cheerfully and talked to him the way you would talk to a large, rowdy dog. "Calm down, fella. This is no way to treat Mr Rafferty."

The fighter came out of his stance and stood there looking around absently. He seemed vaguely disappointed, but peaceable enough.

The new guy was shorter than the goon and I; five-eleven perhaps, and slender, with curly black hair and crinkly blue eyes and a nice tan and six hundred shiny white teeth. He put out his hand. "Rod Cayman," he said.

I looked at Cayman's hand and nodded to him. "You got here just in time," I said. "I thought I was going to have to

94

hurt him."

Cayman pulled his unshaken hand back and smiled again. Behind him the pug did a silent "haw-haw-haw" laugh.

"See ya," I said, and walked away.

Cayman trotted to catch up. "Uh, one moment, please, Mr Rafferty."

I didn't stop. Cayman turned to face me and began to do an odd shuffle-trot, sideways-hop step to keep up. Funny thing was, he made it look almost graceful.

"I bet all the girls say you're a wonderful dancer," I said.

"What? Uh, pardon me, could we stop for a minute?" He showed me his pretty teeth again.

"Thirty seconds," I said, and stopped. "After which I'm off to lunch."

"Thanks," Cayman said, and the smile melted into a concerned look. "I'm very sorry about Dave," he said. "He, well, let's face it, he forgets himself sometimes. He was a boxer, you see, and I think there was maybe some brain damage or something. I didn't see what started him up like that just now. I was on the phone or I'd have …" He shrugged and held up his hands. "What can I say? I'm sorry."

"Fifteen seconds," I said.

"Please," he said, "I'm asking, right? And look, I'm not grabbing you—"

Funny he should say that if he'd missed the beginning of my scuffle with Dave.

"—I'm not grabbing, right? I'm just saying that Judge Gortner would like to speak with you."

"Gortner?" I said. "Presumably he's related to the juvenile slimeball I rousted yesterday?"

Cayman winced and looked over his shoulder. He pulled

his lips back in a grimace and said carefully, "Judge Gortner is Jerry Gortner's grandfather, yes."

"If I go see the judge, will he curb the little bastard's violent impulses?"

Cayman winced again. "Please," he said, "don't talk about Jerry like that in front of Judge Gortner. It would be, ah, counterproductive. But, yes, I do think it's possible you might find the meeting could be, um, useful." The teeth appeared again, each one glinting hopefully.

"Think, possible, might, could be?" I said. "That must be a new record for ass-covering." I turned around and started back up the street toward my office. "Okay, I'll go. Two minutes."

I went up to the office, took off my blue sneakers, put on a pair of high western boots. It was a gimmick I'd learned from Cowboy. I didn't particularly like walking around in cowboy boots, but they could be very handy at times

I tucked my best blackjack down the left boot, found the little .25 imitation Beretta in my desk drawer, and slipped that into my right boot. It wasn't much gun, but it would do for very close work.

I located my smallest blackjack, a palm-sized leather and lead-shot slapper, and shoved that into my right hip pocket. As an afterthought I got the ball bearing from Thorney's house and took it too.

Then I went down to the street, got into the Continental, and we set off to meet the judge.

I wondered if he was any tougher than his rotten little grandson.

I bet myself he would be.

CHAPTER 18

"I think you and Judge Gortner will get along fine," Cayman said. He showed me his teeth again and fiddled with the knee of his trousers, preserving the crease.

Cayman and I were sitting—lounging, actually—on the backseat of the Continental. The boxer, Dave, drove. He was a helluva good driver. He never seemed to use the brakes or the accelerator, but the car always flowed into the gaps, almost before the gaps opened. We were invariably in the fastest-moving lane, and we caught more than our fair share of green lights.

I wished I could drive like that. Hilda sometimes claimed my driving resembled Arnold Schwarzenegger tenderizing meat. A patent untruth, obviously, but still ...

Dave slipped the Continental around a blue Dodge that had gone straight through three intersections with its right turn signal on.

"My congratulations," I said to the back of his head. "I like to see ugly, tough guys do things smoothly and precisely. It gives our public image a nice boost."

Dave said, "Hunh?"

I said he drove well; I didn't say he was literate.

Rod Cayman snagged a car telephone off the console and tapped away importantly. While he waited for someone to answer, he made sure I noticed what he was doing but pretended not to notice me noticing him. There must be a high workload involved in being that phony.

"It's Rod, Caroline," Cayman said into the phone. "We're on our way." Pause, nod. "Yes, he's with us. Bye." He put the phone back in its clip.

I said, "What kind of Judge is Gortner, anyway?" I had begun to wonder about a judge who would send a pair like Dave and Cayman after me. "What court?"

Cayman put on his PR face and said, "Judge Gortner isn't on the bench at the moment, actually. The honorific is used by his many associates as an indication of their respect and high regard." He smiled smugly.

Then I got it. "What you're trying to say, without saying it, is this: Thirty years ago, Gortner was a part-time city judge handing out traffic fines in Snake Navel, New Mexico. He just liked being called 'Judge' so much he's hung on to the title ever since."

There are more of those ersatz judges running around Texas than you'd think.

Rod Cayman sniffed and looked out at the traffic.

Up front Dave's shoulders bounced a couple of times.

"Don't pout, Rod old buddy-pal," I said. "Now I'll say something nice. You did a good job finding me so quickly. How did you do that, pray tell?"

Cayman exhaled through his nose and said, after a pause,

"We got your name from that senile old fool who claimed Jerry assaulted him."

"If you sicced the hulk here on to Thorney, you better be tired of having all those teeth, pretty boy."

Cayman shifted a few inches closer to the door on his side.

"Mr Thorneycroft gave me your name quite willingly, I assure you."

Dave turned his head ten degrees and wheezed over his shoulder, "'At's right. Besides which, I don't thump old men, no matta who's paying."

After that, the conversation seemed to pale. We rode the rest of the way in silence.

We went to Gortner's home, not an office building as I had expected. It was an older house, large, nicely kept, on a very large lot. It was near, but not quite in, the Turtle Creek area.

Dave stopped the Continental on an immaculately raked gravel drive. We all got out. Cayman led the way around the house, past several trees that might have been willows, across a large slate patio in the back of the house, in through a set of French doors and to an office close by. For the last part of the trip, we were joined by a regal blond woman in her thirties. Cayman called her Caroline and tried to be jolly. She ignored him. So far, of all the judge's employees, I liked Caroline the best.

Dave sat down in a cane chair outside the office; the rest of us went in.

"Judge Gortner, Mr Rafferty," Caroline said, then she left and closed the office door behind her.

"Well, well," Gortner said, bounding out from behind his desk. "This is, indeed, a pleasure, indeed it is." He wanted to shake hands and do all that ho, ho, ho, how-do-you-do business. We did, then he waved me into an armchair facing his desk.

Gortner had an honest-to-god, high-backed, black-leather judge's chair behind the elegantly polished teak desk, so there was no doubt where he'd sit. Rod Cayman quietly went to a small couch off to one side, took out a notebook, and looked attentive.

Judge Gortner was a big, bluff, and hearty man in his late fifties. He vaguely resembled John Connally, the Texas governor back in the 1960s who was wounded when John Kennedy was shot. Gortner had wavy gray hair, a faint tracery of broken veins on his small nose, and an open expression on his face that said: Trust me, I'd never lie to you.

Sure he wouldn't.

Judge Gortner leaned back in his expensive chair and frowned delicately. "I understand we have a small problem concerning my grandson Jerry. A schoolboy prank, I believe."

"This is not a small problem. Jerry and his friends attacked the man's house. They did a fair amount of damage to the house and they injured the man. They could have killed him."

Cayman piped up with, "Absolutely ridiculous. A few pebbles, a broken window, and a senile octogenarian who hates young people. Furthermore, there is nothing to prove young Jerry was even—"

"Judge," I said, "I came here to talk to the organ grinder. What say we get rid of the monkey?"

Gortner pursed his lips, then nodded. "We won't take up any of your time, Rod. Thank you so much."

Cayman slapped his notebook shut and left. His jaw was set tightly. Prediction: Whoever was below Cayman in the local pecking order was due for a bad afternoon.

Judge Gortner put his elbows on his desk and said, "You know, Mr Rafferty, Rod may have a point. It's not hard to see how an elderly gentleman might, well, become overly excited in the face of, shall we say, youthful exuberance."

"No, let's not say 'youthful exuberance.' I accept that the boys were not trying to kill the old man. But it was only blind luck that they didn't. Also, there's a background of harassment and vandalism here. Some of that might have been 'youthful exuberance,' but not this incident. This was an attack."

Judge Gortner nodded soothingly and said, "Let's just go over the facts of the matter, Mr Rafferty. First, you've accused Jerry and other, unnamed, youths of harassment. Have you eyewitnesses, photographs, statements, anything at all, to support that claim?"

"No."

"Have you any evidence to support your contention that my grandson damaged this man, uh, Thorneycroft's house or injured his person?"

"I have his slingshot."

"You mean you have *a* slingshot. *Someone's* slingshot. But, Jerry's? I don't know about that." He shook his head slowly. "Do you have any purchase documentation? Photographic or taped evidence? An *independent* eyewitness?"

"No."

"I see. And isn't this the same old man who recently fired

a high-powered rifle, endangering his neighbors and passersby?"

"I have the sudden feeling Jerry Gortner was already gone when the cops showed up that night. I'm willing to bet his name is not on the police report."

Gortner smiled contentedly and spread his hands wide. "Now, I ask you, considering all the evidence, why would anyone believe Jerry was involved in yesterday's incident? I should say, yesterday's *alleged* incident."

"Personally I find it significant that you had me picked up and brought here. The DA might, too."

"Mr Rafferty, are you here? Why, I believe my appointment book and diary, not to mention my staff, would confirm that I'm alone right this minute. Working on a speech, I believe."

"All right," I said. "I get the picture. You've decided the kid is going to get away with it."

"Be practical," Gortner said. "And, after all, what are we talking about? As Rod said, a few pebbles and a broken window."

That made me mad. "I'm having a helluva time making you understand that we are *not* talking about a few pebbles and an inner-tube slingshot. Those kids had hunting sling-shots—weapons, effectively—and these things." I stood up and dug the ball bearing out of my pocket. "They leave big dents in things like houses and heads."

Gortner had a polished stone paperweight on his desk. I picked it up and weighed it in my hand. Almost two pounds. Probably heavy enough. Judge Gortner looked suddenly apprehensive.

"Relax," I said. I put the ball bearing down on Gortner's

desk. It began to slowly roll away across all that beautiful teak. The bearing didn't get very far, though, because I whacked it with the stone paperweight. That made a dent in the desktop that held the shiny metal ball while I hit it twice more, a bit harder each time.

"Look at this," I said, and lifted the bearing out of the dent. "When this bearing came out of your grandson's high-tech slingshot, it left a bigger dent than that."

I put the bearing back in the depression in the desktop and bashed it again. The stone paperweight broke that time. I used the biggest fragment, hammered the bearing, checked the depth of the dent and hit the bearing again. That time the paperweight fragment broke.

"Well, hell, I'm out of paperweight, but that's almost the right size dent."

The office door banged open. Dave, Cayman, and Caroline rushed in. There was a certain amount of *oh, my goodness* and *what's going on* and *are you all right, Judge* chatter. Most of the dialogue came from Cayman and Caroline. Dave just looked like he wanted to fight again.

Gortner waved at the three of them. "I'm fine," he said. "Mr Rafferty was, er, conducting a demonstration, that's all." While he talked to them, he looked at the dent in his desktop.

I handed Gortner the ball bearing. He took it carefully, with his thumb and forefinger, and fitted it into the dent. Then he took it out and looked at it again. Finally, he looked up at me. "Are you sure about this?"

"Look at my face," I said. "Would a man with a face like this lie?"

Gortner frowned. "I didn't realize this," he said. "I wasn't fully informed."

I couldn't tell whether he was acting or not. Some of those professional Texans are pretty good.

"Well, for god's sake, get that kid slowed down, will you? Before somebody gets badly hurt."

He nodded, still examining the ball bearing, then said, "Thank you. Rest assured I will deal with the matter. Dave, take Mr Rafferty to wherever he wishes to go. Now, shoo, all of you. I want to think about this."

———

I sat up front with Dave while he drove me back. A few blocks from my office, Dave said, "How 'bout someday we get togedda down at the gym, huh? Mix it uppa couple a rounds, whaddaya say?"

"I don't fight for fun, Dave."

"Aw, c'mon. Be a sport."

"Forget it," I said. "It wouldn't work. If we fought your way, with rounds and rules and all that, you'd wipe up the floor with me. If we fought my way, we'd either put each other in the hospital or I'd forget myself and shoot you."

Dave oozed the Continental to the curb in front of my building as smoothly as a cat sliding on wet glass. "Well, okay," he said. "Damn shame, though. Not many guys worth fightin', ya know?"

"Yeah. Well, thanks anyway, Dave." I got out of the car and it slid away into the passing traffic.

Then I realized I still hadn't had lunch, so I set off in another attempt to walk to the barbecue place.

That time, it worked.

CHAPTER 19

"If I fired every brush jockey because some tight-assed housewife claimed he stared at her boobs, I'd be out there cleaning pools all by my lonesome," Larry Davis said. He slapped the armrest of his wheelchair and slipped briefly into his black stallion routine. "Honky rednecks done love to see that, wouldn't they? A crippled spade they could roll into the pool for grins."

Friday afternoon, late. I was back at Aqua-Tidy, in Larry Davis's kitchen. I'd originally come out to run down an Ortega angle, but once there, I'd settled in like a lost house pet. It was the most pleasant time I'd had since I left my house that morning. And why go home now? Hilda had a business dinner scheduled, the freeways would be clogged with rush-hour traffic, and Larry seemed happy enough with the company. So he should. After all, I was being a thoughtful guest. We were drinking my beer.

I'd decided on Budweiser for my next beer of the week, partly because I liked the label. I know that's a stupid reason to select a beer, but there you go. Advertising legends have been built on flimsier foundations.

"Seriously," I said. "Luis Ortega moved into your rental room upstairs because he was kicked out by his girlfriend, Maria. A friend of hers saw Luis getting it on with one of your clients."

Larry Davis frowned and opened another Bud. He didn't seem too worried about body mass today. He said, "On *LA Law* don't they call that hearsay evidence?"

"Shut up with the legal crap. I'm expounding a theory here. Now, the point is this: Luis thought he was a cocksman. Remember the underwear trophies in his closet? So maybe he came on to the wrong woman one day. No, wait a minute, make that the right woman married to the wrong guy. Because this guy, when he found out, didn't do the normal things. He didn't yell at the wife or say 'Hey, now I can screw around, too,' or find a marriage counselor or get drunk and punch out Luis's lights. Instead he got mad. He got bad mad. He hung back and followed Luis and learned where he could find him. Finally, when he was ready—presumably when he had set up a good alibi elsewhere—he came around, conned me right out of my socks, and whammo! Bye-bye, Luis."

"Whew," Larry said. "You sure do work at it, don't you?"

"And I'm not finished yet. Sub-point A. The fake bounty hunter who actually made the hit might not be the husband. He could have been a hired hand."

"Am I wrong or would that complicate things even more?" Larry asked.

I sighed and drank beer. "Damned if I know. In some ways, maybe it would. But in others … Look, how many guys could—not would, but could—find a hired killer? Hopefully, a guy like that would stand out. He'd be connected, he'd have a record, things like that." I said all that with much more confidence than I felt.

Larry said, "Maybe so, but then he'd be harder to crack. A person like that wouldn't exactly collapse in remorse and tell all, would he?"

"I'm trying not to think about that part," I said.

"Keep trying. So what do you want from me?"

"A list of the people whose pools Luis cleaned in the past, oh, say, two months?"

Larry nodded. "No problem. At least, it's not a problem for me. Might be for you, though. There's gonna be a hundred or so names on that list."

"Individual calls, maybe. But won't a lot of them be repeats?"

"Not as many as you'd think. Betcha it's over eighty names," he said.

"Eighty?"

"Luis was part-time, like you said. He didn't have a regular service run; he just did whatever was on the board when he came in."

"Wonderful." I got us each another beer.

"The accountant comes Monday," Larry said, "So we'll be into the books, anyway. You need the list any sooner than that?"

"I wish I did, but no, that's fine," I said. "There's no shortage of loose ends I still have to run down. I want to check the girlfriend's family, a possible gambling angle, stuff like that."

"Must be jest excitin' as all get-out being a honky private

in-vestigator." He took a long pull at his beer and said solemnly, "You get to thump uppity niggers much?"

"It varies from week to week," I said. "Right now I'm working on a local government case. Some black dude running a business out of his house. But, hell, I don't think he's a real honest-to-god black. Probably got a name like Muhadje el-Khumquad. I think he's a Libyan terrorist."

Larry shook his head sadly. "Hey, man, don't even say that kind of thing out loud. Those clowns from the council hear that, they'll believe it."

CHAPTER 20

Saturday morning Hilda and I went for a drive. We took her car because the BMW's radio worked. We were planning to make a full day of it. Drive, talk, brunch with the beautiful people, and maybe later go out to White Rock Lake for the dinghy races.

But first I wanted to check on Thorney.

"Five minutes, that's all, babe," I said to Hilda.

"Uh-huh," she said.

Thorney hadn't seen the vandals since Thursday, when we had rousted the Gortner and Wisermann boys. He told me in a distracted way, mostly because he was staring at Hilda, who looked terrific as usual.

"Hey, I'm over here," I said to Thorney. "Gawk at me while you tell me about your call from Gortner's goons."

"Sorry," he said, and slicked down his hair with a big hand. "Well, yesterday morning, this young fellow came to the door. Smiled all the time and said he worked for that Gortner boy's grandfather. I didn't trust him for one minute. He reminded me of an old Australian saying, what was it, oh, right, 'flash as a rat with a gold tooth.'" Thorney nodded happily. "I haven't thought of that for years, but it sure fits that fellow. He was a rat with a gold tooth, all right."

That had to be Rod Cayman.

"Was there another man with him?" I said. "Big guy, a boxer?"

Thorney shrugged. "There was someone in the car, out at the curb. He never got out. Anyway, the rat fellow carried on about me signing something and getting fifty dollars for my trouble."

Hilda bristled. "You didn't …?"

Thorney laughed, a big booming roar that filled the old house.

"Never," he said. "I told him to get off my property. He got kind of smart-alecky then, and he said who's going to make me, and I said me and Rafferty. He said who's Rafferty and I told him. Why?"

I explained about Rod Cayman and Dave and Judge Gortner and how I hoped I'd done some good but halfway doubted it.

Thorney grinned widely. "Well, now, sonny-boy, you said when those kids knew you were hanging around, they might stop. Didn't figure they'd go running for their poppa, huh?" He laughed again, another rolling boomer that became infectious.

While Hilda strolled around Thorney's living room, looking at mementos, Thorney pulled me aside. "What's the story here?" he asked. "You two are married, but she still uses her old name?"

"We're not married."

Thorney frowned and pursed his lips. I think he disapproved. Hilda turned then and asked him about an old medal in a glass frame. Within ten seconds Thorney was grinning foolishly, basking in the sun of Hilda's presence.

Most of us did.

Before long Hilda and I had been there for an hour. My "five minute" stop had turned into a combined nostalgia trip and navigation lesson. Any chance of brunch in yuppie heaven grew slimmer by the second. Hilda was a great sport about it.

Thorney got out his sextant and went over the parts and adjustments again. I remembered most of them. Then he led us out to the backyard, found a sunny spot, and handed me the sextant. "There's nothing mysterious about this," he said. "You measure the angle between the horizon and the sun, stars, moon, whatever, then look up the numbers in the books."

Dallas backyards being notoriously short of sea horizons, Thorney poured oil into a flat pan. He said the oil, being liquid and shiny, would make a "flat to the world" mirror. I could use the sun's reflection in the oil exactly like a sea horizon, as long as I divided the sextant angle by two and— well, Thorney understood how it worked.

He saved my right eye by reminding me to use the sextant filters, then waited patiently while I fumbled through a long series of wobbly sights.

Back inside he averaged the sights into one potentially workable one, looked up this and added that, and finally drew a position line on a printed form he called a "plotting sheet."

"Now what?" Hilda asked. "Don't you have to put that on a map?"

"Chart," Thorney and I said simultaneously.

"Picky, picky," Hilda said.

Thorney said, "Not really. I can mark where we are on the plotting sheet."

He did. The X he drew was quite a way from my position line. "Well, it'll come," he said. "Sixty-five miles off isn't bad for the first try."

Hell with him. I thought it was wonderful.

"Hil, babe, isn't that amazing? Finding where you are, where you're going, with only—"

Hilda looked wary. "Are you working up to one of those male honor-code things?"

"Not exactly," I said. "But now that you mention it, if you consider—"

Hilda pointed to a group of wavy printed lines in the corner of the plotting sheet. "What's this funny-looking thing?" she said oh-so-brightly. Hilda could deliver the fastest non sequiturs in the west. She sometimes called the process "hiding Rafferty's soapbox."

At twelve-thirty, we made a big platter of grilled cheese sandwiches and ate them while going through Thorney's memorabilia. Memorabilia, hell, the man was a walking museum. Periodically he'd drag out another batch of treasures.

Thorney had been everywhere and done everything. He was an oil-company rep in Mexico during the revolution in the late twenties. He had geological reports, and photos of swarthy men with bandito mustaches and huge sombreros, and a moldy old serape that made Hilda sneeze until he put it away.

He had joined the merchant marine in the thirties and

later sailed on World War II convoys to England and Murmansk. After the war, he and five others bought a boat and sailed it from California to Australia, then went into the desert to mine opals.

For me, those nautical bits and pieces were the most intriguing. Thorney's large dining-room table slowly disappeared under a pile of old charts, yellowed plotting sheets, and shippy gadgets like parallel rules and curved brass dividers. There was a shoebox of old boat photos, too. Thorney pulled out a handful and showed them to Hilda and me.

"That's her," he said. "The *Rosinante*. Forty-four feet overall. Built in Boston in 1911."

It was the ship I'd seen in the picture on Thorney's living-room wall. "Gaff ketch," I said for Hilda's benefit.

"Gesundheit," she said.

"You'll have to make allowances," I said to Thorney. "She doesn't speak boat."

At the bottom of a mildewed briefcase, Thorney found a letter-sized envelope with a penciled date on it. He opened it and grinned.

"Well, I'll be ... I thought I'd lost this." There was a navigation form in the envelope. Thorney smoothed it out on the tabletop.

The printed form had room to calculate the two different sextant sights needed to determine a ship's position. Both parts of the form had been filled out. The writing was readable but not very neat. A few figures had been Xed out, there were scribbled notes in the margins, and there was a coffee-cup stain in the upper right corner. Across the top in broad, smeary pencil strokes, someone had written BOUNTY?

Thorney sat with one hand on the old paper and looked past me at something or nothing. "We sailed from Long Beach, like I told you, down to the Galapagos Islands, then through the Marquesas and Tuamotus to Tahiti. From there we headed west, toward Australia. One day, a couple of months later, I took these star sights at dusk, worked them up, and plotted our position, just like every other night. Then I crawled into my bunk."

He unfolded one corner of the form that had been bent over and carefully smoothed it, pressing it slowly against the tabletop with his big right hand. "I couldn't get to sleep, though, because something was bothering me. Then bingo! it hit me. We were abeam Tonga that night—that's about halfway between Tahiti and Australia—and almost exactly where the *Bounty* crew mutinied."

I said, "Damn. Captain Bligh and Fletcher Christian? Seriously?"

Thorney nodded. "I was almost certain at the time that it was the place. I kept this and checked the history books later." He held up the form. "We passed right over the spot an hour after I took these sights." He grinned a little sheepishly. "I spent most of that night on deck, thinking about it."

"I'm sorry," Hilda said. "I think I saw the movie, but I don't ..."

Thorney and I looked at each other. He waved at me to go ahead. "Hollywood made Bligh into a monster, Hil. Most people don't realize what a great sailor he really was." I had to stop and think for a moment. Thorney nodded encouragement.

"Okay, I remember now. They kicked Bligh off the ship. Some of the crew chose to go with him, though. Fifteen or twenty, I'm not sure exactly. They had some food and water, though not much. And they stopped somewhere, but ... help, Thorney."

"They went ashore for water," Thorney said. "On one of the small islands near Tonga. Natives attacked them and killed one man, so Bligh ordered the lifeboat back to sea. You go on now," he said to me. "You're doing fine."

"Okay. So there they were. It was an open boat; they were short on food, and this was, oh, 1790 or thereabouts. Club Med hadn't discovered the South Pacific market then. The natives were, as they say, restless. There was no safe place to stop so they didn't. They sailed that overgrown rowboat more than three thousand miles—"

"Four thousand miles," Thorney said. "To Timor in New Guinea."

"And they all made it. That's right, isn't it? There were no further casualties?"

"That's right."

I said to Hilda, "That was probably the most significant small boat voyage in the last three hundred years. And Thorney sailed over the very spot where it began. Imagine the feeling of being there, the link with the past. I'm jealous as hell."

Thorney smiled. "It was good."

"Some guys have all the fun," I said. "Would you consider adopting me?"

CHAPTER 21

Sunday morning. Early. Early early, in fact, when there's only the smallest gray hint in the sky to tell you another day will be along soon now, if you can just hang on for a little while longer.

I read somewhere that if hospital patients made it to this point they were likely to make it through the whole day; the lonely dark hours were the dying time.

Perhaps the rising sun cheered the hell out of hospital patients but it didn't do much for me. I sighed and rolled over for the seven hundredth time.

Hilda squirmed beside me and moved a smooth, sleep-heated arm across my chest. She pushed her forehead against my shoulder. Her forehead was hot, too.

"Sorry, babe," I said. "Go back to sleep."

I dozed off, too, off and on, mostly off.

An hour later, it was still early, but bright outside. I was on my back, counting the little diamond patterns in Hilda's bedroom drapes when she woke up.

"Um, good morning, big guy," she said, and grinned

cheerfully. Just like that. Boom. Asleep, then awake. Amazing.

"Hi, babe."

Hilda scratched her black mop of hair, then stretched lazily. "You didn't sleep very well, did you?"

"No problem."

"Uh huh. What kept you awake? Cats fighting? The bed too hot?" She lurched up onto one elbow and leaned over to rub her nose against mine. "Or deep, dark, heavy thoughts?"

I sighed and grinned. Well, I sort of grinned. "Dark, heavy thoughts, I guess. I think I'm having a midlife crisis. Bet you didn't know I spoke yuppie."

"Well, first of all," Hilda said, "I don't go along with this 'midlife' business. Let's see now, for at least a quarter of my life so far, I was a little kid. Then there was a long spell as a teenager. Part of that was good, but part of it—yuck! Anyway, that's half or more of my life to date gone right there. I figure what counts now is my *adult* life. I may already have some of that behind me, but I'll tell you what; I'm just getting warmed up good."

She smiled and playfully screwed a fingernail an inch deep into my side. "And, my fierce and scowling true love, so are you."

"Well, sure," I said, "but what if you run out of time to do all the things you want to do? And don't forget, babe, everyone slows down eventually."

Hilda nodded seriously. "Even Thorney."

"That's right. Of course, he hasn't slowed down very damned much for a man his age, but still … Besides, he already got to—oomph!"

That time she used her fist instead of a fingernail, and she gave me a good shot in the ribs. "Rafferty, you're jealous! Of Thorney!" She shook her head, her eyes wide. "I can't believe this. You, the guy who … Rafferty, don't you understand—I mean *really* understand—that you've already done things other people would give their …" Hilda smiled at me the way mothers smile at children planning careers as space rangers. "I love you," she said.

Then she sat up and put her hand lightly on my chest. "You're only feeling what everyone feels eventually, especially men. Rafferty, the truth is that you're never going to sail off on a grand adventure to an idyllic South Sea island. You have to face that." She smiled again. "It's called growing up."

"I've heard about that," I said, "but I'm not quite ready for it."

"I know, dear, and I'm glad. I think."

———

Later on that morning, we sat at Hilda's breakfast counter drinking coffee, eating doughnuts, and idly watching *Sunday Today* on the little kitchen TV set.

"There," I said, pointing. "Did you see that? She crinkled again."

"Missed it," Hilda said. "Damn."

"You'd see it if you hadn't bet me she didn't do it. I tell you Maria Shriver crinkles her nose just before the commercials." I reached out and poured us both more coffee. "She does have a dynamite jawline, though. Gotta give her that."

"Maybe she's a preppie," Hilda said. "A preppie might crinkle her nose."

"Naw," I said. "Preppies have names like Buffy or Muffin. Who ever heard of a preppie named Maria?"

"Who, indeed? Hey, big guy, are you working today?"

"I don't think so. I'm kind of stuck, to tell you the truth."

"Maybe that has something to do with your case of the megrims." Hilda took another doughnut and pushed the plate toward me.

"Thanks." I took another doughnut, too, even though four is usually my limit. "Well, maybe not stuck, exactly. I have a long list of Luis Ortega's last customers to check out." I explained the jealous husband/horny housewife theory. "Somehow, I don't think Sunday is the best day to knock on doors and say, 'Hey, lady, have you screwed any good pool cleaners lately?'"

Hilda nodded solemnly. "Phone McNair-Anderson first thing tomorrow. I'm certain they'd appreciate your sensitive insights."

"I'm ignoring that. Anyway, Thorney's problem is on hold now. All I can do is wait to see which way Judge Gortner jumps."

"Surely he'll talk to that boy," Hilda said.

"I figure he'll either pull the kid's chain or start a campaign to canonize Saint Jerry." I shrugged. "Who knows?"

On the TV screen, Maria Shriver crinkled her nose. Hilda pretended she'd missed it again.

———

We went for the drive we'd missed the day before and had a late lunch at an outdoor restaurant Hilda had heard about. The food was okay. At least they didn't give you two asparagus spears, a radish, and a splash of sauce on a huge plate, call it Salade de Whatever, and charge like a wounded bull.

There was a travel agency across the street from the restaurant. They had a gigantic Club Med Moorea poster in the window. Hilda saw me looking at the sea, sand, and palm trees. "Would you like to change places?" she said. "From this chair you could ogle a reasonably attractive blonde at the corner table. She doesn't have Maria Shriver's jawline, of course, but ..."

"No thanks, babe, I'll tough it out here."

"Be strong."

Wouldn't you know it, we were caught leaving the restaurant by a couple Hilda knew. They invited us to a cocktail party later that afternoon.

"Nothing fancy. Come as you are, darlings," the woman cooed.

"Marvy," I said, but they all pretended I hadn't.

Hilda had just sold the party givers eight thousand bucks worth of Victorian batwing bird feeder—or some goddamn thing—so we put on our customer-relations heads and trotted off to sip and soiree with the beautiful people.

I was very restrained and decorous. Even Hilda said so later. But this one guy got all excited when we were introduced. He was a sales consultant, he said, but he seemed to think he was Conan the Barbarian. He worked out, and lived on the latest body-building wonder diet. He told me the names of all the stuff he ate and the pills he took and how much he could bench-press and how his lats and pecs had improved and ... It was boring as hell.

Then he wanted to know how often I had to fight and run

and shoot and all that, and it went on until he talked himself into a challenge.

He wanted to arm-wrestle, for Christ's sake.

Our hostess went pale. Hilda got a trifle tight around the eyes, too. Maybe they thought I lacked couth. I can't imagine why.

I manfully declined to arm-wrestle.

Conan called me chicken.

I declined again.

Conan bet me a hundred dollars.

I took him outside and we arm-wrestled across the hood of Hilda's BMW. His breath smelled like mint. I beat him five times straight and put his hundred bucks in my pocket.

Funny thing was, it didn't improve my mood all that much.

CHAPTER 22

Monday, I got up early and really hit it. The Mustang and I were only a rust-colored blur as we rocketed around Dallas. Busy, busy, busy.

I found—eventually—a west Dallas street guy I'd used as a snitch in the past. I wanted his help with the Ortega gambling angle. But Diego didn't think any action Luis could have tapped was big enough to warrant a hit if he welshed.

"Hey, Rafferty, you playing with yourself, man. No way. Black eye, sure. Busted leg, maybe. A little cutting, possible. But shotgunned by an Anglo? No fokking way, man."

"Does this mean you don't want to earn the fifty bucks by checking it out, Diego?"

He grinned. "I didn't say that, did I? I get back to you, man. Count on it."

He diddly-bopped away, singing out Hispanic rap-style greetings to people he knew or pretended to know.

Diego was the most indiscreet snitch I'd ever seen. Yet again I wondered how he stayed alive on the street. Unless that snitch persona was a con and everyone knew it but me.

Naw, couldn't be. He'd been right about the truck driver in that insurance case last year. On the other hand ...

Hell with it; Diego would find what he'd find and I'd believe it or I wouldn't. Why worry now? I climbed back into the Mustang.

The engine didn't want to start at first. When it finally fired up, it made that hissing noise again. Uh-oh. I pulled out into the traffic, anyway. Some days, simply being in motion was as good as it got.

———

I went downtown to the cop shop to talk to Ed Durkee and Ricco. Ed was on a day off; Ricco was in the coffee room, eating a jelly doughnut and carefully not spilling coffee on his garish sport jacket.

"Hey, Rafferty," he said. "What's up?"

"I need a favor."

Ricco nodded sagely. "This don't surprise me," he said. "When do you not need a favor?" Ricco's affected speech pattern went with his clothes. I bet he had a "© Damon Runyon" tattoo somewhere.

"Come, come," I said. "Think of the warm inner glow you feel in your heart from fulfilling your chosen role as a dedicated civil servant."

"What the fuck are you yapping about now?"

"Well, scratch 'civil,'" I said. "You wanna swap tidbits of information or not? There might be a clue hanging around loose."

Ricco took another bite of doughnut and shrugged. "Maybe. What you got?"

"The Ortega thing. I found Luis's common-law wife."

Ricco shrugged again. "Big deal. So did we."

"Congratulations. Here comes the tricky part. They had a, oh, call it a strained relationship. In fact, call it 'Frankie & Johnny' with a mariachi sound. Luis 'done her wrong.' And there is a platonic boyfriend who's very annoyed about that. Well, not a boyfriend, really, more like a would-be protector."

Ricco's eyes narrowed. "You think the boyfriend had something to do with Ortega?"

"Not really. For one thing, he is not the shit-kicking bounty hunter who faked me out. And I'm pretty sure he's only what he appears to be, but ... How about you let your fingers do a little walking through the records?"

"What am I, your personal goddamn records clerk? Maybe I ought to just go roust this stud myself."

"Calm down. That's why I haven't told you who he is yet." I explained to Ricco about John From Next Door's protective attitude, how Maria Hermosa might need him, and my opinion that John was probably cleaner than Mr Sheen. I left out the part about Maria Hermosa being pregnant. Ricco wasn't the kind of person you'd tell that to.

"Okay," Ricco said around a final slurp of coffee. "I'll play your silly game. If Records don't have a package on this guy, I'll leave him be. What's his name?"

"And while you're at it, how about Maria's family? Have you found any hot-blooded brothers; maybe a father or uncle with a violent temper?"

Ricco shook his head. "Already been down that road, Rafferty. There ain't no one out there doing a family revenge number for the Hermosa ginch. The story is that she, Mama, and Papa came up from Mexico two years ago. Just the three of them. Legal and all, too, which has to be an unnatural act for greasers."

A uniformed cop came into the room and shoved coins into one of the soft-drink machines. He gave Ricco a pointedly neutral look and ignored me.

"Where's Maria's father now?" I said.

Ricco said, "Yeah, well, the Hermosas haven't exactly prospered here in the home of the free and the Anglo. Last year Papa—uh, Papa's not real smart, you see—Papa buys this bottle supposed to be gen-u-ine Scotch. He gets it from one of his greaser buddies, right? Party time! Only it ain't real Scotch; it's rubbing alcohol and iodine and, I don't know, goddamn sheep dip, maybe. The stuff almost turned Papa's lights out. As it happens, he ain't dead, but he also ain't quite alive enough to know that."

"Okay, then—"

"Hang on," Ricco said. "Next thing you know, Mama Hermosa's busy lighting candles in the cathedral, when blooey! Stroke city. So now, Mama *and* Papa Hermosa got their brains turned to salsa. They're both stretched out somewhere soft, doing vegetable imitations on my tax money."

The uniformed cop stared at the back of Ricco's head for long moment, then carefully took his cold drink out of the machine and left. He took slow, deliberate steps and held his back very straight.

I said to Ricco, "Your warmth and sensitivity never fails to amaze me."

"Yeah. Anyway, forget the Hermosa broads relatives and revenge. What's the boyfriend's name?"

Whoops. "Oh, ah, I can't remember offhand," I said. "I'll give you a call."

"What are you trying to pull? Was this all a con?" Ricco curled his lip.

It was too embarrassing to tell him I really didn't know John's last name. I just got up and walked out.

With dignity, though. With great dignity.

———

Claude Cannerly was a tall, skeletal man in his fifties who knew every person in Dallas who (a) was a politician, (b) wanted to be a politician, (c) knew any politicians, or (d) could spell the word *politician*.

Okay, so I'm exaggerating. But not much.

"You met Judge Gortner, eh?" Claude rumbled. He had a low, soft voice surprisingly deep for his pigeon chest. "Business or pleasure? And whose business or pleasure was it, yours, or his?"

We were standing on a street corner near the county courthouse. Ambience-wise, I found the setting disappointing.

"Claude, isn't political gossip properly done in smoke-filled taverns? You know, the back booth, furtive looks, and talking behind your hand. Where's your sense of tradition?"

He looked surprised. "You read too many books, Rafferty. Besides, out here, people see me talking to you. They'll want to know who you are. It gives me something to trade." A bus went by; Claude coughed, then said, "What about Judge?" He said "Judge" like it was a first name, not a title.

"Oh, it was business, sort of, and both of ours, in a way. He's not a real judge, is he?"

Claude shook his head quickly. "Of course not. He's a lawyer, though. Some of those would-be judges can't even say that."

"Hooray for Gortner. Is he honest, Claude?"

Claude laughed. "How long is a piece of string? Why? Did he promise you something?"

"No," I said, "but he might. I want to know what it's worth if he does."

"Good point." He frowned for a few moments, then said, "Judge Gortner's as honest as anyone in his line of work. More important, he's old Texas, so if he looks you in the eye and shakes your hand, he'll probably do what he says."

"What exactly is his line of work."

A short, fat man strode purposefully along the sidewalk. Claude flapped one hand at him in greeting, then said, "Judge is a fixer, a professional go-between. He calls himself a consultant, but mostly he makes phone calls—Judge knows everybody in three states—and he introduces people."

"Big deal," I said.

Claude nodded. "Bigger than you think. Look, suppose you want to build something or do something. Maybe it's a project so new that no one knows what to expect; maybe it's so different that folks are nervous about it. The thing of it is, if your project is touchy in any way, you need Judge Gortner. Pretty soon, he's out there talking to people, patting backs, squeezing elbows, explaining to the right people how the common folks just downright *need* whatever it is you've got. Judge calls that tenderizing the market.

"And he'll set up meetings and business lunches for you,

meetings with the people who can help you. Judge will tell you who should get what subcontract and which charity needs a donation and whose wife wants an invitation to what. Eventually, you'll most likely get whatever it is you want. Oh, you'll have to give a little, maybe set aside some park land or whatever, but there's an up side, too. If there's any state or federal money out there—grants, special loans, tax relief, whatever—Judge'll find it for you." Claude waved his arms expressively. "Politics, that's all. And Gortner's a politician."

A car horn bipped softly; Claude grinned and waved at a gray Mercedes going past.

I said, "My dealing with Gortner is on a more personal family level. I'm more interested in him as a man."

"Understood," Claude said. "You can trust Judge, I'd say. Not Tom, though. Watch out for him."

When I looked blank, Claude said, "Tom Gortner. Judge's son."

"This is turning into a family saga. I've only met Judge and his grandson Jerry. Tell me about the missing link."

Claude licked his lips and leaned forward. "Tom is Judge's only son. Spoiled rotten as a kid and he never outgrew it. Terrible Tommy, they used to call him. He barely got out of high school—that was back when they still had passing and failing—and then he flunked or partied himself out of three or four colleges. I swear, Rafferty, it almost broke Judge's heart when Tom came home from Austin with his tail between his legs. Since then, why, nothing much has changed. Oh, maybe Tom's not putting his tit in the wringer quite so often these days, but he's not completely over the habit. When he does, Judge bails him out."

"What does Tom do?"

"Judge has him appointed to this and that," Claude said. "Tom would be in his late thirties now, I guess. He's presentable enough, got this boyish kind of face and he smiles real pretty. So Judge doesn't have much trouble boosting him onto quango boards and getting him committee seats. I think he's on some ag department board at the moment. Something about land use, or—hell, it doesn't matter. Tom will make money at it."

"How? Director's fees? Expenses?"

Claude sniffed. "The normal money, sure, but Tom sweetens up the take by selling his vote. To all comers, all at once." For Claude, that would be the ultimate sin. Imagine, a politician who wouldn't stay bought.

On the walk back down the street, Claude said good-bye and scurried into the courthouse; I went on. I got lucky for a change and beat a parking cop to the Mustang by half a block. And when I twisted the key, the engine started right up without making that noise.

Aha! Things were looking up.

———

I drove all the way out to Maria Hermosa's apartment building just to read John From Next Door's mailbox.

Barcola. His last name was Barcola. I phoned Ricco.

"That guy's name is John Barcola," I said. "I just remembered."

Ricco snarled but finally said he'd check it out and let me know.

Aqua-Tidy next, where Larry Davis was on his second

beer after a long session with his accountant. He gave me a list of the swimming pools Luis Ortega had cleaned in the two months before he went to that great chlorine plant in the sky. There were eighty-three names on the list. Whoopee.

Some of the names sounded vaguely familiar, but then again some of the names were pretty common. There were three Joneses, several Smiths, and a pair of Browns, for Christ's sake. The addresses were all over the place. Whoopee again.

Fought the rush-hour traffic home. Like a dummy, I took the freeway where I zoomed along at speeds approaching thirty miles an hour. Well, occasionally I zoomed. More often I was stopped dead. Finally pulled into Hilda's driveway at six-forty-five. As I reached for the ignition, the Mustang made that noise again.

Damn!

CHAPTER 23

The first shot skittered off the pebbled walk and howled away somewhere. The second bullet made a baseball-size crater in the forehead of a mannequin wearing the baggiest shorts I'd ever seen.

By then Thorney and I were down behind a long stone planter box, trying to find a position where the human body was less than two inches high.

It didn't seem a particularly pleasant way to spend a Tuesday morning.

An hour earlier, I'd gone to Thorney's house. Just to check on the old guy. There had been no further visits from vandals, he told me, and he was just going shopping, did I want to come along?

Why not? So we boogied off to go hang out at the mall. Like awesome, okay?

Now someone had turned the mall into a shooting gallery, in the old county-fair sense of the word. And what kind of crummy mall was this, anyway? How were we expected to hide behind such a puny little planter box?

In the odd way your mind works at such times, I realized that when I had reached out to push Thorney down, he had already begun to drop. He was pretty quick for his age.

Off to our right, voices came from other hiding places. A woman's voice shrilled up and down the scale wordlessly. A second voice, a man's, just went up. "No, no, no, no ..." he shouted. Another man yelled, "Call the police! Someone call the police!" That voice was steady and purposeful.

Hopefully, one of the clerks in the dozen nearby stores would have already thought of calling the cops, but you never know.

There was another dull boom and a sharp *skree* as a third slug ricocheted off the top of our planter screen. Thorney wriggled and twisted more tightly into the angle between the low wall and the walkway.

"You okay?" I said.

"Goddamn it," he said testily. "Somebody dropped an ice cream cone over here. I'm lying in it, that's all."

It's not hard to tell who has been shot at before and who hasn't.

"He's over that way I think," I said, pointing through the planter. "By the exit tunnel. Keep your head down, for god's sake."

I'd been shot at before, too, at various times. None of those occasions had been particularly good and this time was just about as bad as it got.

Unless it has happened to you, it is hard to realize how demoralizing it is to be unarmed, curled into a ball, and shot at by an unknown, unseen attacker. There is no focus, no one to fight, no *way* to fight back. All you can do is lie there and stay calm and be ready to take advantage of whatever happens next. Which is not easy.

I hate that feeling.

"What are you squirming around so much for?" Thorney said grumpily. "He can't shoot through all this brick and dirt."

"He wouldn't have to shoot through it," I said, "if he just came across that little courtyard and around the corner down there."

The screams and shouts went on in the background while Thorney digested that little tidbit. "I don't suppose you brought a gun with you," he said finally.

"You 'don't suppose' entirely correctly."

A woman shouted from one of the stores, "The police are on their way. Stay down, people. Just another few minutes."

The man yelling "no, no, no" switched to "thank you, thank you, thank you."

Thorney grunted, "No shots for a while. I wonder if he's gone."

"Well, don't stand up and look, Rambo."

He turned his craggy head just far enough to give me a dirty look.

Perhaps three minutes later, we heard the sirens. Then there were running feet and hoarse shouts. Soon a bullhorn-distorted voice told us everything was fine now, but we should stay put while the officers cleared the area.

Which meant the shooter had gotten away.

Thorney and I scooted up and sat leaning against the planter. The long muscle down my right shin twitched and jumped uncontrollably. I felt like running around the block or fighting someone or—it didn't matter much what I did;

anything to get rid of that nervous energy and the dull, brassy taste at the back of my throat.

Thorney felt it, too. He swallowed loudly and shuddered. He grinned a wobbly, lopsided grin and rubbed his left knee. "Getting kind of old for this falling-down stuff." Then he draped his wrists over his raised knees and stared at them. "I don't know how long it's been since anything like this happened to me," he said. "I'm out of practice."

"You don't get used to being shot at, Thorney."

"Hmmph! Only some nut," he said. "Or a holdup."

"Don't bet on that!" I said it more angrily than I intended. "He was after us."

"Naw," Thorney said.

"Think about it," I said. "There were only three shots, they were all aimed at us, and when the shooter got short on time, he cut and ran. That makes it a thinking man's attempt at a hit. Loonies shoot at random targets, and they almost always wait around until the cops come to kill them. It's like they're committing suicide, but they want company."

"Hmm," Thorney said. "You might be right."

"Trust me. He was shooting at us. What bugs me is I don't know which one of us was the target."

I found myself wondering what heavies were on the Gortner payroll besides Dave, the boxing chauffeur. I had hoped my demonstration with the ball bearing had impressed Judge Gortner enough to quell the teenage terrorism problem. Had he only upped the ante instead?

No, that was crazy. No one would escalate a problem from teenagers breaking windows to shooting up a shopping mall. Come on!

So say the shooter was after me. The phony bounty

hunter was still out there; maybe I was getting closer to him than I thought. But why try for me now? A shopping mall was a lousy place for a hit; it was crowded with witnesses, it had limited escape routes for the shooter and reasonable cover for the victim.

And, dammit, he could have tried for me anytime, but this was the only place Thorney had been out in public since the vandalism problem blew up. Which seemed to validate the first premise: the shooter wanted Thorney, not me.

Come to think of it, it didn't have to be Judge Gortner who was after Thorney Maybe it was Judge's son, Tom. Maybe he—

"Anyone hurt here?" The cop asking the question was a burly, redheaded guy. He glanced at us quickly, then swiveled his head back and forth to look up and down the mall. "It's all over now. You gentlemen can stand up."

We did. Thorney needed a hand up and he limped at first, favoring his sore knee.

There were eighteen or twenty of us who came out from behind walls and columns. No one had been hit. The cops chivied us into two lines and an officer went down each line, taking notes and asking everyone what they'd seen. Other cops went into stores to interview people there.

When the cop working our line got to Thorney and me, we told him what we'd seen: nothing. Then I left Thorney with strict orders to stay near the cops while I found out who was ramrodding the investigation.

His name was Jefferys. He was a stocky, balding, black lieutenant, and he was busy. My winning smile and PI license bought me only five minutes of his time.

The time limit was no problem; Jefferys didn't know

much. The shooter was a man who was either medium height or tall; he wore a track suit or a shirt and jeans or overalls colored dark gray, black, or blue. He had also worn a ski mask or a beret and a scarf or he had a big, bushy beard and sunglasses. He carried a shotgun, a rifle, a machine gun, or, incredibly, a samurai sword.

Jefferys sighed and said, "I mean, really, who needs eyewitnesses when all you get is this kind of shit."

"It was not a shotgun," I said. "And if it was an automatic weapon, he used it on single fire. Judging from the ricochets, I'd say a rifle, shooting a hot, fast load."

Jefferys riffled quickly through a notebook, found the page he wanted, and said, "Okay, well, thanks, but we already found two .270 shell casings." He turned to another page. "Oh, and there was a car double-parked by the entrance with the motor running. We think that's how he left."

"Do you have anything on the car?"

Jefferys put the notebook away and said grimly, "Just think of it as a rainbow made by General Motors or Ford or Chrysler but maybe it was a Jap import, okay?"

"Gotcha," I said. "Thanks."

He had already turned away to talk to a uniformed officer. I went back to where I'd parked Thorney.

He was standing near two patrolmen, eavesdropping on their conversation with a woman who kept saying she had been "almost killed."

She was a trim-looking, excitable brunette who had been trying on a tennis outfit in a sports store. One of the ricochets had apparently gone through the front window, traveled the length of the store, and finally punched through both walls of the changing room. The woman swore up and down she had felt the breeze when the bullet went past her "um, derriere" just after she put on the "darlingest little tennis dress ever."

She was still wearing the short frilly dress. Like the two young cops, Thorney gave close attention to the site of her almost-wound. She repeated her story two more times; Thorney bent way over and carefully eyed her backside each time.

Finally I said, "Come on, you horny old goat. Let's go get a drink."

He gave me a deadpan look. "Beth would raise hell if I was to have a drink after all this excitement. My heart, you know."

"Who's gonna drink it, you or Beth?"

He nodded and fell into step with me. "That's a good point," he said. "And after that, what?"

"After that, we run in a couple of shooters for our side, then I go find the bad guy. Just like in the movies."

Thorney nodded. "Fine. After you find him, I'll cut his balls off."

"You know, Thorney," I said, "I really am thinking about that adoption thing."

CHAPTER 24

Organizing protection for Thorney was easy. As soon as we arrived at my house, I phoned Cowboy and Mimi. But it was not easy to explain who the opposition was. Or who I thought they were. Or even who they might be.

The only players I could identify were a smarmy pretty boy, a punchy boxer, two gawky teenagers, and a silver-haired, kindly grandfather. I told Cowboy all that on the phone, which was not much fun, because I knew I sounded like a little kid. *Hey, there are monsters in my bedroom closet, really and truly.*

"We could jest shoot anybody we happen to see," Cowboy said. "That make you feel any better?"

I said, "You know how complicated these things get at times. Just think of this as one of those times."

"Hell's bells, Rafferty." He pronounced it *hay-ell's bay-ells.* For some reason his drawl was thicker on the telephone. "It's jest that if we knowed who the bad guys are, then we wouldn't have to hole up nowhere. We could go kick ass instead."

"Can't be helped, Cowboy. And I don't know how long this might take, either. Are you and Mimi available for, oh, say, up to a week?"

"Shore. Mimi's sister is here, but that ain't no problem. She's catchin' a plane back to Louisville this afternoon, anyway. Airport's kind of on the way to your place, so it'll all work out fine."

"Good. Which sister? Marie?"

"Naw, this is Mimi's kid sister, Myra. Don't think you've met her. She looks like Mimi, but she's taller."

"Oh." I could have guessed that much; *everybody* was taller than Mimi. "My place later, then. Oh, and the target is an old man named Thorneycroft. You'll like him."

"That don't matter," Cowboy said. "If you want him to stay alive, he stays alive whether we like him or not."

How's that for guaranteeing your work?

Thorney and I roamed around my house, not doing anything in particular, getting in each other's way while we didn't do it. At that time I was renting a small cottage on Palm Lane, out by the Dr Pepper plant. There wasn't much room in the little house, certainly not room enough for two large men with time to kill.

While I was busy doing nothing, I found a note I'd written to myself the night before. It was a list of Ortega case things to do. I had to find out if Diego had earned his fifty bucks and I had to work through the customer list and I had to see what Ricco had learned about John "from next door" Barcola and—

"Hmmph," Thorney snorted. "Of all the ..."

He had turned on the TV in the middle of a newscast. They were running a Middle East film story. A group of men in civilian clothes cavorted around a dusty street, celebrating something by firing AK-47s into the air. They were firing long, long bursts, twenty rounds or more. It was definitely amateur night at the war; they must have burned out a dozen gun barrels while we watched.

I said, "You suppose there are any birds left in that part of the world?"

Thorney harrumphed again.

I sighed and shoved the Ortega case list into my pocket. "Now, then, Mr Warmth," I said, "let's talk about what we're going to do with you."

"Do with me? What am I, some shirttail boy? You damn well don't have to 'do' anything with me."

"Thorney, stop and think, will you? Until I can find out what the hell is going on, you're better off out of circulation."

"You don't know he was shooting at me in the first place," Thorney said. "Suppose I spend two weeks hiding in some cellar, then we find out he was after you all along? Or that it had nothing to do with either of us, like I said before."

"You are becoming petulant and a pain in the ass," I said. "Cowboy and Mimi will be here soon, then I can go to work. I think we'll put you into a motel."

Thorney shook his head and sighed dramatically. That was probably meant to tell me I was overreacting. He didn't refuse to cooperate, though, which seemed to be Thorney's version of a ringing endorsement.

I dug an old sports bag out of the bottom of the hall closet and filled it with various things that went bang. Thorney spotted the little Ithaca pump with the short barrel. Well, shortened barrel. Okay, sawed-off barrel.

"Aren't those things illegal?" he said.

"Yep. Loud, too."

After a while Thorney fell asleep in his chair. I watched television. Daytime television to boot. Well, the idea was to kill time. Why not bore it to death?

About three o'clock I saw Mimi come up the walk. There was no sign of Cowboy.

Thorney was awake at the moment, and it wouldn't hurt him to meet Cowboy and Mimi in their, um, natural element. I hauled my gun bag into my lap and became very busy with it.

The doorbell rang.

"Hey, get that, will you, Thorney?"

"Haw." He smirked. He hauled himself out of the chair and walked stiffly toward the door. "First you want to wrap me up in cotton, then you're sending me out into the street, practically."

"Just answer the door, will you?"

"Keep your shirt on," he said, and swung open the door.

Mimi stood on the step with her western hat held in front of her. She wore jeans and boots and a fringed western-style jacket.

"And what can I do for you, young lady?" Thorney asked. He was suddenly courtly and avuncular.

It was a natural mistake to feel macho and parental around Mimi. She's only four and a fraction feet tall, after all, and she has this round, cheerful face and big, big eyes. She looks so damned innocent.

"Afternoon, sir," Mimi said. "Could you kindly direct me to—" Then she saw me and nodded cautiously.

"Come on in," I said. "Everything's okay."

"Oh, good," she said, and stepped inside. She put her hat on the coffee table. The 9mm Beretta she'd been concealing behind the hat went into a holster on her right hip.

Thorney stared at her.

Mimi trotted over to my chair and pushed her cheek out to be kissed. "Hey, you growly old tomcat," she said. "Where you been? Haven't seen you for months!"

"Hi, Mimi. Cowboy jumped the back fence, did he?"

Mimi nodded and opened her jacket. She had an Uzi slung under her right arm. She unclipped the sling and laid the Uzi on the table beside her hat. "We didn't know for sure what was going on, so …"

Thorney shuffled backward until my easy chair caught him behind the legs. He sat down. He didn't say a word. It was an interesting change.

I went to the kitchen and opened the back door. Cowboy slipped through the opening and smiled lazily.

"How do, boss-man. Mimi in already?"

"Yeah. Come on through. You want a beer, coffee, anything?"

Cowboy shook his head. He carried a riot shotgun, the police/military version with a pistol grip but no stock. That was all I could see, but I was fairly sure that was not his only weapon.

In the living room I introduced Cowboy and Mimi to Thorney. They both "how do"-ed politely; Thorney pointed at Cowboy. "Hang on," he said. "I've seen him before. In an old movie, maybe."

"James Coburn in *The Magnificent Seven*," I said.

"That's it!" Thorney said.

Cowboy sighed. He hates that.

Mimi giggled and scratched her forearms where the throwing knife sheaths chafed her skin.

CHAPTER 25

With the pleasantries over we went to work. Cowboy and Mimi had arrived in two pickups, which made us a three-vehicle convoy to Thorney's house.

After we'd opened and checked through the house, Cowboy and Mimi each pulled back to cover a different end of the street. I stayed with Thorney.

He'd gotten a little testy as the day wore on; he tried to give me a hard time. But he finally packed a bag, and we locked up the house. He kept forgetting which doors he'd already locked and I think we shut off the water main three different times, but what the hell, it was a pretty tough time for the old goat. He was entitled.

We left then, with no sign of the opposition. We didn't pick up anyone on the way either—with three cars, it was easy to be sure.

By four-thirty that Tuesday afternoon, we had Thorney tucked into an upstairs room at a Harry Hines Boulevard motel. I'd never been there, but Cowboy recommended the place for hiding out. We took two connecting rooms where a pair of longish corridors met at a right angle. From the door of either room, you could see anyone approaching while they were still twenty yards away.

"We've looked at a whole bunch of these places, Cowboy said, "and I reckon this one's got the best killin' zones in town."

We let Thorney pick which room he wanted; the other became the guard barracks, command bunker, whatever. Cowboy and I reminded each other to park well away from the motel. I went over the ground rules with Thorney; stay away from the windows, no room service, and live out of a suitcase.

"If we have to evacuate," I told him, "there won't be much time."

Cowboy tossed two bags into a closet. "Damn straight! I ain't waitin' for no toothbrush packin'."

Mimi assembled shotguns and stacked them in corners with a box of shells beside each one. Then she laid her Uzi on the bed and looked around the room with her hands on her hips. "Not bad," she said. "Nice and homey."

I didn't feel all that homey. It had already been a long day and it would be longer. I was suffering from Hilda-deprivation. I went to Thorney's room and dialed Gardner's Antiques.

She was out. Damn. I didn't leave a number.

I phoned Beth Woodland next; I didn't want her to think Thorney was missing and drag the cops into this. Beth was good about it, even when I wouldn't tell her the name of the motel. I also toned down the shooting and deleted Cowboy's comment about the five-star killing zones. Then I gave Thorney the phone and went into the other room.

Cowboy was coming back from a trip to his pickup. He lugged a large canvas bag that clanked solidly when he put it down. He took an industrial-size electric drill out of the bag and fitted a masonry bit into the chuck.

Mimi had already marked Xs on the wall on each side of the room's main door; Cowboy began to drill holes there, leaning hard against the drill as the bit squawked its way into the concrete blocks.

When he had finished drilling, Mimi took one of those rechargeable vacuum cleaners out of the tool bag. She used it to suck up the concrete dust and chips.

Cowboy banged masonry anchors into the holes and bolted two heavy metal brackets to the wall, one on each side of the door. When he had grunted the bolts down tight, he went to the tool bag and removed a solid steel bar about three feet long. He held the bar horizontally across the closed door and lowered the ends into the brackets. The bar made an impressive clunk as it settled into place. Nothing short of a tank was coming through that door.

I said, "Now, there's a man who hates room service."

Cowboy dusted his hands and thumbed his big hat back on his head. "Well, now, Rafferty," he said, "I never did like this siege shit, but if we're gonna do her, by God let's do her right."

"Don't drill in the other room yet. Thorney's on the phone."

Cowboy grinned. "I did that room a couple of months ago. We was babysittin' a nervous bookie; that's when we found this place. All I got to do is dig the putty out of the holes and bolt the whatnots on."

"You ought to peddle this mobile Maginot Line gadget, Cowboy. The bookie could give a personal endorsement."

Cowboy took the masonry bit out of the drill and wound the power cord around the handle. "Wal, it sure did keep him cosy and safe for that week. Then he decided it was safe to go back on the street." Cowboy shook his head and *tsk*ed, *tsk*ed.

"And?"

Cowboy put the drill in the bag and looked around to see if he'd forgotten anything. "Oh, a couple days after he paid us off, they blowed up his car."

"Was he in the car at the time?"

Cowboy looked at me quizzically. "Well, of course, he was in the car! Otherwise, they wouldn't have blowed it up now, would they?"

Silly me.

After Thorney finished talking to Beth Woodland, Cowboy fitted another gizmo to that door. I made a phone call.

"Judge Gortner's office," a pleasant voice said.

"Well, hello there, you sweet thang. Put me through to Judge, darlin'."

I don't care what you say, when you're imitating a down-home, friends-and-neighbors, southern politician, you cannot be too hokey.

"I'll see if he's in, sir," the voice countered quickly. It might have been Gortner's secretary, Caroline. "May I tell him who's calling?"

"Why, shore you kin, sugar," I said. "This's Daniel J. Fendermann, way over here in Waycross, Georgia." I chuckled with what I thought was a conspiratorial air. "Fact is, that's Mayor Fendermann, tell you the honest-to-God truth. Now then darlin', Ah need to speak with Judge about a … well Ah suppose you could call it a delicate political matter."

Across the room, Mimi rolled her eyes.

The phone was briefly silent. *Oh, damn, she knows who the mayor of Waycross really is.*

Then she said, "Certainly, Mr Mayor. One moment for Judge Gortner."

I hung up then and turned to Cowboy. "He's there and he's where we start. Shall we let Mimi watch the store while you and I go do that little thing?"

Cowboy test-fitted the security bar and nodded. "Shore nuff. My, we are coming up in the world. Gonna go thump a judge."

"This is only a fake judge, and he may not even be the bad guy. Still, it's a place to start."

"Suits me," Cowboy said. "Hell, maybe this job won't be as borin' as I thought."

CHAPTER 26

"Goddamn muffler sounds like a zillion horse farts all at once," Cowboy grumbled. "Whyn't you ever get this car fixed up decent."

We were in my Mustang on the way to Judge Gortner's house. I said, "Well, I've been seriously considering seat covers."

"'Bout time," Cowboy said. "It looks pretty tacky with this duct tape all over the place." He lifted his fancy riot gun out of his lap and carefully put it on the backseat.

"You've missed the point. Duct tape is surprisingly cool on a hot summer day. Very refreshing."

"Oh, I'll bet," Cowboy said. "All the new models gonna have duct tape as standard equipment next year, huh?" He pried an enormous Ruger revolver out of a shoulder holster under his jacket. He flopped the cylinder out and checked the loads.

I said, "You know, I have a shotgun with a shorter barrel than that howitzer."

Cowboy sniffed. He pushed the Super Blackhawk's

muzzle somewhere down by his left hip, then levered the massive hand cannon back into the shoulder harness. The process resembled a man shoplifting a step ladder.

"So, boss-man," he said, "what do you want done with this Gortner dude's hard men? Are we talking shoot or stomp or mollycoddle?"

"There probably won't *be* any hard men, Cowboy."

"Sounds like mollycoddle to me," he said. "Doggone."

"What can I tell you? I only know of four people at the house where we're going. There's Gortner; he's a talker, not a doer. There's a blond woman, tallish, handsome. She's the office manager or appointments secretary, whatever. There's a guy named Cayman. He's too pretty to be anything but a talker."

Cowboy retrieved his shotgun from the backseat and held it vertically between his knees. "Where you takin' me, Rafferty? Spring trainin' camp for wimps?"

"Well, Dave's no wimp. He's an ex-pug. A little slow, maybe, but he's built like a leather sack full of rocks. Don't try to box with him. Now, I don't see him either carrying a gun or going up against one, but I could be wrong." I shrugged. "Oh, Gortner's wife may or may not be there. I don't know."

Cowboy said, "'Course, depending on this and that, the mall shooter might be in there. Or a couple dozen heavies."

"Or an armored division," I said. "With tactical nukes."

"Damn right," Cowboy said. He squirmed in his seat. "You know, I purely love this line of work."

We crunched onto Judge Gortner's pretty gravel drive a little after six o'clock. I drove all the way in and stopped opposite the front door, behind a pale green BMW four-door.

We got out of the Mustang—it didn't make the hissing sound. Was that an omen?—and went up three steps to a broad, columned porch. Cowboy held his riot shotgun loosely by the handgrip, letting it dangle and slap lightly against his leg. I'd left my shotgun at the motel and had only my old .45 tucked in the back of my belt. Classic understatement, that's my style.

We were still ten feet from the front door, barely halfway across the porch, when the door opened and Rod Cayman stepped out. He didn't see us at first, and when he did, he didn't recognize me.

Cayman tried a big smile and a booming greeting first. He had trotted out only fifteen or twenty teeth and three words when Cowboy flipped the shotgun up to point at his face and said, "You hush, now."

Cayman's voice stopped dead, his smile froze in a grimace, and his eyes slowly rolled back up into his head. He collapsed like a puppet with the strings cut.

Cowboy clucked his tongue and said, "My, my, my. Ain't he the fearsome one?"

"We'd better do something with him," I said. "If we don't, he'll wake up soon and go screaming down the street."

"Got my K-tel handcuffs," Cowboy said.

"Do it."

Cowboy had a dozen large plastic cable ties curled up inside the crown of his big hat. He tied Cayman's wrists and ankles together, then rolled him off the porch into the surrounding bushes.

The front door was still ajar, so we walked in.

"Whooee," Cowboy said. "Man, could you stack a bunch of hay in here!"

"Here" was a marble foyer two stories high. Arches to the right and left led to the rest of the ground floor. Straight ahead a wide staircase climbed and curved its way to a second-floor landing.

"If you'll keep an eye on things down here," Cowboy said, "I'll do the top floor." He started up the stairs, surprisingly quietly for a man wearing boots.

Cowboy had been gone three minutes, maybe four, when there were footsteps in a room beyond the left-hand archway. Dave the boxer appeared, carrying a dark gray suit on a clothes hanger. He saw me, stopped, and looked at the suit as if to decide whether he should drop it, throw it, or what.

By then I had the .45 out and it was all over.

You'd be surprised how often professional boxers make that mistake. They're waiting for a bell, I think, or for someone to yell, "Round One!"

"Dave." I said, "there's nothing personal in this, but I can't fight you now." I held out the .45, not quite pointing it at him. "There's only one way I can go today, so let's not mess around, okay?"

Dave nodded. "I gotcha," he said in his high, wheezy voice. "Listen, I don't get paid that much, hey? So, uh, tell me what I'm s'posed to do."

I told Dave to lie facedown on the foyer floor. He did. Soon Cowboy came downstairs and used his cable ties on Dave's arms and legs. Then he said to me, "I'm one up on you, boss-man. Want to make it twenty bucks a head?"

"Who was up there?"

"I don't know, some woman singin' and splashin' in the tub. I locked the bathroom door."

"Well, you're not one up on me, then. Locking a door doesn't count. And your first one fainted, for god's sake. Ten bucks a head, and we're even now."

"Oh, fair enough, I s'pose. Now what?"

"Hang on," I said to Dave, "Judge is still here, isn't he?"

"Yeah," he wheezed. "Inna office where you was before." He breathed in and out noisily.

"What about that blonde, uh, Caroline?"

"She … she left twenny, thuddy minutes ago." Dave's wheeze had become labored. I finally realized why. Face-down with his arms tied behind him, most of his weight was crushing down on his chest and stomach. I rolled him over onto his side.

"Oof, thanks," he said. He snuffled in a few dozen cubic yards of air. Dave was tough as old steak, but he sure was a dumb son of a bitch.

"Is there anyone else in the house?"

"Naw," Dave said. "Cayman left awready, too. Hey, you sure you didn't hurt Miz Gortner."

Cowboy answered him. "The bath lady? Hell, she don't know she's locked in yet."

"Well, okay then," Dave said.

Dave had told the truth. We didn't find anyone else when we checked the rest of the house.

"Show time," I said, and opened the door to Judge Gort-ner's office. He was lounging in his fancy judge's chair, holding a half-filled Scotch glass, and watching the evening news on a TV set built into a bookcase.

When Cowboy and I walked in, Judge jumped. A dollop of Scotch slopped onto his dignified tie.

Cowboy killed the TV set and flopped into a deep black leather armchair. He laid the shotgun across his knees and pulled his big hat down low on his forehead.

I sat down opposite Gortner and smiled at him.

He didn't smile back.

CHAPTER 27

Judge Gortner had good nerves. Except for that one jump when I had startled him by opening the door, he never wavered. For a long moment he looked at Cowboy, seemingly asleep in his armchair, then he turned to me with a bland expression on his face. Only the bunched muscle along his jaw showed he was less than totally relaxed.

Without taking his eyes off me, he slowly reached out to an intercom unit on his desk. He pressed a button and said, "Dave, would you come in here, please?" His voice was slow and even. He released the intercom button and leaned forward with his elbows on his desk blotter. He could have been a character portrait. *Waiting for Dave.*

After a very long three minutes I said to Gortner, "Well, how about that? I guess Dave must be tied up at the moment."

He blanched. "What have you done to Leonie?"

"If that's Leonie upstairs in the bathroom, she doesn't even know we're here."

He nodded slowly and glanced sideways at the telephone.

"No," I said.

He nodded again and eased himself deeper into his high-backed chair. He put his arms on the armrests, lowered his chin and scowled at me through his eyebrows. "Well?" he said. He really was very good at that.

"Who was the shooter you sent after Thorney?"

He frowned even more. "I don't know what you're talking about. What does that mean, a shooter?"

"Okay," I said. "Be difficult. You do remember Thorney, the old man your grandkid picks on?"

Gortner started to argue about "picks on," then he nodded. "Yes, all right, the old man. What about him?"

"Someone tried to shoot him today."

"Ridiculous! If you think I would ..." He clamped his mouth into a tight line and glared at me. High indignation. But was it real?

"Why shouldn't I think that?" I said. "Last week your trained gorilla tried to bounce me around on—"

"Whaatt?" That was out of character for Gortner; maybe we were getting somewhere. Maybe.

I told him about *Rocky 27*, the street-theater routine Dave and Cayman had gone through outside my office. I went through it quickly. I don't like situations like that, where I'm probably being conned, and while I'm telling them something they already know, they're using the time to think up the next lie.

And Hilda thinks I'm out here having fun.

Judge Gortner listened to the story of my sparring with Dave, then said, "And because Dave, er, exceeded his author-ity, that's why you have broken into my home tonight?"

"Of course. What do you expect? A knock on the door

and 'Beg pardon, Mr Judge, sir, did you hire the gentleman who tried to kill Thorney and me today? No? Okay, then, you have a nice day.'" I shrugged. "How was I supposed to know who you had stashed away in here?"

Gortner said, "I see. Well, I'm sorry about the incident with Dave."

I gave him a little while, then said, "Would you care to expand slightly on 'sorry about that'?"

He shook his head. "I can administer my own staff organization, thank you."

"Well, you'd better get hot, for Christ's sake!" Now I was angry, for several reasons. I had a niggling suspicion Gortner was telling the truth but I couldn't penetrate that slick facade to find out. And, of course, if he was telling the truth, if he or his family *hadn't* sent the shooter after Thorney, then I was in trouble. Because I didn't know where to go from here.

I said, "So you keep this pro head-knocker around, but if he—how did you put that?—if he 'exceeds his authority,' it's not your fault? Bullshit. Which makes me wonder who else you have in your little zoo. Have you noticed anyone running around here with a rifle and their fingers crossed?"

Gortner grimaced and wiped his mouth.

"Maybe that was only little Jerry, apple of your eye and all-round bad-ass grandkid. Did you buy him a rifle to replace the slingshot I took away?"

Gortner pursed his lips and blinked both his eyes at the same time, knotting his eyebrows and cheeks for an instant. It looked more like a nervous tic than a blink.

"I don't hear you talking to me, Judge."

There was an antique student's lamp on Gortner's desk. It had a swiveling glass shade and a brass frame. The lamp made a loud noise when I threw it against the far wall. Hilda would have cried if she'd seen that.

"Wasn't me," I said. "King's X. 'Sorry' makes it all right."

"Easy boss-man," Cowboy said from under his lowered hat. "No need for that. The man's gonna tell you now."

Gortner wiped his mouth again and nodded quickly, almost nervously. "Uh, yes," he said, "perhaps I should be, well, a trifle less secretive."

How can Cowboy tell when they're going to crack like that?

"Rod Cayman is the problem, I'm afraid," Gortner said to his desktop. "He's a very ambitious young man, but not, ah, entirely straightforward."

"He's out front in the bushes, by the way," I said. "In case you want to be groveled to, later on."

Cowboy snorted. "Candy-ass."

I wasn't sure whether he meant Cayman, Gortner, or me.

Gortner didn't seem to care where Cayman was. He went on in a sorrowful monotone. "Perhaps I'm getting old; I never used to have problems like this. Well, you're not interested in that. Ah, it seems my grandson, Jerry, realized he was in trouble after you and, uh, the old gentleman caught him and his friend. Jerry and his father don't, er, get along very well, so Jerry phoned me to ask for help. He thought he had been arrested or something and had escaped or … well, he's young and he was upset and confused. I calmed Jerry down and assured him everything would be all right. Then I asked Rod Cayman to find out what had happened, who was involved, and so on."

Gortner seemed to realize he still had a drink on his desk. He picked up the glass and took two quick gulps.

"Perhaps Rod thought I expected independent action; perhaps he misunderstood my instructions. I don't know. In any case, he reported back to me. I know now that was a very sanitized version of Jerry's misdeeds, but I didn't know that then. I understood you were acting as, uh, Mr Thorney-croft's agent and I thought that you might be, well, more logical and less emotionally involved than he. So I told Rod to set up an appointment for you. I assumed we'd be able to, um, work it out."

"Meaning you'd show me how well you had the kid's ass covered and I'd give up."

He shrugged. "It was … That's the way it's …"

"Uh-huh," I said. "Why did you send Dave after me?"

"I didn't!" Gortner said. "Not the way you mean, at any rate. Look, you have to understand about that. A few months ago, Rod brought me a proposal based on one of those reha-bilitation programs, a fresh start for ex-convicts or something."

"Well, well, well," I said.

"Oh it's not what you think," Gortner said. "Dave isn't a real criminal. There was an unsanctioned prizefight; Dave's opponent died in the ring. This was over in Mississippi, as I recall. Or Alabama. In any case, a zealous county attorney had Dave charged with manslaughter. He served only five months."

"Quoth the loyal Rodney."

"No, no," Gortner said. "I know that for a fact. I checked Dave out myself before I agreed to let him work here in my house."

"As what?"

"Oh, well, he drives, runs errands, a little bit of everything, really. Rod drafted a job description that calls him a personal protective consultant, but that's only Rod's way of—"

"Come on," I said. "What Dave really does is make Cayman feel like a big man when he rides around in your Lincoln."

Gortner sighed. "I'm beginning to think you're right. And I'm now finding out that Rod has, ah, manipulated Dave into aggressive acts that I do not condone."

"Why haven't you fired this geek, Cayman, then?"

Gortner looked grim. "There are, uh, other considerations to be weighed."

I laughed at him. From his expression, he didn't like it much. "Did too many cute deals, did you? And now you can't dump Cayman without making someone mad."

Gortner said, "I wish it was that simple."

"Hoo-boy," Cowboy murmured from under his hat. "Now we gettin' down to the nut-cuttin'."

"Cayman has something on you, then," I said. "Something messy."

Gortner looked even grimmer. "I assure you, this has absolutely nothing to do with your Mr Thorneycroft."

"Okay, then, tell me what you did—if anything—about Jerry after I showed you the ball bearing last week."

Gortner had been avoiding my eye, but now he raised his head and faced me squarely. "I had my son and my grandson in this office that same evening. I showed Tom what you showed me." Judge put the tip of his finger into the dent I'd pounded into his desktop. I don't think he even realized he was doing it. "And we both made it quite clear to Jerry that such behavior would not be tolerated in the future."

"Will that stick?"

"I'm sure it will. Down deep, my grandson is not a bad boy."

I'd have felt better if he'd said something like *he's a rotten little bastard, so we'll keep him locked in the attic from now on.*

"Let's hope you're right about that," I said. "My immediate problem, though, is this: If you didn't send a shooter after Thorney, who did?"

Gortner shook his head. "I assure you, I have no idea."

"Would your son feel protective enough about Jerry to have Thorney killed?"

I was only fishing for an unguarded response; you don't ask a man if his son is capable of murder and expect an objective answer. Strangely, though, Gortner seemed to consider the question seriously.

"No," he said finally. "I don't believe Tom feels strongly enough about *anything*, even his own son, to consider that sort of action." There was just a trace of wistfulness in his voice.

So where do you go from there?

I stood up. Despite appearing to be asleep, Cowboy beat me to my feet.

"Your wife is locked in a bathroom upstairs," I told Gortner. "It will frighten her less if you let her out."

Judge Gortner nodded and said, "Thank you."

We left. We were barely out the door, though, when Cowboy said, "Go ahead, boss-man. I'll catch up." He turned and went back into the office.

Dave was still sprawled on the cool marble floor of the foyer. He was motionless and his eyes were closed. For a moment I was afraid he'd suffocated, after all.

Then he woke up. "Hey," he said, blinking.

I cut him loose; he sat up and yawned. A faint sound drifted down the staircase. Dave looked up quickly. "Gortner is on the way," I said. "He wants to go up for her."

Dave nodded and I left him there, sitting on the floor, rubbing his wrists and ankles.

Outside, Rod Cayman was long awake. He'd squirmed out of the bushes and belly-wriggled thirty feet down the gravel driveway. When I freed his arms and legs and rolled him over, he had so much gravel in his pockets, he rattled.

Cayman could not or would not stand up; he sat with his legs outstretched and trembled. I had to drag him off the driveway to make room for the Mustang.

Which started on only the third try and chugged lustily until Cowboy appeared in the front door. He came striding across the deep porch, slapping his leg with the shotgun. Rod Cayman gave a tiny shriek and made a hurried hands-and-knees scramble back into the bushes.

"Would you believe," Cowboy said, jerking a thumb at the quivering bushes, "ole Judge is gonna pay me five thousand dollars—*five thousand*—just to run that wimp outta town? I got to git a certain photograph and legal document, too, but that ain't no hill for a high-stepper." He looked at me. "Which shows you how little ole Judge knows 'bout hiring people like us."

"I don't think I wanted to know that," I said. "I'm running out of leads." I drove down to the curb and pulled out into the street.

"Hell," Cowboy said, "when he offered to pay that much, I said I'd break the wimp's leg for free. He said no. Man's got your problem, Rafferty. He's just too sentimental."

"Couple of softies, that's us," I said.

Cowboy squirmed down in his seat, cradled his riot gun, and dropped his big hat over his face. A moment later, he said, "Don't know how you expect to ever amount to anything."

CHAPTER 28

Cowboy and I took a sackful of hamburgers, fries, onion rings, and beer—Rafferty's Cuisine à la Siege—back to the motel. By then it was well after eight o'clock. Thorney and Mimi were hungry and anxious to know what had happened.

First, though, I phoned Hilda's house. No answer. Damn. My answering service had no message from her, either. But Diego, my west Dallas snitch, had phoned twice. He'd call again. I told the service to tell Diego to name a time and place to meet. The girl on duty was new; she thought that sounded so exciting, "like Mike Hammer, you know."

Good grief.

While I was on the phone, they had all gone into the second room and spread out the food. Thorney sat at the motel desk; Cowboy and Mimi were on the bed, eating off their laps. I settled onto the floor with a beer and two hamburgers.

While we ate, I told Thorney and Mimi about our "heroic raid on Fort Gortner." Trying to lighten it up didn't help much. By the time I had finished, I was annoyed at how little we'd accomplished. That feeling, the detritus of greasy paper and cardboard boxes, and a rising tide of indigestion all seemed to fit together.

I wished I was somewhere else, holding Hilda's hand.

Thorney started to speak, stopped abruptly, and burped. "'Scuse me! Ate too fast." He thumped himself on the chest and winked at Mimi. "Didn't know you were workin for such a crude old man, did you, little lady?"

Mimi simpered at him; Thorney grinned like a fourteen-year-old. God!

But, good, too. As long as Mimi had him calmed down and smiling he was less likely to get mulish and do something silly.

But Thorney wasn't all that calmed down and smiling. He said to me, "You're saying you struck out, is that right?"

"Sort of," I said.

"Sort of, my a—uh, foot!" A sidelong glance at Mimi; he really was a courtly old bastard. "You *think* that Gortner fella hired whoever shot up the mall today. So you went off tonight and scared hell out of people and tied them up and I don't know what all. But you still don't know for certain one way or the other. I call that striking out. What do you call it?"

Cowboy whistled softly. "The man likes it with all the hide and hair still on, don't he?"

I said to Thorney, "All right, goddamn it, I call it striking out, too."

Thorney gave one of those old-man "damn right" nods and looked superior.

I said to Cowboy, "Without resorting to Chisholm Trail analogies, tell me what you thought of Gortner. Was he shining us on?"

Cowboy clucked his tongue thoughtfully. Finally he said, "I think he tole us the truth, mostly. And I don't reckon he set up the shooter, which is what you're really askin'. Howsomever, jest 'cause I think it, that don't make it so."

"That's about the way I read it, too," I said. "Goddamn it."

"Now don't get your dobber down, boss-man," Cowboy said. "If this sort of thang was easy to work out, there wouldn't be no need for folks like us."

"I can never remember," I said. "Was it Camus who said that, or Billy Graham?"

I tried Hilda's house again. Still no answer. I tried the answering service. Nothing from Hilda, but Diego had called again. *Meet me at eleven o 'clock where,* nervous giggle, *Large Tony got knifed in '85.*

Diego liked his little games. But I knew where he meant, and I was armed well enough to go there tonight.

Thorney complained. He wanted to go, too. Mimi distracted him with the announcement that her father still had his grandfather's army-issue Krag-Jorgenson rifle from 1900 or whenever. Thorney took the bait; they drifted into a conversation about cavity magazines and high bullet weight/low muzzle velocity ballistics.

I ducked out of the room and did a quick perimeter check of the motel grounds before walking two blocks to the parked Mustang. Then I left for my rendezvous with Diego. I told myself this diversion into the Ortega case was only temporary. First thing in the morning I'd be hot on the trail of the shopping-mall shooter.

Sure I would. Just as soon as I figured out where to start.

Diego's rendezvous site had deteriorated since I'd last seen it. The derelict hotel was still there, inhabited now by a gang of black and brown street kids who resented having the Mustang parked across the street. Maybe it was a crack house; maybe they just felt territorial. They came out to chase me away.

Not one of them could have been over fifteen, but at the same time they were ageless, like prowling carnivores in a dank and crumbling urban jungle. They had a frenzied nerviness that worried me.

They bopped around the car, catcalling and inventing elaborate raps I could barely understand. Two of them ran over the car. Literally. Up onto the hood, over the roof, and down the trunk. Another pair were lined up, too, but I held the shotgun up and cocked it. They went back to circling and rapping.

At ten to eleven, four more kids arrived, laughing and shouting. They carried jacks and mechanic's tools. Cheers from the assembled multitude.

They were going to strip the Mustang with me in it.

As they surrounded the car again, I realized that, once the Mustang was disabled, they wouldn't stop until they'd pulled me out. And then ...

When they heard the starter grinding, they howled and banged on the car. The engine started, I popped the clutch and got the hell out of there.

The kids jeered. A brick crunched into the trunk lid. I wondered if any of them were shaking, too, and decided they weren't. And that was the most unnerving part.

I got home, bone weary and twitchy, at eleven-thirty. There was a note from Hilda on my pillow.

10:45 pm

Hi, big guy!

Dropped by to share a pot of my finest pea soup and my tender alabaster body. The soup was marvelous. (Yours is in the fridge. Blue Tupperware thingo, second shelf, on the left.)

The bad news is, I have a bitch of a morning schedule. A terribly earnest porcelain maniac from Chicago arrives bright and early in the a.m. with an offer for the Devereaux collection. So, my missing loved one, I'm taking the body home now, still tender, still alabaster, still (sob) unshared.

Love,

Hilda

P.S. Eat your heart out, Ugly.

P.P.S. Please be careful doing whatever you're doing.

Aarrgh!!

CHAPTER 29

A telephone that rings at four a.m. rarely brings good news. The one beside my bed that dark and gloomy morning was no exception. I came out of a restless sleep thinking the caller might be Hilda.

No such luck; it was Diego.

"Hey, Rafferty, man, sorry 'bout dat meet. Dey was a buncha wild animals dere, man. Dem freaks, dey scare me, man. I cut out."

I let the phone fall onto the pillow and twisted my head around to fit it. "I cut out too, Diego. It was either that or kill some of them."

"You shoulda, man. Dose wild kids, dey—"

"Shut up, Diego. What do you want?"

"Hey, man, be cool, okay? Choo wanna meet someplace? I foun' out 'bout that Ortega cat."

"Go ahead," I said.

"Hey ... What 'bout my fifty, man?"

"One: I'm not going back into that goddamned jungle

tonight. Two: You don't get paid until I hear what you have, anyway. Three: I'm good for it."

"I doan know, man …"

"Four: Good-bye." I fumbled for the phone and pushed down the disconnect button.

Sometime later I woke up and realized I hadn't put the phone back on the hook. So I did. Then it rang.

"Whisper in my ear, Diego."

"Choo a hard man, Rafferty. Choo doan care nothin' about poor Diego, out here on da street, tryin' to—"

"Repeating item four, good—"

"Wait a minute, man! Okay. Ortega was strictly small-time. Thass why it took me so long. Man, nobody ever hearda this dude! But when choo got Diego el Zorro on de job, man, choo got de best!"

"Are you stoned? What's this Zorro business?"

"Hey, man, dat's my street name now. Diego el Zorro. Espanol, choo dig? Diego the fox. How 'bout dat?"

"Diego, will you, for Christ's sake—"

"Okay! This morning, yesterday morning, I doan know, Tuesday, anyway, I foun' dis man. He is a nephew of my father's fren, Cristobal, and he used to hang aroun' wit' Luis Ortega on the street, gambling and like that."

I stretched and rubbed my face. Needed a shave. "Tell me about the 'gambling and like that.'"

There was a second's pause; I could almost see Diego in a phone booth somewhere, shrugging eloquently. "What 'bout it? Dat's the whole point, man. Ortega din't bet hardly at all. Cristobal's nephew say he used to brag about bettin', but he lie, man, he lie like a rug. Oh, sure, Luis go to cockfights, but he only bet ten, twen'y dollars. Or fi' dollars on a pool game.

Rafferty, choo barkin' up the wrong tree, man. Nobody gets shot over a fi' dollar pool game."

"You're really making my day, Diego. Look, could this guy be covering for Luis? Or for somebody Luis welshed on?"

"De word on de street is, Cristobal's nephew and Luis was pretty tight, man. I think it's de truth."

"Shit," I said. I hadn't really expected the Ortega gambling angle to pan out, but even so …

Diego whistled appreciatively and called out something in Spanish. They called back, faintly. There were street noises in the background, too. Then his voice boomed again. "Hey, Rafferty, my fren, you oughta see the gorgeous *puta* workin' thees corner. She just did a t'ree minute car job, man. What a pro! T'ree minutes!"

"Don't stand too close. Some of those bugs can jump."

"Hey, I doan come 'round dere and insult your sister, do I?"

Don't ask me; he has a strange sense of humor some-times. I said, "I'll get your fifty to you," and hung up.

I set my alarm, then went back to sleep until the clock chirped in my ear. From Hilda's note, I assumed she was meeting that six-thirty flight. Minus driving time and dressing time that meant …

She answered on the second ring. Her voice was cautious. "Hello?"

"Best pea soup in all Christendom, I'd say."

"Rafferty! How are you?" She sounded bright and hugely alive, even at that hour of the morning. Suddenly Wednesday became a day worth living through.

I said, "Sorry about last night, babe. Yesterday was pretty screwed-up. I kept missing you on the telephone." I sat up and jammed the pillow behind my back. "I didn't think to phone here last night. What a dummy."

"That's all right," she said. "I missed you, though."

"I missed you, too. Tonight. And I'll tell you all about it."

"I don't think I like the sound of 'all about it,'" she said, "but tonight, yes."

"I'll call you later. Hey, I know you're meeting a plane, so—"

Hilda said softly, "You're going to think this is silly and feminine, but last night I missed simply having a meal with you almost as much as I missed the sex."

"Boy, if I ever said that, they'd kick me out of the Federated Thugs and Gumshoes Guild."

"Oh, really?"

"Sure. They'd probably burn my ceremonial blackjack, too, and put a notice in the newsletter: Rafferty's a sissy."

"Uh-huh," she said.

I said, "You do have a point, though."

"Relax, big guy," Hilda said. "Your secret is safe with me."

"But seriously, cookie, you are going to come across tonight, right?"

She laughed and hung up.

I slept well, after that, and didn't get up until about nine.

Midway through my second cup of coffee, Cowboy phoned. "Boss-man, how about you meet me across the street from Gortner's house? Somethin' going on out there I think you ought to see."

CHAPTER 30

There were two guards in front of Judge Gortner's house. They wore neat, pressed security-company uniforms. Each guard wore a police-style gun belt and carried a baton and personal radio. They looked fit and alert. Perhaps without realizing it, they stood in identical hand-on-hip postures as they stared across the street at Cowboy and me, leaning against his pickup. Not far from each guard, there was a long florist's box leaning against a tree.

Cowboy thumbed his hat an inch higher on his forehead. "Ten bucks says them boxes ain't roses," he said.

"No bet." I'd once carried a shotgun around for a week in a box exactly like that.

"They was setting up shop when I first got here," Cowboy said. "That was eight-thirty or thereabouts." He chuckled softly. "Come out here to see ole Judge 'bout that little chore he wanted done. But them two heroes there, they said as how Judge wasn't seeing nobody this morning."

The guards stared at us across the empty suburban street. Cowboy kept his voice low. "I watched for a little bit—there's a couple more of 'em inside—then I found me a phone booth. Old Judge, he didn't want to talk to me on the phone, either. That's when I called you."

"These guys are pretty good, you know," I said. "Amateurs would have already come over here and tried to shoo us away."

Cowboy nodded. "Yep. The curb's their perimeter, I'd say, and they ain't gonna be suckered outside of it. Ex-military, both of them, prob'ly." He slowly swiveled to face me. "'Course that don't mean we couldn't get past 'em."

"I know that. But we'd have to kill at least one of them to do it. That seems a bit drastic."

Cowboy shrugged.

"Time spent on reconnaissance is never wasted," I said. "Let's check out the back."

We drove around two corners, then counted houses from the corner until we found the one that backed onto Gortner's lot. I rummaged around in my wallet, found my Dallas Water Board Inspector business card, and tucked it into my shirt pocket.

I walked down the driveway toward the garage behind the house. No one challenged me. Two side windows were open, the back door could not be seen by any of the neighboring houses, and the garage was empty. And wide open. Burglars get all the breaks.

The backyard was large and well kept. There was a timber fence on the rear property line with a low mass of white-flowering bushes on this side and Judge Gortner's backyard on the other.

The ground rose very slightly from the fence to Gortner's patio. I could see the back door where Cayman, Dave, and I had entered. Six feet from the door, another rent-a-cop stood at parade rest, alert for the approach of marauding Visigoths. His shotgun lay on a wrought-iron table; there was no need for gimmicks like a florist's box in the privacy of the backyard.

Welcome to Fort Gortner. Now I knew how the Indians felt when the Seventh Cavalry wouldn't come out and fight.

As I went around to the front of the house, a maroon Buick station wagon pulled into the driveway. A woman in her late forties looked at me strangely as I walked past her car.

I waved to her, smiled, and shouted, "Water grumbles main inspect sog bog none okay now thanks—and have a nice day." I kept moving down the block; Cowboy picked me up around the corner.

"I've been thinkin' on it," Cowboy said. "I believe we could get in there without hurtin' no one."

"Uh-huh," I said.

We drove down Gortner's street again on the way out of the area. A van with HOME SECURITY ALARM SYSTEMS painted on the side was parked at the driveway entrance. A red-haired man stood beside the van and argued with one of the guards while the other guard talked on his belt radio.

"Well, now, I was gonna say we could steal us a limo, but if they gonna be that picky, we'd best forget the whole thing," Cowboy said.

"It doesn't matter," I said. "I wouldn't know what to do while we were in there. Not for the seventeen whole seconds it would take until the entire Dallas Police Department landed on our heads."

"Yup, there is that little problem."

"Got an idea," I said. "Find a phone booth."

We went to three phone booths, in fact, before finding one with a phone book. Luckily, Gortner is not a popular name in Dallas. There were only two listings: Gortner, L. V. , and Gortner, Thomas R. I wondered what L. V. stood for. Lyndon Victor? Leon Vauxhall? Leslie Vladimir? Maybe that was why he called himself Judge.

The address for Gortner, Thomas K, was near Thorney's house. We pulled up in front of it five minutes later.

It was a nice house, newer than Judge's place, and flashier, but the guards were the same—uniforms, florist's boxes, and grim stares.

"Wal, now," Cowboy said, "how 'bout that? Somebody's got 'em a big cookie cutter says Security Guard on it, and they jest stamp out however many they need."

"Hell with this," I said. "You'd better get back to keeping an eye on Thorney. The private army could mean Gortner's ready to go to war."

"It could do," Cowboy said.

"But it might only mean that we scared him last night, and he's realized how vulnerable he is."

"Yeah, it could mean that, too," Cowboy said.

"I don't suppose you'd care to venture an opinion?"

"Naw. You're the one does all that intellectual shit. When you work it out, lemme know who you want alive and who you want dead, okay?"

CHAPTER 31

Hilda said, "Dear, don't you understand how much you and Cowboy frighten normal people?"

"Now, there's a vote of confidence," I said. We were sitting on the couch in Hilda's living room. Most of the lights were off; a jazz record wailed gently in the background. We were holding hands and talking mostly, with occasional short breaks to neck and fool around a little. Just a couple of wild and crazy kids.

"No, seriously," she said. "Think about it from this man Gortner's viewpoint. You and Cowboy went storming into his house—no doubt with guns drawn—tied up his staff, imprisoned his wife, and gave him the third degree in his own study. That is what happened, isn't it?"

"Well, sort of ..." The inside of her left arm, three inches above the elbow, was amazingly soft and warm.

Hilda said, "After that, any normal person who could afford them would hire guards. I imagine it was terrifying for him. For all of them."

"It didn't bother Dave the boxer. He fell asleep."

"Well, he's a thug, too, isn't he?" Hilda said. She lightly dragged her fingernails down my forearm. "Which reminds me. If this Gortner man is a big Mafia Chieftain or something, shouldn't he have enough muscle men already? Why would he have to hire guards from an ordinary security company?"

"Yeah, I wondered about that, too."

Hilda said, "So there."

"The trouble is, babe, I can see Gortner doing almost the same thing if he *was* behind the mall shooting, once he'd realized Thorney had some firepower on his side, too."

"I still don't think so. Besides, you don't think anyone would shoot at Thorney because their grandson might get into a little trouble, do you? I don't."

"I know," I said. "It doesn't make sense. But it also doesn't make sense for this super slick political fixer to have a heavy like Dave working—"

"Which you said he explained," Hilda said.

"Well, he sort of explained that. The thing is, Hil, the whole Gortner clan is hunkering down. Father and son are both behind secure perimeters. Gortner won't even talk to me on the phone."

"Hah," Hilda said. "Under the same circumstances, neither would I."

"The son, Tom, has taken an immediate, indefinite leave of absence from that fancy committee or board or whatever it is."

"Says who?" Hilda stopped scratching my forearm and started on my leg. Nice.

"Claude Cannerly, my political snitch. And Jerry, the grandson with the slingshot, didn't go to school today.

Because—get this—he's transferring to some upmarket military academy out East."

"How in the world can you find out things like that?"

"I lie to people. You see, it didn't seem logical they would turn the house into a fort, then send the kid out to school. So this afternoon, I called and told the kid's mother I was the assistant principal and was Jerry sick or what? She said her husband had already phoned the school, why didn't I talk to my own staff, and she would advise where to send Jerry's transcripts when they had, quote, 'finalized their decision.' She probably gets that kind of watermelon talk from her husband and father-in-law."

"She told you all that on the phone?"

"Sure. It's crazy what people will tell you if you act dumb and let them lord it over you. Telephones are wonderful things." I moved my leg a little, so she could scratch it more easily.

"And you're sure Thorney is all right? This must be very hard on him, getting shot at, then being cooped up in a motel with Cowboy and Mimi."

"He's okay for now," I said, "but he's too stubborn to put up with it for very long."

"Try to spend some time with him, dear. He likes you."

"I like him," I said. "I'm doing the overnight shift tomorrow, so Cowboy and Mimi can have a break. Mostly, though, babe, I need to be on the street, finding the shooter, so Thorney can go home."

"I know, big guy." After a long, soft while, she said, "Did the shooting frighten him. "

"Thorney? No way. He's tough as an old boot."

"Yes," she said, and snuggled closer. "So what happens now?"

"I think now I reread my copy of *So You Want to Be a Private Detective* and look for ideas."

"No, silly, that's tomorrow. I mean, what happens right now?"

"Oh. Go home and hit the sack, I guess. I'm pretty tired."

"On the other hand," Hilda said, "you could rip off my clothes, push me down on the floor, and have your lustful way with me."

"Oh, well," I said, "I could probably stay awake that long, if you really—oomph!"

CHAPTER 32

The next morning, Thursday, I went straight to the cop shop and found Jefferys, the lieutenant running the mall shooting investigation.

Jefferys had assembled all the paperwork into a workable stack by then. It was a big stack. "But that means nothing," he said. "A guy spends all day shoveling out a stable, he ends up with a big stack, too."

There were interview reports from the eyewitnesses; fat lot of good they were. Eyewitnesses are notoriously inaccurate most of the time, but this batch was ridiculous.

And there were interview reports from the shop owners and workers and from those of us who had contributed only by falling down and staying alive. Those reports made an impressive pile, but when you boiled them down, they were no more useful than the eyewits.

There was very little physical evidence. Three cartridge casings and three slugs. Which was a start, Jefferys claimed.

"Ballistics says if I find the rifle, they can identify it by matching the ejector and firing-pin marks. But until then? Without the rifle? Hah!"

The getaway car had been found, huzzah, huzzah, and it was definitely the one that people had seen parked, idling, by the mall entrance. Absolutely, positively, by God. Bless his bureaucratic persistence, Jefferys had impounded the car and showed it to every eyewitness on his list.

"It's an '85 Honda Accord, ugh? Blue, kind of a sky blue," Jefferys explained wearily, "but did any of them, even one, say Honda in the first place? They did not. Did anybody say sky blue? They did not. And when I showed them the car, what did they say, every single goddamned one of them?"

I said, "What they said was, 'That's the car, officer. Just like I told you.'"

Jefferys squinted at me. "Were you ever a cop?"

"Long time ago. Nothing's changed. I suppose next you're going to tell me there weren't any useful prints on the car."

"Consider yourself told."

"Shit."

"Yeah." He rubbed his chin and said, "My kid's got this T-shirt. It says LIFE'S A BITCH, AND THEN YOU DIE. I get a case like this, I feel like the guy who painted that T-shirt."

"Whoops, there's more," I said.

"There's more," Jefferys said.

And life truly is a bitch sometimes; the Accord had been stolen from the mall parking lot.

"You wouldn't believe it," Jefferys said. "Dumb bitch left her car keys in the ignition 'because'"—he put on a gratingly high falsetto—"'I was only gone for a teensy-weensy little minute, officer.'"

"This *is* the same mall we're talking about."

Jefferys nodded rapidly. "Same mall, same parking lot. Okay, the Accord was parked down the other end, a hundred yards away, maybe, but even so ..."

"Where did he dump it?"

"Right back where he took it! Almost, anyway. I'm telling you, this guy had balls like ..." He made the sort of cupping gesture more often used to describe Dolly Parton's chest. "He must carry 'em around in a wheelbarrow." He shook his head and sighed. "Best I can figure, he lifted the Accord, drove it to the other end of the mall, went in, shot up the place, came out, drove *back* to where he'd started, parked the Accord, and walked away."

I said, "Or got into his own car."

"Well, sure, he got into his own car. 'Walked away,' that's a figure of speech. Nobody walks into or out of a shopping center. Not carrying a rifle, anyway. His car was probably parked close to where he left the Accord. That would have made it easier to transfer the rifle."

"Well, then, did anyone see—"

"Don't start!" Jefferys held up both palms. "I'm a pretty good cop, okay? So I thought about that, too. And I talked to a guy in the center management office who knows this kinda shit, and I asked him how many parking spaces there are in that lot. And he told me a big number. A big, big number. I wrote it down somewhere. Then he told me what their fancy computer says is how many different cars go in and out of any one parking space in a typical day. And that's also a pretty big number. I wrote it down, too. Now, if I understand all I know about probability theory, you multiply the big, big number by the pretty big number and then you have one chance out of *that* number of finding the right car. And, I promise you, Rafferty, *that* number is enormous. Ee—goddamn—normous." He looked at me brightly. "You want to know how many cars that is?"

"No, I don't want to know how many cars that is."

"I didn't think you would."

———

Next, I went to my office. Beth Woodland came over immediately. She was worried about Thorney, but she was very brave and very levelheaded about the whole screwy mess.

"I won't ask questions," she said solemnly. "Just promise me one thing. Promise me you won't let anything happen to Thorney."

"I promise, Beth."

She nodded twice and tried for a smile, which didn't come off. As she left my office, her back was stiff and her head was up and she walked in a very straight line, taking small, careful steps.

I picked up the phone and went to work.

Two hours later, I had struck out at proving Judge Gortner was the kind of guy who hired shooters. Apparently he was no more than he seemed to be: a slick political fixer who must have been shocked by how easily Cowboy and I had barged in on him. That's what the good guys told me; the bad guys never heard of him, which was the same song, different singer. I realized I was swearing a lot. Worse yet, I was repeating myself.

Around noon, I checked the office beer supply, then phoned a place in the next block that delivers sandwiches. Their food wasn't all that good, but not having to go after it was worth something. On a day like that, it was worth quite a bit.

Lunch came. Feet on the desk, beer, pastrami on rye, much thinking but no fresh ideas. Lunch went. I swore some more. It still didn't help.

I wadded up the sandwich papers and made a perfect foul shot into the wastebasket. As if to signal the score change, the phone rang.

It was Ricco. "Rafferty, you wanna know this stuff about the Hermosa broad's new boyfriend or not?"

It was the wrong case, but what the hell. "Make it good, Ricco. I need a win today."

"Tough. We got nothing on John Barcola. I even did a little scraping around, more than I said I would because—"

"Because you're so committed to truth, justice and the American way."

"Tell you the truth, I was bored. Anyway, he's a welder, I found out. Works the night shift at a pipe plant just across the river. Steady job, good credit rating, what can I say?"

That's the kind of day it was. Everybody was coming up as understudy to Mr Clean. What *can* you say?

By the middle of the afternoon, I had come around to thinking that what Hilda said—and what I had been wondering deep down since last Tuesday morning—might be right.

Maybe I was the target, not Thorney.

It made sense in a way. In the course of doing business I occasionally did things that angered the kind of people who had other people killed.

But it didn't make sense in another way. If someone was trying to whack me, why did they try on the only occasion I was out in the open with Thorney? Why then and at no other time?

Unlike Jefferys, I didn't know zip about probability theory but my hardware-store-giveaway calculator worked out that there were three hundred thirty-six hours in two weeks. More button punching told me the hour I'd spent in public with Thorney was less than one third of one percent of that time.

And *that's* when somebody tried to hit me?

Come on!

Suppose it was Wells, the fake bounty hunter?

Okay, suppose that. One: Why would he bother? I was only the stupid hick who let him get away after he killed Luis Ortega. He was clear and clean. There was no reason for him to want to take me out.

Two: Back to the one third of one percent argument. If it had nothing to do with Thorney—and Wells sure as hell had nothing to do with Thorney—why would he shoot at me when I was briefly with Thorney and *at no other time*?

Three: Even if I was wrong, if it was Wells, he would prove it by trying again. Until then Thorney had to stay tucked away.

It wasn't Wells. No way.

It probably wasn't anyone after *me*.

But.

But, for the moment, that was the only thing I had to work on. I picked up the phone again.

I spent all afternoon with that hard phone in my ear. It was a waste of time. I couldn't find anyone who wanted to put my lights out, or anyone who'd heard that somebody else wanted to put my lights out, or anyone who'd even heard a rumor that somebody wanted ... etcetera, etcetera.

Again, all the good guys said that and all the bad guys agreed with them. A couple of the bad guys—and one state cop—offered to punch me out, and Freddo Lombard had a unique suggestion about me hang-gliding down an elevator shaft. He was still miffed because I'd rained on his freight-theft parade.

But Freddo's all mouth, everybody knows that.

The point was, by the time I dragged myself out of the office, butt-weary and ear-sore, I was reasonably sure there was no organized effort to get me.

Which did not do one damned thing to help me work out what the hell was going on.

CHAPTER 33

"Why don't you marry her?" Thorney said.

It was my night to motel-sit with Thorney. We'd eaten Chinese food I'd brought, and watched the evening news. Now we were sitting around talking, like recruits sit around the barracks, shining shoes and talking about women. Wonderful. Thursday Night Dead.

I'd just explained to him about Hilda and me, about how we had different houses, but we lived at both of them. From time to time. Sort of. Depending.

"I don't know," Thorney said wistfully. "I don't understand how people think now. Used to be if a man and a woman were in love, they got married and raised kids. Simple. What's wrong with that?"

"Nothing."

"Well, marry her, dammit! Hilda's a fine lady. You should make an honest woman out of her."

"Thorney, it just doesn't work like that anymore. You know that."

"Oh, I know it," he said. "I know it."

I'd brought a bottle of Scotch, too, and we were each having a small sip now and again. The Scotch, on top of the uncertainty, and the boredom, was getting to Thorney a little.

"Nothing's the same today." He waved his glass and slopped some onto his pants. "I wish I'd bet somebody fifty years ago there'd be hom'sexuals marching in parades, women working and men home cooking, single women raising kids and some of them only kids themselves. I could have gotten damn fine odds on a bet like that." He screwed up his seamed, square face and looked puzzled. "Lot of changes."

"Were you ever married, Thorney?"

He poured himself another inch of Scotch and waved the bottle at me. I shook my head. "Never got married," Thorney said. "Came close a couple of times, though. Maybe I should have."

"Oh?"

His eyes lit up as he said, "Lucinda Bayless. Lucy. She had blond hair and big blue eyes; she looked a little like that Doris Day, except she didn't have freckles." He smiled. "But then I went to Mexico. And that was no place for a woman, not during the revolution. Later on we still might have, but I joined the merchant marine, and ... See, girls couldn't wait around in those days. They worried about being called old maids." Thorney sipped his Scotch. "We were loading teak in Rangoon the day Lucy married a fellow from Tulsa. Railroad man. He treated her all right, I guess." He took big bite of his Scotch this time. "Lucy died ten years ago last August. Still a pretty woman, even then."

"Sorry."

"Nothing for you to be sorry about," he grumped. "You asked; I told you. Don't make a goddamn meal out of it." He looked around the room and curled his lip. After three days in those two rooms I didn't blame him. "I'm tired," he said. "G'night."

"Night."

He trudged off into his room and went to bed. Five minutes later he was snoring. There was a nasty-sounding rasp and a gulp at the end of each inhalation. He hadn't seemed as spritely as usual, either. Maybe I should get a doctor in tomorrow unless he was better.

I got a book out of my bag—I was rereading *The Caine Mutiny*—and opened it. After I read the same page four times, I gave up and watched TV with the sound turned down low.

The next thing I realized, the room curtains were leaking sunlight and Cowboy was knocking on the door. My clothes felt like I'd worn them for a week, my neck hurt from falling asleep sitting up, and my mouth tasted like the entire Russian army had marched through it. Wearing sweatsocks.

CHAPTER 34

Thorney was still in bed as Cowboy and Mimi settled in and I, still barely awake, settled out.

I went home and let the shower pound on my head for twenty minutes. That helped my stiff neck some, and breakfast did its bit, too. I'd worked my way up from crummy to so-so by the time I phoned Hilda's house.

Missed her. Sharp slide back toward crummy.

With impeccable timing I set off for the office in the dying gasp of morning rush hour. It was a long trip downtown with a carbon-monoxide headache as a bonus. And when I walked from the parked Mustang, it hissed again. What next?

I trudged into my office and told myself to get busy, to flash into action, to accomplish something today. Myself gave me a funny look and said *oh, sure*.

In her office next door, Beth Woodland looked up and arched her eyebrows in question.

"Nothing new," I mouthed, and grabbed for my telephone. That was an easy move, almost instinctive. In my racket most moves start with, or involve, the telephone.

Then I noticed my finger was frozen over the buttons. It was pointing but not pushing. The finger seemed to belong to someone else.

And I realized with a sudden sick lump in my chest that I had no idea who to call next. Or what to do next. Or where to go next. I was stuck. Stopped deader'n a wedge, Cowboy would say. This was not a pleasant feeling.

I found myself still poised over the phone, and I forced whoever's finger that was to do *something*. It tapped out Hilda's office number.

"Babe, I'm having a little problem here."

"It sounds like it," she said. "Talk to me, big fella."

"I've run out of places to look for the bad guys, Hil. I owe money to every snitch in town and I still don't know anything. I'm hurting."

Her voice was slow and thoughtful. "Perhaps it can't be pushed like that. Rafferty. Could you simply wait and see what happens? After all, Thorney is safe, isn't he?"

"Safe enough, but he's getting moody, and I don't think he's very healthy. You should have heard him breathing last night."

"I'm sure he has a doctor you could call."

"Yeah, but it's not just Thorney. *I'm* getting buggy, babe. I am definitely not in what you might call 'wait' mode. I am more in your basic, 'beat the shit out of somebody' mode."

"I see," Hilda said. "Well, what can I do to help you?" She was already doing it, of course. We both knew that.

"You wouldn't have anybody over there I could thump on, would you?"

"Darn!" she said. "If only you'd called ten minutes earlier."

"Them's the breaks, I guess." I listened to her breathe for a few minutes, then said. "Thanks Hil."

"I love you, Rafferty."

"Bye, babe."

"Bye. Be careful?"

"You got it."

We hung up, and I left the office, not good yet, but better. Definitely better.

Outside, I stood on the sidewalk for a while and glared at passing cars and people. I halfway wished someone would come along and shoot at me. At least then I'd have something to do.

No one did. That's the way it is some days; nothing seems to go right.

Finally, feeling strangely weary, I retrieved the Mustang and drove across town to Harry Hines Boulevard and the hideout motel. On the way I wondered how to explain to Thorney that because my brain had gone out on strike, he couldn't go home yet. And I didn't know when he could. And I didn't know when I *would* know when he could. I didn't like me very much for that.

Gradually, I noticed the Mustang was hissing again. Big deal. What's one lousy snake when you're up to your ass in alligators?

As usual I parked in a strip center lot two blocks away, walked to the motel, and started up the driveway. Which brought to mind an old complaint. Ever notice how many motels don't have people-type sidewalks? Whoever designs those things must think humans are incapable of motion when severed from their rolling stock.

Hilda calls such careful societal analysis "pettifogging," but I figure someone has to think about these things; it might as well be me.

There was an out-of-state Dodge wagon in front of the motel lobby door with the rear gate up and a family putting three or four small overnight cases in the back. They hadn't carried those little bags to the parking lot; maybe the motel designers were right.

I was fifty feet from the lobby door, passing a flower bed of bushes—would that make it a bush bed?—when tires squealed out on the street. One of the kids in the Dodge-loading party chirped something high and piping, then a car engine strained loud and tight and a bright green MGB with the top down squirted out of the passing traffic and raced up the motel drive.

There was a wicked speed bump on that driveway; I'd almost tripped on the damned thing a couple of times. The MGB hit it full-tilt. The low green car lurch-hopped twice and landed awkwardly, slowed to half speed. Well, that was the idea of speed bumps, after all.

There were graunches and grindings and engine roars, then the MGB suddenly darted forward and, just as suddenly, locked all four tires in a raucous slide to a nose-low stop.

Toby Wells rose out of the MGB, all six feet plus of him. He seemed even bigger as he stood up on the seat and aimed a familiar Remington twelve-gauge shotgun at me.

CHAPTER 35

By the time Wells pulled the trigger, I was down on the ground. Almost down, anyway, and it didn't take long to finish the job. The shotgun pellets went over me and made a soft, tinny *rattle-splat* against the brick building. It seemed odd to be able to hear that small sound, what with the shotgun going off and the Dodge kids screaming in the background.

There were other noises, too, like the hard rasp of my own breath and the scrape of my clothes against bushes and bricks as I dove into the garden plot and scrambled along the base of the wall.

The shotgun boomed again; several leaves and one small, bright red flower dropped in front of me. Brick dust drifted into my face.

Crawling along, I banged my knuckles hard against a rock, and discovered I had the .45 in my right hand. I couldn't remember pulling it out of the back of my belt, and I wondered how I'd done that while moving on all fours, without falling on my face.

As I reached the end of the planted area, the mother and children from the Dodge ran, bent over, into the motel. The father was sitting beside the big wagon, with his back to the rear wheel. His head was lowered; his chin nearly touched his chest. Hit, maybe.

The shotgun went off a third time and took out a window somewhere. I squirmed behind a low, decorative concrete pot and peeked around the side of it.

Wells was visible from the belt buckle up over the hood of the Dodge. He was apparently still standing in or on his little car. I fired at him twice, but I was in an awkward position and trembling after the high-speed crawl. I might as well have thrown the gun at him.

Wells flinched, though, and he ducked out of sight. While he was down, I scuttled out of the bushes and duck-walked to shelter behind the Dodge's front wheel. I looked under the car, saw the MGB's wheels, but no feet or legs. Then I heard muttered words from the back of the station wagon.

No! I thought Wells was behind me. I nearly broke something getting turned around and bringing the Colt to bear.

It wasn't Wells. It was the Dodge father. He was praying. "Our Father, who art in heaven," he said rapidly, over and over. "Our Father, who art in heaven, our Father, who art in heaven."

I poked the .45 around the front of the Dodge and pulled the trigger, not aiming because I wasn't brave enough to stick my head out, just shooting to keep Wells's head down, too.

There was a moment or two where nothing happened, then a window shattered way up above us. A bedside table drifted down lazily, landed on one corner, and collapsed like a foldup toy. Chunks of glass clattered down around the wreckage.

Cowboy leaned out of the missing window in Thorney's room. He held his riot shotgun in both hands. There was no expression on his face as he fired and worked the slide, fired and worked the slide, chug-chugging rounds down at the MGB. He might have been in a factory, stamping out tin cans or plastic fire engines. It was long range for a short-barreled shotgun and almost straight down. Chug, chug. It sounded great.

Wells bellowed in outrage. I sneaked a look. He was sitting down in the car again, pushing at the gear lever jerkily. I snapped a shot at him; part of the dashboard suddenly distorted. Wells popped the clutch; my next shot punched into the trunk behind him.

The MGB spun in a tight circle and bounced over the speed bump. As it lurched, Cowboy fired again; Wells's left hand on the steering wheel became red and ill-defined.

Wells screamed again, in pain that time, the sound barely noticeable over the other shouts and the traffic noise and the after-ring of the shooting. The little car kept moving, accelerating into traffic, and out of sight.

And it was over.

I stood there for a moment, tingling, buzzing with the combat juices. I noticed my hands and knees were filthy, and I'd lost a big chunk of flesh when I banged my knuckles. I put the .45 away and spit-washed my hands.

Mother Dodge and the kids came out and surrounded Dad. He hugged his family and they all cried. I watched them and knew I should feel terrible about their innocent involvement. At least part of that was my fault. And I did feel bad, a little, but only a little. Mostly I felt alive now, and energetic; eager to get out and bust this thing wide open now that I knew what I was working with.

Then I tried to feel guilty about feeling so good, but I couldn't work up much of a guilt trip about that, either.

I'd have to think about it later; it was time to go, while people still ran around, shouted, and talked themselves into the conflicting stories that would keep the cops busy for days.

I walked around the outside of the motel to the rear service door we'd selected earlier. In the background the sirens were beginning. The closest one was still a long way off.

The loose boards in the motel back fence came away easily. I stacked them neatly at the base of the fence. Then I leaned against the building and waited.

Forty feet away another service door opened. A Vietnamese man in a white T-shirt and apron came out, carrying two full plastic garbage cans. He looked at the gap in the fence, dumped the garbage into a nearby dumpster, and looked at the fence again. Then he looked at me. He didn't stop moving, though, and he went back inside without saying anything.

The door beside me banged open. They came out. Mimi first, with her Uzi barely disguised by the bath towel she had draped over it. She scanned the immediate area and nodded at me.

Cowboy was six seconds behind her with two bags in his left hand, another draped over his shoulder, and Thorney's upper arm clutched firmly in his right hand. He was moving Thorney about twice as fast as Thorney wanted to go. The old man was pale and shaken. We squeezed through the fence, then I took one of the bags and Thorney's other arm. We picked up the pace quite a bit.

Ten minutes later we were a dozen blocks away, headed south.

"Goddamn!" Cowboy said. "I hate these hurry-up bug-outs. Now I got to make me two more of them door whatz-its." He looked at me and a grin slowly spread over his leathery face. "It was kinda fun while it lasted, though, hey?"

Cowboy, Thorney and I waited in a hamburger joint while Mimi caught a cab back to where their pickup was parked. We drank coffee and drifted in and out of, mostly out of, conversation. Thorney, especially, didn't want to talk. He drank his coffee and chewed his lip a lot. And sighed several times.

When Mimi pulled in and honked, we went out and shifted their gear and guns into the pickup.

Cowboy shrugged. "Just call. I'll come a'runnin'."

Mimi held her cheek up for me to kiss, but she went to Thorney and squeezed the old man's waist for a long time. He patted her awkwardly, his immense hand seeming absurd on her small back.

"Bye now, Thorney," Mimi said, backing away and looking up at him. "You take care now."

Cowboy and Mimi drove off; Thorney and I got into the Mustang. He said, "Uh, Rafferty, about our talk last night. When I told you to marry Hilda."

I picked at the cracked vinyl on the dash.

"Seeing you down there, dodging that shotgun, I figured

it out," he said. "You don't want to make that fine woman bury you someday."

"If you say so, Thorney. Let's go home."

Five minutes later he said, "You're wrong, you know. Married or not it'd be just the same for Hilda."

"If you say so."

CHAPTER 36

"Now it's just a hunt, babe. And I'm good at that. He's out there; I find him; it's over. Simple."

Hilda said, "He tried to *kill* you, Rafferty. There's nothing simple about that."

It was six o'clock. Out front the showrooms of Gardner's Antiques were dark. Hilda and I sat in her office, side by side on a gigantic monstrosity of a horsehide sofa. We were sipping white wine—Hilda's office drinking is more upmarket than mine—and I was still mentally reorganizing the structure of the case.

"Well, okay, not *simple* simple," I said, "but simpler than it was." I drank more wine. "Are you sure you don't have a beer around here anywhere?"

"Chardonnay or mineral water, sport. Take your pick."

"If people were supposed to drink this stuff, it would come in six-packs, Hil, believe me. But," I said, moving the wine-glass out of her sudden reach, "I'll drink it anyway. Now, as I was saying—"

"Rafferty, my love, you've been saying it for thirty

minutes! The mall shooting never had anything to do with Thorney, and this Wells person must be on that list of pool owners or swimmers or whatever."

"Well, probably on the list. Connected to Ortega's Aqua-Tidy job, anyway. Won't be long now."

Hilda put her hand on my arm. "I only wish you weren't quite so ... enthused because you're going to hunt—your word!—hunt this man like an animal."

"Eight hours ago, he was hunting me," I said.

"I know, dear, and believe me, I dislike that much more. But you should hear yourself." She sipped her wine and smiled at me. Wistfully? Ruefully? "You sound like a Little Leaguer before the big game."

"Speaking of kids, did I mention that with Jerry Gortner shipped off to military school, Thorney's vandalism problems are over?"

"You mentioned it once or twice."

"And you were right about Judge Gortner, Hil. He was never involved in the shooting. It's funny, though. He reacted so—"

"Imagine waking up to find a rattlesnake on your chest," Hilda said. "You'd react. And so would most people if you and Cowboy attacked their house."

"Maybe so ..."

"Trust me, Ugly." Hilda finished her wine and stood up. "Come on, big guy. It's food or fall-down time for me."

"Thimble-belly," I said. "Wanna go to my place? We can pick up steaks on the way; I'll make potato skins. Double cheese and heavy on the sour cream?"

She grimaced. "Cardiologists resurface their tennis courts because people eat like that."

We ate out instead, at an Indian restaurant not far from her store. I told Hilda that curry had a strong taste so you couldn't detect the trillions of tiny cholesterols hidden in there. She didn't believe me.

It was a good evening. Quiet, which was what I expected. Wells wouldn't be back right away, not with his left hand turned to hamburger. Even so, I was careful. I made Hilda sit behind a column in the restaurant; I got the car out of the parking lot myself; I checked each car that stopped beside us at traffic lights; I kept my car gun, the .45, in my lap. Nothing very special, just the normal precautions anyone takes when a nut is after you with a shotgun.

———

Nine o'clock Saturday morning. I sat in my office, holding a list that outlined the final working months in the short and horny life of Luis Ortega.

According to my theory, one of those Aqua-Tidy customers was Wells, the ersatz bounty hunter who had a hot temper and a wife with an itch between her big toes. Had to be. Betcha.

It was a long list. Three-and-a-quarter typed pages. Eighty-three names and addresses.

Maybe I'd had too much of Hilda's fancy wine last night; maybe chapattis slow the blood flow to the brain. For some reason, I couldn't come up with a good way to work through the list.

There were so damn many people! Door knocking would take forever. And I would have to see only the men in each house to make that work. Unless wifey answered the door in a negligee while hubby fired a shotgun in the background.

The telephone was the quickest way to whittle the list down to a manageable size. My only problem was deciding on what pitch to use.

Good morning, and speaking of adultery ...

Or maybe *Hi, I'm doing a survey on shotgun killers?*

Or even *Please mail a recent photo of yourself in a cowboy hat to Box—*

Then Beth Woodland burst in, laughing and grinning and wiping her eyes. "I just came from Thorney's house and he's okay and you're wonderful and, and ... thank you very much!" She hugged me, then stiffened and backed away hurriedly. She grinned, embarrassed. I think she, too, felt uncomfortable about that hug. It was a trifle too reminiscent of Honeybutt and Hotstud McGoodbuns.

"Anyway," she said brightly, "Thorney says thank you, too, and he wants you to come over."

"I'll do that," I said. "Really. But I still have to—"

"Of course! God, what a dummy I am. That man is after *you*, not Thorney, so ... May I help?"

I handed her the Aqua-Tidy customer list and said seriously, "Sure. Phone these people. Ask whoever answers if they are, perchance, a tall fellow who likes to shoot people."

"Okay," she said quickly. "And—I know you're only kidding about what I should say—is it okay if I pretend to be a nurse? I could say I have the test results on his hand injury. Because Thorney said the man's hand was hurt, and I think—"

Rafferty's Rule Fourteen: To feel really dumb, be a smartass once too often.

Larry Davis had given me only names and addresses, so I looked up the phone numbers and she made the calls.

Beth was in the wrong business. She'd have made a great conwoman. "Good morning," she said each time, with just the right flavor of professional disinterest. "This is the clinic. About the tests on your hand, the doctor wants you to ..."

She got the first bite on the sixth call. I was ready to hit the street, but it turned out the guy had lost three fingers in an industrial accident and was halfway through a physio-therapy program.

After she'd hung up from that one, I said, "I thought we'd nail this down easily, but now I wonder. Come to think of it, having a busted hand is a pretty good reason not to clean your own pool."

"What's the next number?" Beth said briskly. I hoped that insurance guy paid her well; she was a hard worker.

At noon I went out for hamburgers. While I was gone, she went back through the busys and no answers. She wouldn't stop for more than ten minutes to eat. By four-fifteen her doggedness had paid off. She had eliminated the last name on the list.

Which did not mean we were finished.

I totaled up the separate lists I'd kept. "Okay, that's forty-six we can forget about—for now, anyway. There were nine apartment buildings. The managers all have both hands, but Jack the Ripper could be living there and how would we know? There were twenty-three busys and no answers; they have to be re-called. And, wonder of wonders, five people bit on the injured-hand medical-report gimmick. Two you've pretty well cleared up; but three need checking out."

Beth rubbed the back of her neck and rocked her head

from side to side. "Ouch. It's a lot of work for just three names, isn't it?"

"Yep. And if I strike out on these three, we'll have to work through that big batch you never reached. Do you mind?" I gathered up the list and picked up my jacket.

"Oh no. Anytime." She got up, too, and as we left the office, she said "Are you going out right now to, uh, check out those people? On a Saturday night?"

"You bet schweetheart. Ya see, it ain't all fast cars and a schlap inna face with a forty-five."

"Oh, cute," Beth said. "Ricardo Montalban, right?"

"Forget it," I said.

CHAPTER 37

Door-knocking is a very slow way to gather information. You spend so damn much time going someplace, and once you're there, you usually find out you've wasted your time. Police departments are good at it; they have all that manpower. When there's one of you, it's sheer drudgery.

At last count there was only one of me.

But the three hand injuries had to be checked out, so ...

I went to the most likely sounding one first. In his conversation with Beth, Harold Locklear had claimed it was a dog bite. Oh, yeah. You wouldn't believe how often emergency-room doctors dig shotgun pellets out of "dog bites."

A woman answered the door. I told her I was the district rabies control officer for U.S.O.D.C.P.—I have no idea what that meant—and waited, smiling, with the .45 held behind my back while she yelled for Harold to "come out here."

When Harold showed up, he was nineteen years old and definitely not Wells. But I was already inside by then, and fumbling to put the .45 away before they saw it. So I had to look at an ugly black and brown creature chained to a tree in the backyard. I don't know what it was about Harold, but that dog went berserk when it saw him.

So okay, *that* one was a real dog bite.

———

"Yes?" the second man said when he answered his door. His left arm was in a sling. His hand and wrist were heavily bandaged. But he was short and square and black.

I said, "Uh, did my wife come here and ask to use your phone?"

"No," he said, leaning forward to look out past me. "Why? Is something wrong?"

"Car broke down. She went to look for ... but she's been gone for ... well, thanks, anyway." I started to turn and leave.

"Are you sure—"

A soft voice called from inside the house. "What is it, Ross?"

"Nothing, dear." Then, to me. "No one's come to the door but you." He shrugged. That jiggled his arm and he winced.

I pointed to his bandages. "Dog?"

"Ross?" The woman sounded concerned; now there were footsteps coming closer.

He looked at his hand and sighed. "Skateboard. Believe me, leave those things to the kids."

As I went down the steps, he was closing the door and saying to his wife, "... funny day. Crazy telephone calls, then—"

———

They were having a party around the pool at the third address. It was a large, noisy party, and it absorbed me without question. I worked my way around to the booze table, where a sour-looking man in his forties seemed to be the unofficial bartender.

With a totally neutral expression he gave me a Scotch on the rocks and the news that, yes, Barney, "he's over there by the diving board," had suffered a gunshot wound the day before.

Well, well, well. Except ...

Except Barney wasn't Wells. Barney was a stumpy, bald man with a drinker's red nose and a booming laugh. He didn't seem at all perturbed that he'd lost two fingers.

The guest/bartender held up a plate of chips and crab dip until I took some. He eyed the swirling throng morosely for a while, then said, "Barney's such a dumb son of a bitch. He did it himself, you know. Rabbit hunting." He shook his head wearily. "Couldn't even take a shotgun through a wire fence without shooting himself."

He gestured at the crab dip; I shook my head.

"Barney's a dentist," he said. "I mean, come on! Will people go to a dentist who has two fingers missing?" He sniffed. "He can't see it coming, but I think his practice will suffer. He won't be able to afford parties like this a year from now."

"It'll be your turn, then," I said. "Let him drink your booze."

He shook his head. "No way. Barney's an asshole."

"I see."

"I only screw his wife sometimes, that's all."

Oh, no, I thought, what have we here? Barney wasn't

Wells, the bounty hunter, but if his wife was messing around …

I said, "What would Barney say about that, if he found out?"

"*Found out?* Barney likes to watch." The man shrugged. "Like I said, he's an asshole." He thought about that for a moment, nodded, and added, "She's quite a nice person, though."

He gestured at the crab dip again; I shook my head again. When I put my empty glass down and moved away, he raised his hand in a casual farewell.

I let the chattering mob float me toward the way I'd come in. Barney was still whooping it up by the diving board.

———

Sunday, before I went to work, I stopped at Thorney's house to see how he was.

He was pretty damned angry, that's how he was.

"Look at that!" he roared. "You said this crap was over."

Someone had sprayed red paint on his front steps. Not much paint, no dirty words. Little kids, I thought. Thorney didn't care how little they were.

"Miserable, pus-gutted, stinking …"

"Do they have courses in swearing for sailors?" I said. "Look, it's not Gortner or his gang, that's obvious. I'll do what I can today, but you've got to give me a little slack. I'm closing in on that fake bounty hunter."

Thorney glared at his red-streaked steps. "I'll close in on the rotten little …"

I found a hardware store open and bought a can of magic

goop absolutely guaranteed to take paint off concrete. When the salesman shook his head and said, "Good luck," I bought a can of paving paint, too. If Thorney couldn't take the red off, he could paint over it.

I left both cans at Thorney's house, then went to the nine apartment buildings on the Aqua-Tidy list. That took the rest of the day. At each one I'd hang around for a while, blending in, people-watching. It's surprising what you can learn that way.

Four times I was approached and asked, with varying degrees of courtesy, what I wanted or who I was looking for.

The other five times, I gave up first and found the manager myself.

Not that it mattered. Either way it happened, I struck out. I didn't see a single injured hand. The managers didn't know of any, either.

I taught the Mustang's steering wheel a long string of new words on the way home that night. Some of them were especially inventive, I thought.

———

The sky was gray and gloomy on Monday morning. It was trying to rain, but not yet doing a very good job at it when I went up the stairs toward my office.

Beth Woodland was already at her desk on the other side of the big window; she saw me and came over. I put the coffee on. She smoothed out the crinkled Aqua-Tidy list. We went to work.

With a cup steaming beside her elbow, Beth assumed her

nurse persona and began calling the twenty-three numbers that had been busy or unanswered on Saturday.

Most of those people were available now. She went through them fairly fast, but, at noon, there were still eight names she couldn't contact. All morning, there had been only one nibble.

The name sounded vaguely familiar. After fifteen minutes I redialed the number myself.

It was Fall-down Forester running another medical scam. "How goes it, Rafferty? You know, I figured one of the labs screwed up and put my name on a righteous X ray, for once. I'm in the middle of a neck injury claim, but what the hell, right?"

"What the hell, indeed," I said. "Keep smiling through the pain."

The remaining eight numbers were annoying. Three busy, five no-answers.

Finally I got smart and called information. Aha! Since the directory was printed, all three of the perpetually busy numbers had been changed. Those numbers had gone to bucket shops, so it was no wonder they were always busy; those phones were running hot, peddling aerobics classes and bathroom renovations.

The old places, the homes where Luis Ortega had cleaned the pools, now had unlisted numbers.

In a perfect world I'd have been in trouble then. But it's not a perfect world, and I know this guy who likes twenty-dollar bills more than he likes following SW Bell company policy about unlisted numbers, so ...

Beth dialed the numbers. All three calls were answered. All three thought she was crazy. Damn.

I whittled the five no-answers down to two by checking the addresses with the cop shop. After a commendable amount of caution—we spent ten minutes playing "do you know," and he checked my office number in the phone book —a desk sergeant called back and admitted the residents at three of those addresses were on vacation. They had advised the division and requested extra patrols.

"Okay," I said to Beth, "I'll door-knock the last two to make sure. No sweat."

She grimaced. "Will one of them be ...?"

"I doubt it very much."

She went back to her office and I poured the last, tarry cup of coffee into my mug. I was fairly certain I was only going through the motions now. And if these motions didn't conjure up Wells, what would?

Hilda had called this an animal hunt. Maybe I should treat it that way. Maybe I should tether myself like the goat in a tiger hunt. Cowboy and Mimi could pick off Wells when he came sniffing around.

Offhand, that didn't sound like a whole lot of fun.

Get hot, Rafferty, I thought. Hit the street.

Partially to plead for additional suspects, and partially to invite myself over for a beer later, I called Larry Davis at Aqua-Tidy.

"Hey, man, what's happening?" he said.

I reminded him of the wonderful theory we had concocted in his kitchen—

"You concocted, man. I just listened. Like I'm listenin' today while this honky accountant, supposed to be workin' for me, is lettin' them IRS dudes take too many taxes 'way from dis hard-workin' nigger." As he talked, he became angry. Or pretended to be. In the background a deep male voice chuckled easily.

I said, "Honky private cops have problems, too, pal. One of which is that I'm down to the last two names on that list of Luis's customers. You got any others you didn't tell me about?"

"Naw," he said. "Dis heah white numbah-dumpah, he done put down all them names for old Larry."

"I was afraid of that."

"Cain't ketch the dude, huh?"

"Maybe not, but he won't be catching much, either. I hope he plays softball." I told Larry about Wells and his wounded hand. "They won't see him around the ballpark for a long time."

"Uh, tell me again what this bounty hunter dude looks like." There was no enraged black accent in Larry's voice now; it was flatter, and slightly muffled as if he were cupping the receiver close to his mouth.

"Tall," I said. "Big. Dark hair, long arms—"

There was a scuffle on Larry's end of the phone, and hoarse shouts, and a clatter as the phone was dropped.

Nothing for a long time, then scrapes and grunts and finally Larry Davis was back. His voice was angry now, but weary, too.

"You'd better get over here, man," he said. "I found your goddamn bounty hunter."

CHAPTER 38

I dropped the phone, banged on the window, yelled to Beth, "We got him now," and hit the street door like a twelve-year-old on the last day of school.

Ten minutes later, I was only eight blocks away, pushing the Mustang through a steady drizzle and suddenly slow and cautious mid-afternoon traffic. Which was reasonable enough; the streets were like ice.

Then I realized we didn't "have him now" at all. I slid to a stop across from a newsstand with a pay phone. Horns honked through the rain sizzle as I bailed out and ran inside.

But the pay phone was broken, and a chuckling man with dirty glasses held me up for five bucks to use the phone behind the counter. While I dialed, I watched and heard one car after another slip and slither around the double-parked Mustang. Some of them didn't miss it by very much.

Larry Davis answered on the eleventh ring. His voice was flat. "Yeah?"

"It's Rafferty," I said. "Look, I should have told you this before. Call the cops right now, as soon as I hang up, and tell them about the guy. Give them his home address if you have it. Because now that he's running, he'll only go home once, if at all. The cops can get there fastest; I'm still downtown. Got that?"

"Uh, yeah, I got it, but—"

"I'm on the way," I said, and hung up.

As I stepped outside, a gray Daimler slid toward the Mustang with an ominous air of inevitability. It finally oozed to a stop an inch short of expensive noises. As I opened the Mustang's door, a superbly dressed woman of perhaps sixty lowered the Daimler's window and suggested I do several things that ladies of her generation weren't supposed to know about.

———

"I called them," Larry Davis said, "but I don't know if it did any good."

He sat in his wheelchair uneasily. He wriggled and fidgeted and seemed to hang on to the armrests more than usual. He'd been pushed over, he told me, chair and all. It had taken more than twenty minutes to get the chair upright and work his way back into it. When I had phoned him from the newsstand, he was still on the floor.

I tried to imagine how naked and defenseless he must have felt. I don't think I could handle that.

"Have the cops been here?" I said.

He shook his head. "Not yet. They said they'd send somebody, though."

We were in Larry's office this time. He was drinking bourbon; I was looking at a business card. Wesley Tasot, it read. Larry pronounced it Tass-oh. According to the card, Tasot was a "field accounting consultant" for an Oak Cliff firm.

"It's a small company," Larry said. "A CPA runs it, I think. They have this package deal where a guy comes around to balance the books, work up the figures for all the dumb reports you gotta do, prepare tax returns, all that stuff." He pointed at Wesley Tasot's card. I hadn't realized before that his fingers were as long and skinny as his wasted legs. "He was the one who did my work. Every Monday, regular as clockwork. And Wes seemed like a nice-enough guy. Man, I sure hope he hasn't fucked up my taxes or anything like that."

"What made you realize he was the fake bounty hunter?"

Larry took a big swallow of his drink. "What didn't? Once I finally woke up. Mostly, though, it was his hand. He had a glove on his left hand. The glove was full of cream or anti-septic, don't know what. Smelled medicine-y, anyway. Wes said he'd been playing with a German shepherd he has, and it got too excited and chewed up his hand."

See what I mean about "dog bites"?

"That hand hurt, too," Larry went on. "I could see how tender it was, from the way he jumped when he bumped it. Then on the phone you said that about the bounty hunter dude getting shot in the hand and ... well, boom! Everything was so clear all at once. Wes doesn't talk country like you said, but he's the right size and looks. His initials, too. Wesley Tasot. Toby Wells. W. T. and T. W."

He took another drink. "Anyway, I just knew, that's all. I guess I gave myself away, though, because he looked at me funny and then he pushed me over and ran." He looked at his watch. "Where are those cops? How long can it take?"

"His house is the important place. You did give them his address?"

He nodded. "I didn't have it, but he's in the book. In DeSoto, though. Will they go way out there before they've come here? Because I don't think they understood what I was telling them."

"Uh-oh. With another police department involved, I don't know. And it might be too late, by now."

What the hell. I dialed Tasot's number and listened to the phone ring.

It rang for a long time. As I was about to hang up, a woman answered. "Hello," she said in a lethargic tone.

"Afternoon," I said. "Mr Wesley Tasot, please."

"He's, uh, he's not here right now," she said.

"What time do you expect him?"

"I, um, I'm not sure. He … well, he may not be coming back." There was a long pause when I could hear her breathe, then she hung up with a gentle click.

"He's been and gone," I said to Larry.

"Well, shit!" he said, and pounded his chair's arm with his fist.

"Don't worry about it. Tell me what you can about him before the cops finally show up and get in the way. What's the connection between Wes Tasot and Luis Ortega?"

"Luis and Wes's wife, I'd say. Wes used to … look, I can't recall a specific remark, but the way he talked about his wife, I'll bet that's it."

"Okay, but how did Luis crack on to Tasot's wife?"

"Like you thought! He cleaned their pool. Look at this." He wheeled himself over to his desk and picked up a hardbound desk diary with a torn slip of paper sticking out of it. The diary cover had been labeled ORTEGA.

"Each of the pool cleaners has one of these," Larry said. "It's a payable hours log, job assignment form, and daily work sheet, all rolled into one. Here now—" He opened the ORTEGA diary where the slip of paper was. The left-hand page was a day almost three months ago. Two-thirds of the way down the page, someone had written WES with a smeary felt-tip pen. There were other names and addresses written in a different hand with a ballpoint.

"See, I write these up every morning," Larry said, "so the cleaners know what they're doing for the day and what order to do it in. Otherwise, some of those dummies would be going back and—never mind that, the point is, I wrote in those customers' names, and Luis added this WES note."

He clapped the book shut and tossed it onto the desk. "I remember it now. I'd screwed up the ledger somehow; posted a batch of receivables wrong, I think. Wes put in a couple of hours overtime sorting out the mess. The next day I told Luis to clean Wes's pool when he had the time. Free, naturally. It was a way to say thank you. So Luis had a chance to get something going with Wes's wife, like you thought. And it was a one-time, non-billable job so Wes never showed up on the customer list. Hell, even if I'd made up the list I gave you instead of having Wes do it, his name wouldn't have been on it."

"Did he know why you wanted that list?"

"Oh, sure. You can thank ole motor-mouth here for that; Wes knew you were going to investigate the people on the list."

I said, "That was last Monday, right?"

"Yeah," Larry said. "When Wes made his regular Monday stop."

"By Thursday morning he was shooting at me." I realized with a sudden fright that I'd spent that Monday night with Hilda. And another night ... uh, Wednesday. And Friday night, but that was after the battle at the motel, so ...

"Okay," I said finally, "I think I've got it now. He knew—knows—about my office, obviously. That's where all this started. He also has to know where I live because I'm in the phone book, for Christ's sake. But for some reason he hasn't tried anything there. And he may or may not know about Hilda."

The thought of Tasot lurking around Hilda's house made my stomach roil, but when I thought about it ...

"He's an amateur," I said, more to myself than to Larry Davis. "That's why he has left me alone at home. He just doesn't know how to assault a house. Plus, when you think about it, both the mall and the motel shootings were pretty sloppy. And both those times I'd just been to the office. That's where he's been picking me up."

"He's been working, too," Larry said. "He showed up here today just like normal."

"Of course! He has a boss and a schedule to keep. That's slowed him down a lot." The thought of Tasot out there, hunting me, was a little unnerving, even if he was doing it on a restricted schedule.

Rafferty's Rule Two: Be lucky.

Rafferty's Rule Three: If you're going to be stupid, see Rule Number Two.

Larry's drink was long since empty, and being stupid makes me thirsty. I built Larry a fresh bourbon and Seven, found a beer for myself, and answered the door when someone knocked on it.

The cops had finally arrived.

They took a statement from Larry because Wes Tasot had assaulted him, but they weren't particularly interested in much else. Once they found out that Tasot was long gone—from here and from home—and that this was only a subparagraph in a continuing homicide investigation, it was all over. They made a note to refer their report to Ed Durkee; he could decide whether or not to involve the DeSoto cops.

"That'll be tomorrow," I said, "and you're already too late for today. Forget it."

The younger cop didn't like that much. He had his fists on his hips and mouth open when the older cop butted in. "One more thing," he said to me. "Don't you go out there and bother this Tasot guy's wife, okay?" He was round-faced and plump, with a button nose and twinkling eyes. He looked like a butcher, not a cop.

"Me?" I said, aghast. I even put my hand on my chest; how's that for aghast?

"You. The detectives won't want you yapping at that poor woman first, confusing her, and screwing up the evidence."

"You're absolutely right," I said. "Couldn't have put it better myself."

He squinted at me, nodded, and walked out.

I drank the last of my beer, stood up, and said to Larry, "Don't worry about Tasot. He won't be back."

"I know," he said. "Where are you going?"

"To question Tasot's wife. What else?"

CHAPTER 39

DeSoto is a little town south of Dallas. In some ways it's more of a suburb than a separate town, though it is separated from Dallas by three concrete barricades: the Lyndon B. Johnson Freeway, the R. L. Thornton Freeway, and the J. Elmer Weaver Freeway.

Seriously. I wouldn't kid about a thing like that.

DeSoto consists of small pockets of suburban development surrounded by countryside. Some of that countryside is pure north Texas boondocks; some of it has been carved up into the three- and five-acre blocks hearty real-estate hawkers call "ranchettes" or "farmlets."

Wesley Tasot lived in a ranchette. Or maybe it was a farmlet. City boys don't know that kind of stuff.

Whatever it was called, it was a medium-sized brick house with a gravel driveway that needed more gravel or more raking or better yet, both. The house was set well back from the road. It looked lonely and out of place, a dollhouse plunked down on a worn pool table.

Someone had made a feeble attempt at landscaping; a

half-dozen young trees stood in a row across the front yard. The largest tree was six feet tall and slightly bigger around than the stake to which it was tied.

I parked halfway up the driveway and sat, cradling the comforting weight of the .45, occasionally working the wipers to keep the windshield clear. Waiting. I waited because Tasot was an amateur and amateurs do not wait well. The seconds ticking by gnaw at them; they want to get out there and get the dying done.

Everything told me Tasot was gone, but I'd already screwed up too much on this case. It was time to do the right thing for a change. And then, too, I hadn't brought Cowboy as a backup, which may have been yet another mistake. We'd see.

I waited.

The house was quite and still. In what was probably a living-room window, the drapes had been pulled on one side, but not the other. There was a curving concrete side-walk from the drive to the front door, then up two steps. One corner of a hairy welcome mat hung over the top step.

There was no sign of life.

There was an equally quiet three-car garage beside the house, but detached from it. One of the garage doors was up; the space beyond was empty.

Behind me barbed-wire fences left the road at right angles and passed each side of the house and garage, then continued away out of sight.

In the back, just visible between the house and the garage, there was an odd building with no walls. It had a high, flat roof—tilted a little, but flat—held up by six telegraph poles. I finally worked out that it was where ranchetteers stack bales of hay. When they have hay. Then I wondered why Tasot didn't have any hay.

Waiting's not so bad if you keep busy.

After fifteen minutes there had been no sign of anyone hoping to commit mayhem upon the tender body of Mother Rafferty's favorite son. I waited a little longer, anyway.

The feel of the place began to seep in, and I wondered if Tasot owned this place or rented. There was an air of malaise, a feeling that no one who lived in this house cared about it very much.

After waiting thirty minutes, I started the Mustang and drove the rest of the way up the drive. Duty called.

I parked in front of the closed, middle garage door and got out. There were no sounds from inside. I squatted down and stuck my head into the garage a foot above the ground. It's an old cop trick. If anyone is in there, waiting to shoot you, they will expect you to be standing up. Unless it's a cop who's waiting to shoot you, in which case you're in big trouble.

But this time there wasn't and they weren't and I wasn't. The garage was empty.

Empty of people, anyway. There was a familiar red Pontiac parked in the middle bay. Almost two weeks ago Tasot (as Toby Wells) had jumped into that Pontiac's passenger seat and bugged out. Well then, there now, as Cowboy would say.

The empty slot, the one where the door was open, usually had a car parked in it; there was a recent oil droplet where the engine would be. Wherever that car was, I bet Tasot was in it. I hoped the road was rough and his goddamn hand hurt.

The last bay of the big garage was an unused home workshop. A long heavy workbench had dusty cardboard boxes piled on it. Pegboard sheets on the wall were marked with outlines where tools had been hung. There was a table saw, too. Its blade was dark with rust.

This had to be a rental house; whoever set up the workshop didn't live here now.

On my way to the front door, I went all the way around the house, rain or not. The backyard was big, ragged, and empty. If the barbed-wire fences hadn't turned and met way out there, it would have been hard to tell where the yard stopped and the boondocks began.

There was a large patio behind the house, with PVC outdoor furniture here and there. One of the chair seats was ripped. And there was the pool. It needed work, of course. The water was thick and green with algae.

I went around to the front, rang the bell, then stood well off to the side, with the .45 handy. Not aimed at anything, just handy. After the door chimes had faded, there was no other sound. My shirt was wet through now. I shivered slightly in the late afternoon gloom.

There had been no sound or sign of life since I'd arrived. Even when I'd circled the house, no one came out or appeared at a window or yelled or said a thing. I began to wonder what I would find inside.

Finally, though, she came to the door and opened it. She was a slender blond woman, very plain, with her hair pulled back and no makeup. The flesh over her left cheekbone was scraped and puffy; that eye was halfway closed. She looked at me with a resigned expression.

"What?" she said. Not angry, not inquisitive. Just "What?" in a flat, lifeless tone that didn't really expect an answer.

She wore a simple blue dress that resembled a uniform. It dropped straight from a high neck to well below her knees. She clasped her hands in front of her. Her nails were short and plain. Her only jewelry was a plain gold wedding band.

"Mrs Tasot?" I said.

"Yes."

"Who else is here?"

She shook her head. "No one. Wes left."

I stepped forward; she backed away and stood against the foyer wall, like an obedient dog told to stay.

I said, "I'm going to look around."

She nodded. "Yes."

It didn't take long to check the house. It was empty. When I returned to the front door, the blond woman stood passively in exactly the same spot.

"We'd better talk, Mrs Tasot. Would you like to sit down?"

She led the way to the living room, walking with her head lowered and her arms close to her sides. She had a slight limp, favoring her left leg. There was an ugly yellow bruise on the back of her arm; it was days older than her newly blackening eye.

In the living room she went to a couch and sat swiftly, demurely. She made absolutely certain her dress was tucked over and around her legs, then she picked up a photograph from the coffee table.

She looked at the photo fondly for a long time, as if she were alone in the room. Then she said, "This is what I used to look like." She didn't let go of the photo, but she held it up for me to see. "He let me be pretty then."

It was a snapshot taken in a shadowy place where there were drapes and ropes and mechanical odds and ends. I finally figured it out; the setting was backstage at a theater. Wes Tasot and his wife hugged and laughed at whoever took the picture. Tasot wore the outfit he had used to run the Toby Wells scam. He had on the same fringed western jacket, the same hat. The only difference was the exaggerated stage makeup he wore in the picture. The bastard.

"When was this taken?" I said.

"Two years ago," she said softly. "Wes played Curly in *Oklahoma.* That was during a good spell."

Wes may not have changed in two years, but his wife certainly had. In the photo she was relaxed and cheerful and outgoing. Her hair was stylish and her neckline was low and her fingernails were long and bright. She looked like she'd be the first one to go out and the last one to go home. She looked like party-time.

Then. Now she looked like five years in a women's prison.

"Mrs Tasot, I'm going to ask you a lot of questions now. If you tell me the truth, maybe I can stop Wes before he gets himself into any more trouble."

She looked up from studying the photograph. "You'll have to shoot him. I don't think you can stop him otherwise."

"Believe me, Mrs Tasot, that doesn't have to happen."

"Wes will make it happen," she said. "You'll see. What is it you want to know?"

CHAPTER 40

"Mrs Tasot, do you remember Luis Ortega?"

"Yes," she said docilely. "The Mexican boy who cleaned the pool that time."

"Did Wes kill him?"

"Yes," she said, without looking up from her studied concentration on the photograph.

"How?"

"He shot him."

"Tell me how, Mrs Tasot. In detail." She seemed too spacey, too likely to say things because she thought I wanted to hear them.

"Wes put on his ..." Her voice ran down and she raised her hand to her swollen cheek.

"I won't hit you," I said, "and Wes isn't here."

She nodded, slowly at first, then more rapidly. "Yes. Of course. Well, Wes still had most of his *Oklahoma* costume, so he put that on and pretended to be a bounty hunter. He fooled a private detective into helping him. Wes took Luis into an alley and shot him, then he got into the car and we drove away." She sighed deeply and looked at her photograph.

"*You* drove away? Was that you in the Pontiac?"

"Yes."

"Who else was with you?"

"No one. Until Wes got in, of course."

I said, "That's a rough neighborhood for a pretty Anglo woman, alone."

"Wes can do makeup. He's been in dozens of little theater productions. I was supposed to be a teenage boy." She shrugged. "Besides, Wes said if I got into trouble, that was just too bad. I deserved it, he said, for being with Luis."

"That is why Wes killed Luis, then? Because you had an affair with Luis?"

"No."

"Let's go over that again. Why did Wes kill Luis?"

"Because he *thought* I'd had an affair with Luis. He …" A long look at the photo, then, "Wes was good before it happened. Really good. He hadn't hit me for a long time. I was out by the pool, when this nice-looking Mexican boy came and introduced himself. He said he was here to clean the pool. He said it was a bonus from one of the companies Wes keeps books for."

A wind gust clattered rain against the window; she jumped. I smiled at her and nodded, and slowly she went on.

"So I said okay and thanks, and Luis cleaned the pool. I read my magazine and sat in the sun. That's all."

"Luis had a thing about women," I said.

"Oh, he was cute!" she said. For the first time a hint of a smile seeped through. "He flirted, sure, but it was only … Like he'd say, 'Got to have a really clean pool for a good-looking woman like you.' Things like that, sort of courtly, romantic, um, Latin compliments." She looked wistful. "Don't you know what I mean?"

"And that was it? He flirted; you sat?"

"Yes. He never touched me, I swear." More looks at the photo. "But Wes had sneaked home and he'd been hiding inside. When Luis left, Wes came running out of the house. His eyes were odd. He was screaming and crying; I remember he had these big tears running down his cheeks. He came over to me and he grabbed my hair."

As she began to talk about Wes, her voice became leaden again. "Wes pulled real hard, and jerked me off the chaise lounge. It hurt a lot because I landed on my hip. On the tiles. And my hair hurt, too, when Wes used it to drag me across the patio and throw me into the pool."

The day was ending; there were no lights in the room. The gloom may have helped her tell me about that berserk and sunny day by the freshly cleaned pool.

"Wes wouldn't let me out of the water," she said. "He yelled at me and called me names and accused me of doing terrible things with Luis and other men. Part of the time I couldn't understand him. It was just a … gabbling noise. I tried to tell him he was wrong, that I hadn't done anything, but that made him even madder. He jumped in the pool then, and he held me under the water."

She sighed. "Wes has always hit me when I needed it. All husbands do that, I guess. But the afternoon Luis cleaned the pool, that was the only time I thought Wes would kill me. I was scared, really scared. He's so strong you wouldn't believe it. I got away from him twice, but not long enough to catch my breath properly. Finally he got his legs around my waist and he grabbed my hair again to hold my head under. I remember it was all bubbly and blue under the water. Almost peaceful in a way, except that I couldn't breathe. My chest felt hollow, but heavy. It was strange. Then, just when I knew I couldn't stand it any longer, I passed out."

I said, "Mrs Tasot, I promise to you, I *swear* to you, I won't let him do anything like that again."

Her voice went on in the dim room as if I hadn't spoken. "When I woke up, I was in our bed. It still hurt to breathe, and later on I had a fever for days. Wes took care of me." A note of fondness crept into her voice. "He was really good to me. He'd bring me meals on a tray and read to me. One evening he sat on the edge of the bed and combed my hair for an hour. When he wants to be, Wes is a wonderful husband."

"But he didn't believe you about Luis, did he?"

"No. He said he knew that Luis and I had been going to motels and taking off each other's clothes and touching each … he said we did crazy things. Which wasn't true, none of it, but the way Wes said those things, almost crooning them, I didn't think it was a very good idea to argue with him."

"I'm sure that's right," I said. "When did he decide to kill Luis?"

"I don't know. He told me about it a few days after, uh, the pool thing. He said when I was better, when I had my strength back then Luis would have to die so I wouldn't be tempted again."

"Tempted," I said.

"Yes. And so I didn't tempt other men, I had to stop wearing jewelry and perfume. Wes threw it all away. Most of my clothes, too. He bought me new things, like this dress."

"And he worked out a way to kill Luis."

"Yes."

"And you helped him."

"Wes is very persuasive." It was too dim to see her face now, but if it is possible to hear a wry smile, I did.

"Mrs Tasot, the day he shot Luis, Wes came to my office and conned me into helping him."

"Oh, that was you."

"That was me. Why did he pick me?"

"Wes decided to hire someone to get caught while we got away. I thought he meant a crook, the kind of man who beats up people for money. But Wes said he didn't know any crooks, so he'd hire a cop. Well, a private detective. Wes said private detectives were no smarter than real cops and they'd do anything for money."

"But why me specifically? Does he know me from somewhere?"

"Oh, no. But he loves your ad in the Yellow Pages."

"You're kidding me."

"No. Wes thinks the part about 'people sought, crooks caught, wars fought' is a scream."

After a while I said, "How often does he beat you?"

"It depends," she said seriously. "If he has a lot on his mind, he ... but look, Wes is right. I usually deserve it. I do really dumb things sometimes."

"For instance?" I said.

"Oh, well, once I put this big dent in Wes's fender. I guess I wasn't looking. Wes says I never look where I'm going. That time he bent my arm way back until it made a funny noise. Wes said later he should have hit me instead, because what with the X rays and the cast and all, it cost more to fix my arm than to fix the fender."

"Didn't Wes get into trouble for breaking your arm?"

"We told the doctor I fell down the back steps."

"How long has he been killing people, Mrs Tasot?"

"A long time, I think. Eight years ago when we lived in Austin, we were at a party and a neighbor patted me on the fanny. He didn't mean anything by it; he was a little drunk, that's all. Wes hit me that night. And a week later, Frank was killed downtown. Stabbed. The police said he must have tried to fight with a mugger, but ... Wes didn't want to talk about that. He muttered something about Frank having gone to see Dr. Mike, which I never understood.

"Then today," she said, "Wes came home in a big hurry and said that nosy detective—that's you, I guess—was after him and he had to go away. It was my fault, he said. He hit me, then he grabbed a bunch of stuff and left. But he left his private closet unlocked and I found ... Wait, I'll show you."

The room flared with light as she switched on a table lamp. She left the room with that same submissive walk and faint limp. When she came back, she handed me an old, wrinkled manila envelope. There were three newspaper clippings inside.

While I looked at the clippings, she studied her photograph.

One clipping was an article from an Austin paper. The small headline was: MAN MUGGED, KILLED, and the story told about the "mugging" she had just mentioned.

There was another clipping, circa 1971, about a college junior who died in a one-car freeway crash west of Denver. The coroner said suicide, but relatives disagreed.

The oldest, most worn, clipping was dated November 11, 1960. With a TRAGIC HUNTING ACCIDENT headline, and a Eugene, Oregon, dateline, the clipping told how Dr. Michael Koenig had been accidentally killed by a stray bullet while deer hunting. Near the end of the story, after listing Koenig's survivors, the reporter quoted a longtime patient and family friend.

"We were camped nearby," Mrs Wilma Tasot, also of Eugene, said. "My whole family is devastated. We all loved Dr. Mike." A spokesman for the sheriff's office said today the identity of the careless hunter is still unknown.

I said, "Mrs Tasot, you do realize that Wes is sick, don't you?"

"Well," she said reluctantly, "maybe he could use a little help, yes."

I'd unearthed enough ancient history to know Wes Tasot was dangerous. And I knew how he had killed Luis Ortega. Now it was time to catch the loony son of a bitch. I took out my pocket notebook and settled into cop mode.

"What car is he driving?" I said.

"A Chevrolet Corsica. It's a company car. I don't know the license number."

"I'll get that from his office. Does he have a company credit card for gas?"

"No, he buys his own. With cash. Wes doesn't trust the oil companies."

"Where do you think he'll go, Mrs Tasot?"

"I really don't know."

"Would he go to a close friend or relative?"

"Wes doesn't have any close friends. His family lives in Oregon. And Washington, too; he has an uncle in Washington. State."

"Help me, Mrs Tasot. Do you think he'll stay in Dallas and hide, or get out of town?"

"Well, he wants to kill you. He's very angry because you found him. But he talked about going away, too. And hiding." She shook her head helplessly. "I can't tell what Wes will do from one minute to the next."

That was fair enough; Wes Tasot probably couldn't, either.

"He still has the shotgun he used to kill Luis, doesn't he?"

"Yes."

"And a rifle?"

"That's right, a hunting rifle. I don't know what kind it is, though."

"Any other weapons?"

"He has two pistols, but only one of them is real. The other one is a prop, from the Oklahoma production."

"Oh, great. Describe them, please."

"They're cowboy guns, like in the western movies. What do you call them, six-shooters?" She shrugged. "I can't tell the real one from the fake."

"How badly hurt is his hand?"

"How did you know about that? It's pretty bad, but he can use it a little. I'm surprised people would keep a vicious dog like that in an office where ..."

Wes Tasot was a very, very sneaky guy.

I asked her for a recent photograph. She found one and gave it to me. And then I was finished. That's one advantage to being private; a real cop would have been here for another hour or two. And up all night writing the report.

"Okay, Mrs Tasot," I said, "if you'd like to pack anything, please do that now. I'll take you wherever you want to go."

"Go? Why, no. I'm staying right here, thank you."

"Mrs Tasot, there are shelters, there are people who will help—"

"No!" she said, and her hand crept up to gingerly feel her swollen, darkening eye. "If Wes came back and I wasn't here, he'd be really mad."

CHAPTER 41

Ricco nodded importantly. "I said it to Ed; I said, 'That's gotta be Rafferty. Who else would be playing John Wayne in a motel parking lot?'"

"Come on, Ricco," I said. "I'm reporting an aggravated assault. I was the *victim*."

"That was last week," Ed Durkee rumbled, pawing through the stack of papers on his desk. "It took you long enough to get in here."

"True, it's been a couple of days," I said, "but you have no idea how traumatized I was."

"Cut the crap," Ed said. "What have you got?"

I told them about Wesley Tasot and his job keeping Aqua-Tidy's books. I gave them the photo of Tasot I'd gotten from his wife the night before. I gave them the Corsica license plate number Tasot's boss had given me an hour earlier. I told them what weapons Tasot had, why he had killed Luis, how he'd forced his wife to help him, and how he had probably killed at least three other people over the last thirty years. I told them all of it. Everything. I was brilliant.

Ricco whistled. "This Tasot guy is a fucking nut."

"Clear, concise, and straight to the point, as always," I said. "Wes Tasot is, indeed, a nut. Now, what are you going to do about it?"

I told them about Mrs Tasot, too, and how she had stayed at home the night before, sitting in a pool of light staring at a photo of better times. Times that could never return.

"She's pretty flaky right now," I said. "She's frightened, she's far too submissive for her own good, and her mind hops back and forth from Wes tried to kill me to Wes loves me truly."

Ed frowned and rumbled, "But if she lives in DeSoto—"

"To hell with the fancy jurisdictional boundaries, Ed. Call her a material witness or a suspect, whatever. Charge her if you have to. You can always drop it later. Just get her out of that house and into a hospital or a shelter."

Ricco said, "Hey, if she drove the getaway car, Ed, we can probably make her as an accessory."

I said, "But only as an excuse, right? Believe me, she's going to be your best witness."

Ed thought for a minute, then said, "Maybe you're right. Let me find out how far I can go with this, then we'll go see her." He punched out an internal phone number and outlined the problem to whoever answered.

Meanwhile Ricco said to me, "Listen, Rafferty, what's your guess? Is this Tasot guy gonna rabbit or is he gonna hang around, try again to whack you?"

"Who knows?"

Ricco led me toward the door, away from the desk where Ed sat talking on the phone. "Tell you what. If you see this freak, do us all a favor, huh? Blow the fucker away. It'd walk easy as self-defense. We got the Ortega thing and two previous attempts on you. And you know, with the goddamn courts the way they are now ..." Ricco looked tired, which was unusual for him. "Trust me," he said. "You see him; don't wait. Just do it."

"I won't let him hurt me or anybody else, Ricco. I'll take him out before that happens. But I can't sneak up behind him on the street and shoot him in the back of the head."

"Why not? That's what he's trying to do to you."

"Yeah, well, even so ..."

Ricco sniffed and went out the door shaking his head.

Cowboy thinks I'm a candy-ass, too.

———

Tuesday the Mustang died. It hissed twice, stalled and wouldn't start. It cost me two hundred and eighty-seven dollars to have them replace a pile of greasy parts with names I couldn't pronounce. I spoke harshly to the mechanic. Hilda said she hadn't heard some of those words before and would I please not explain them to her.

———

Late on Wednesday a patrol unit found the Corsica in a parking lot at Love Field. Ed wondered if Tasot had caught a plane and was long gone. Ricco said that "park the car at the airport and catch a cab into town" stunt was so old it had arthritis. Besides, he said, most airline flights left from D/FW, not Love Field.

True, but ...

I argued that there was an inter-airport shuttle service. And Tasot was an amateur. Where would he hear of the airport parking-lot gimmick?

Which was also true, but ...

Ricco countered that Tasot was obviously a helluva gifted amateur, and he could have picked up that gimmick from any of a hundred TV shows or movies or books.

And that, too, was true. But ...

It all came down to the same thing in the end. Tasot could be anywhere. Or nowhere. He could be driving, riding, or pedaling anything. Or nothing. We were worse off than before. We'd have to be lucky.

"Which is asking a fucking lot," Ricco groused to Ed and me. "How fucking far behind do we fucking have to fucking get before we get fucking lucky?"

Ricco has this vocabulary problem when he's upset.

CHAPTER 42

"Only adjust upward," Thorney said, "because you want to measure the highest altitude. If you adjust the other way, and measure the sun coming down, you'll miss it. And the next one's not till tomorrow."

It was the sun's daily meridian passage. To capture this celestial quirk, I had to have Thorney's sextant to my eye almost constantly. While keeping it properly adjusted. But only in the one direction, of course.

Thorney had done his pan-of-oil artificial horizon thing again. This time he was showing me how to find our latitude by measuring the sun's height at local noon. He called it a "noon sight" and said it was the easiest thing in celestial navigation.

"I don't know about this 'easy' business," I said. My right hand was sweaty on the sextant. My right eye, too, and it was difficult to keep the two heavily filtered suns balanced one atop the other. "I saw that Hornblower movie, dammit. Gregory Peck squinted through one of these gadgets for two seconds and he knew exactly where he was."

Thorney snorted. "Movies!"

"Maybe he had a little-bitty map stuck inside his sextant," I said. "With a sticker that said YOU ARE HERE." In the sextant telescope the top sun had climbed a little above the bottom one. I carefully twisted the tangent screw; the two suns came together again.

"Any more visits from your friends with the spray cans?" I said.

"Not yet," Thorney said. "But the little snots will be back, I bet."

It was Friday, four long days since Wes Tasot had cut and run. The weather was better; it had stopped raining Wednesday night.

So much for the good news.

Ed and Ricco had used a sizable chunk of the Dallas Police Department's overtime budget on the Tasot hunt. They had come up empty. I wasn't doing any better. And Cowboy had called in a dozen favors without accomplishing anything. Which was surprising, because Cowboy knew people who knew *everything* that happened on the street.

The general consensus was that Tasot had skipped town. I agreed with that. Well, mostly I agreed with that. There was only one niggling doubt.

Tasot wasn't a street person. He was a loner and an amateur and a nut and a damned good chameleon. It made perfectly good sense for him to skip town, but ...

Hell! Tasot's wife didn't know what was driving him; how could I guess?

Sure, he was probably gone. Still ...

On the other hand you can't live your life on "buts" and "stills." I hadn't seen Thorney for a week, since our retreat from the motel. Finding Wes Tasot, then chasing him, however futilely, had kept me from visiting the old goat until today.

I had been wearing my blue windbreaker all week, with the shoulder-holstered .38 underneath it. The thinking thug's security blanket.

When I had arrived at Thorney's house, he had looked at his watch, then dragged me into the backyard for this noon sight lesson. It is true that I did not argue against the project.

Which is why I was now balancing a sextant and two tiny suns in the middle of a conversation about vandalism.

"I can't guarantee it, Thorney, but I think the kids might stop now." The suns had separated again, but not by far. I gently made them touch. Versatility, thy name is Rafferty. "Jerry Gortner's gone; he was the ringleader. Okay, there was a carry-over incident, but you've had almost a week now with no problems. They're weaning themselves off bugging you. Betcha."

"Hah!" Thorney didn't seem impressed by my analysis of the situation. "Times about right," he said. "How you doing?"

"They're not coming apart anymore," I said.

"Give it another minute," he said.

The suns stayed together, delicately balanced like two golden beach balls, then slowly the top disk began to overlap the bottom one. I stopped myself from adjusting the sextant —it was surprising how strong the urge was—and said, "She's off."

According to Thorney, that was the shippy way to announce the sun had started down from its noon peak. "She's off," I said again, just because I liked the sound of it.

"Right," he said. "What's the reading?"

That took a little while to figure out, because Thorney's sextant had an old-fashioned vernier scale, but I eventually did. "Eighty-four degrees, five point seven minutes."

"Uh-huh," he mumbled, scrawling on the back of an envelope. "Index error was three minutes on ... divide by two, plus fifteen-two and ..."

He was right about a noon sight being fast. In less than a minute, he came to "... equals thirty-two fifty point eight. Hey, that's good."

"In English, please."

"Look here," he said, holding out the envelope. He walked me through the calculations. "Thirty-two degrees fifty point eight minutes. That's the latitude from your sight and that's exactly where we are. As close as I can work it out from the atlas, anyway."

"Are you serious?" I asked. I looked at the spidery bundle of brass and glass in my hand. "With this ... gizmo, and the sun, I actually ... That's almost frightening, Thorney."

He smiled at me. Perhaps because I was grinning so foolishly. He said, "It's a good feeling, isn't it?"

"Good? Hell, yes, it's a good feeling. 'Good' is self-evident, like sex is wonderful and don't spar with Mike Tyson. This is a lot better than good."

I felt strangely young and freshly awakened, like I had been allowed to enter a very special place.

I said, "It's only geometry and mathematics, and Hilda says I get carried away with stuff like this, but to think that I could find any spot on earth with this—" I held up the sextant. It looked the same. But I was just a little different now, and I was proud of that.

Thorney clapped me on the back. "Come on into the house. I'll buy you a beer to celebrate."

I knelt down to put the sextant into its wooden box. "Can we do this again tomorrow? To prove it wasn't a fluke?"

When Thorney didn't answer, I looked up. He was staring toward the house, frowning and sniffing.

Then I smelled smoke, too, and we both ran for the back door.

There was no smoke inside, though, and the smell was fainter. We found the fire on the front porch. To judge from the amount of ash scattered around, it had already gone down quite a bit. Actually, it wasn't much of a fire; just a bundle of newspapers wadded up and lighted by the front door.

Thorney said, "They probably rang the doorbell, but we didn't hear it out back."

"Well, it beats an attack by massed slingshots," I said. "See, I told you they were slowing down." A man who can find his latitude with a sextant always sees the brighter side of life.

"Snot-nosed little pukes," Thorney said.

"Relax, you grouchy old fart," I said. "I'll help you repaint this part of the porch." The fire was well down now, and I raised my foot to stamp out the last of it.

"Don't!" Thorney said sharply.

"Okay, it's your porch paint," I said.

Thorney grinned wolfishly. "You never saw this one before? It's old as the hills." He used a hose from the front yard, choked down to a mist. He put out the flames, using as little water as possible.

"Thorney, what the hell—"

"You'll see." Thorney re-coiled the hose and walked

around the house. He came back with a shovel. Working carefully, he scraped up the soggy pile of charred and wrinkled paper. He carried the mess off the porch and down to the curb behind where I'd parked the Mustang.

He dumped the clump of wet papers into the gutter and poked at the mess with the shovel. And, as they say, all was revealed.

The papers had been wrapped around the world's largest collection of dog turds.

Thorney leaned on the shovel and said conversationally, "In my day, we used cowpats. Or horse manure, if there was a stable nearby. It was a Halloween prank, mostly," He chuckled. "You could always count on some fool to stamp out the fire." He looked at the mess in the gutter. "Cowpats were the best," he said.

He looked up, grinning, then he stiffened. "Gotcha now," he shouted, threw down the shovel, and pushed around me.

There were two small boys hiding in the side hedge. They were coming out now, but they were giggling and pushing at each other, which slowed them down. Thorney was definitely not giggling, but he was seven or eight times their age, so he was slow, too.

They were all headed for the same corner of Thorney's lawn and it looked like a dead heat to me.

"Dammit, Thorney, don't do anything stupid," I said and started across the lawn after him.

Then I noticed the taxi in front of the house. It stopped but did not pull into the curb. The driver peered out at me, then reached for something on the passenger seat.

Wes Tasot was back.

CHAPTER 43

By the time Tasot lifted his shotgun from the taxi's passenger seat, I had changed direction, dived behind the Mustang, and clawed the .38 out of its shoulder holster.

I sat there, pressed hard against the Mustang's rusty flank, breathing hard, and mad as hell. Every time this Tasot jerk appeared, I ended up behind a car.

Tires squealed. I peeked over the fender and saw the taxi accelerating away. I almost popped one off at the cab, but those Hollywood going-for-the-gas-tank shots never work. Even if you hit the tank, all it does is cause a leak. More often, they ricochet off the trunk lid and hurt someone who doesn't deserve it.

Chasing him, however, seemed to have a lot going for it. The newly repaired Mustang started first try. And it ran well, too. No hissing sound and lots of power. Hot damn!

I was less than a block behind Tasot's taxi when he turned the first corner.

Tasot helped, though. He was a lousy driver. He'd go around corners with his brakes on, then try to accelerate away on the straight bits. In a six-cylinder taxi that probably had 200,000 miles on it, for god's sake.

Three minutes later, I'd caught him; the Mustang lurched at the taxi's rear end like an amorous stallion. But the cab was wide, and Tasot swerved erratically from one side of the street to the other. I couldn't get around him to force the taxi into the curb.

In the end I rammed him instead. We were on a residential street with fair-sized trees along the curb. I dropped back some, cranked on another fifteen miles an hour, and crunched the Mustang hard into the left rear corner of the taxi. I wanted to spear him into one of those trees.

It didn't work. He went between two trees, up a lawn, bounced onto a low porch, and shoved the taxi's nose through somebody's living-room window.

I wrestled the Mustang to a stop in front of the next house down the street.

Tasot scrambled out of the crashed taxi and jogged easily toward the front door of the house. He had the shotgun in his left hand and a rifle case in his right. He also carried a soft knapsack with both straps looped over one shoulder. There were hard bulges in the knapsack. Boxes of ammunition? Tasot tried the front door. It was unlocked; he went in. I wondered how many hostages he would find in there.

This looked like it was going to be a long day.

I pulled into the driveway of the house next door and drove through to the back. After I'd banged on the door for twenty seconds, a boy about fifteen opened it.

"What's the matter?" he asked. He wore a bathrobe and a towel around his neck and he smelled of Vick's. No prize for guessing who had a chest cold and a traditional mom.

"There's a man next door with a gun. Several guns. Call the police. Tell them ..."

He listened carefully while I told him what they would want to know first. He had an intelligent look and he repeated the message accurately.

"Who lives next door?" I said.

"Old Mrs Hodstetter. She's a widow."

"Is she home now?"

He said, "I don't know. Maybe."

"Call the cops now. I'll be out front."

I backed the Mustang down the driveway into the street and cautiously, leaning way down, nosed up the Hodstetter driveway. Then I got out and went into my familiar snuggle-up-to-the-fender routine. I took the .45 from the glove compartment with me and put the .38 back under my jacket. A hide-out gun is always nice, but mainly I wanted the .45's firepower. If bad came to worse and I had to shoot Tasot, I wanted to knock him down properly.

But I don't want to shoot this guy, I thought. Please? First, he's a nut, and second, he's carrying a fake pistol mixed in with all that legitimate artillery.

So how did that siege turn out?

Damnedest thing. After I wasted the sucker, we found out his pistol was a fake. Har de har har. Pretty funny, huh?

That's it, guys. I don't want to play anymore. I'll sit here and watch and tell the cops where he was.

And where the hell were the cops, anyway?

As if in answer, the first siren began, faraway and faint in the afternoon calm.

"Rafferty! Hey, Rafferty," Tasot called from the house.

I didn't answer him. Taunts shouted over car fenders

were TV cop show clichés. I didn't have anything to say. In a few minutes a trained hostage negotiator would come. He'd talk to Tasot until they were both sick of it.

"Come in here, Rafferty," he shouted. "Or I'll shoot the old woman." There was a feeble wail that cut off abruptly. Old Mrs Hodstetter was home.

"I'm not kidding, Rafferty. Come in here."

No way. If he could get me in there by threatening the old woman, he could make me give up my guns by threatening the old woman. And then where were we? He would have two hostages, not one, and Mrs Hodstetter would be no better off.

"I'm counting," Tasot crooned. "Eight … seven …"

There were three, possibly four sirens now, but they were disturbingly distant.

"… six … five …" Tasot chanted slowly.

Why hadn't he started with ten? Or five? Only a nut would start with eight. And Tasot was a nut and that was the whole goddamn problem. Who knew what the crazy bastard would do? Especially if I didn't buy a little time for the old woman.

I stood up and walked around the Mustang, moving toward the corner of the porch, letting the big Colt dangle at arm's-length.

The front door slammed open. Tasot brought a thin, elderly woman in a floral dress out onto the porch, holding her backward against his left side with his arm around her throat. His left hand stuck out awkwardly; it was only a lump of gray, fraying bandage. The shotgun was in his right hand, and he held the muzzle snugged firmly into the hollow at the back of her neck.

Tasot saw me; he seemed startled. I had a sudden flash that he hadn't expected me to come in, so he had come out instead. Why?

Tasot smiled. Some of the tension went out of his stance. He wore gray sweats and blue jogging shoes. He needed a shave and his hair was dirty. But otherwise he hadn't changed much from his Toby Wells guest appearance. He was still a rugged-looking, down-home, big son of a bitch. With a shotgun.

Thank god he didn't have one of the pistols. At least I knew that shotgun worked.

"Hey, Rafferty," he said. "I was beginning to think we'd never get together." He moved along the porch toward me. The old woman missed her footing; he dragged her along without seeming to notice. He kept the shotgun pushed carefully against her head.

I smiled at him. "Hi, Wes. What do you say we let Mrs Hodstetter relax while we talk about this?"

Damn it, I didn't know what hostage negotiators were supposed to say. I only knew things like *freeze, turkey* and *grab some wall, sucker*. I was out of my element.

But Tasot wasn't. He seemed to draw strength from the situation. Perhaps it was the excitement; perhaps it was because he'd finally shed all the pretenses and controls and balances. Whatever the reason was, it gave him an invisible lethal buzz, like the electric feeling around some power lines.

I didn't feel that way at all. I felt naked and vulnerable, despite the pleasant weight of the .45 in my right hand.

Tasot hauled the old woman to the edge of the porch. He stopped twelve feet from me and a foot higher. I could hear Mrs Hodstetter now; she was whimpering very, very softly.

The sirens were closer now. Six blocks? Eight?

Tasot cocked an ear at the same sirens. "It's time, I think," he said calmly. "Good-bye, Rafferty."

The .45 was already cocked. I worked the grip safety more tightly into the web of my hand.

Tasot smiled at me, almost fondly, then he suddenly shoved the old woman away from him, back down the porch. She landed on her hands and knees with a loud sob and folded into a fetal position. She began to cry. She was well clear of our lines of fire.

For three, perhaps four, seconds after pushing her, Tasot remained half-turned away. The shotgun wasn't aimed; it pointed at the sky as much as anywhere. Tasot had an arrogant winner's grin on his face. It grew broader as he gracefully flowed out of his push-pose, supported the shotgun barrel with his left wrist, and turned, swinging the muzzle to bear on me.

I raised the .45 then and shot him twice in the upper chest. He went down, grunting, but with that sardonic half-grin still in place.

I went to him. He was already dead.

Mrs Hodstetter was unhurt, as far as I could see. Then I began to understand what had happened. I checked Tasot's shotgun. It was empty.

After that I sat with the weeping old woman, rubbing her back and telling her everything was all right now.

Neighbors began to appear cautiously, but no one came onto the porch.

When the cops finally arrived, they handcuffed me and took me downtown.

CHAPTER 44

Ed Durkee said, "He had enough ammo to hold out for a week. Box of .44 mag, box of .270 for the ride, and *three* boxes of double-ought buck he somehow 'forgot' to put in the shotgun."

"He committed suicide, Ed," I said. "He pushed the Hodstetter woman out of the way, then he used that empty shotgun to make me kill him."

"Yeah, well, he used you all along, didn't he?" Lieutenant Durkee sat behind his desk like an ad for wrinkled brown suits. "He conned you into helping him with the Ortega hit, then when he got caught anyway, he used you to check out."

It had not been easy to convince the uniformed cops that Ed and Ricco would like to know I was sitting in a holding cell. Finally I told them I would confess, but only to Lieutenant Durkee. They went for that. It was late afternoon now, growing dim outside, and the general mood in Ed's office wasn't much brighter.

I said, "I wonder when Tasot decided to shift gears? Originally, he wanted to kill me—"

"No," Ed said. "Originally, you were only the fall guy."

"Okay. But after he knew I was looking for him—even if I didn't know who he was—he wanted to kill me. Then he changed his mind and made me kill him. When? And why?"

Ed shrugged. "Who knows?"

Ricco pulled a toothpick out of his mouth and peered at the frayed end of it. "I told you before," he said. "The guy was a fucking nut."

"Thank you, Sigmund Freud."

Ed pawed through the pile of papers on his desk. "Ricco's an animal, but he's right. I've got a report here somewhere from that consulting shrink we use. Tasot's been loony-tunes since he was a kid. Sociopathic, the shrink says, with a fancy alphabet-soup subtitle." He gave up the search and leaned back in his chair. "The point is, there won't be any charges or any hassle for you. It was a good shoot."

"No kidding. But thanks, Ed."

Ed looked up. "Did you know he'd offed the cab driver? Body was in the trunk."

"No. When did he do that?"

Ricco said, "Some time after ten-thirty this morning, going by the cab company dispatch log."

"Did you find out where he's been hiding?"

"No." Ed stretched. I heard a joint pop. "What scares me is that next week somebody's going to call and say they haven't seen their neighbors since the night when those firecrackers went off. Then we're going to find a house full of bodies."

"Could be," I said. "Damn! When he flipped out, he went all the way, didn't he."

"I told you," Ricco said. "He was—"

"... a fucking nut!" Ed and I yelled at him.

"Yeah, right," Ricco said.

We sat there for a while, not saying much. Ed and Ricco were probably trying to work up the energy to attack the paperwork. I wanted to find Hilda and several drinks and a meal, in that order. Just as soon as I could get myself started.

Ed's phone rang; we stared at it. It kept ringing anyway. Ed answered it, then handed the receiver to me.

It was Beth Woodland, all but incoherent with rage and frustration. "Thank god! Those damned ... I've called *every-where*! They kept transferring me—Is Thorney all right?"

"Why wouldn't he be?"

"He's in jail!" she wailed. "And I can't find out why or where or ..." She caught herself and said in a tight voice, "Please help me, Rafferty."

"Sure. Where are you?"

"At the office. Please hurry. I'm worried about him."

"Sit tight. Five minutes."

It's nice to have friends on the force. In three minutes, not five, Ed had learned that Beth was right. Thorney was in jail.

A hysterical neighbor had called the emergency number, shrieking that a "big man was attacking her ten-year-old son."

So that's the way the call had gone out. On the scene, though, the uniformed squad saw that Thorney had only spanked one of the firebugs—he was faster on his feet than I'd thought—and anyway, his arson complaint easily trumped the neighbor lady's bitching.

It would have ended there, just another neighborhood feud, if Thorney hadn't gotten on his high horse. He took a poke at one of the cops.

It was only an old man's wobbly swing and all it did was

knock the young patrolman's cap off, but keeping the peace is keeping the peace, so the bottom line was: Thorney went to the slammer.

"Look," Ed said to me, "they put him in to cool him down. That's all. The officer doesn't want to file charges on him; I can bounce the old guy out from here. Go get him and take him home, okay?"

I phoned Beth and told her. "Oh, thank God! What do I have to do?"

"Meet me in the jail office, schweetheart. We'll bust da big man out before you can shay Malteesh Falcon." It really had been a long day; my Bogart was even worse than normal.

"Okay," Beth said. "I'll be right there."

———

I beat Beth to the jail office and I was glad I had. When I arrived, they were booking in an unrepentant sex offender. That wasn't very pretty. And a siren yelped somewhere close, and somebody kicked over a mop bucket, which turned half the lobby into a skating rink. Then a half-dozen sweating, cursing officers wrestled a screaming junkie down a corridor and into a room somewhere. "Hill Street Blues" in western boots.

Things had just calmed down when Beth rushed in, red-cheeked and nervous, balanced between the embarrassment and the excitement of getting Thorney out of jail. I waved her over; we stepped up to the counter together.

When I told the desk man who we wanted, the quiet chill was worse than all the jailhouse sounds I'd ever heard.

"Look, I hope he's okay," the desk man said. "I'll call Parkland in a minute, when the ambulance has had time to get there."

Beth gasped and sank talons into my arm. "What happened?" I said.

The desk man's eyes were very old for his years. "We're still trying to work that out. He had an attack of some kind. Heart, maybe, or a stroke. But nobody cut him or anything like that."

"He was sitting quietly in a cell and he keeled over? Is that what you're trying to tell me?" My voice had somehow become high and strained.

The second man behind the counter opened a desk drawer and put his hand inside while he watched me closely.

"No," the man at the jail desk said. "There were eight or ten other people in the holding tank, too. Like I said, I don't know for sure yet, but one prisoner says a junkie pestered the old man for smokes. They argued and the, um, Mr Thorneycroft ... fell down." He shrugged helplessly. "I'm sorry. He's probably all right. I hope so."

"You damned well better."

———

Eleven minutes later Beth and I ran into the emergency room at Parkland Hospital to find a fuzzy-cheeked resident writing up the report.

Thorney had been dead on arrival.

CHAPTER 45

I wanted to post bail for the junkie, then beat him up. Hilda talked me out of that. She was right about that. She usually is.

A week later they read Thorney's will in a lawyer's office downtown. He left me his sextant.

I have never used the sextant at sea, and I guess I never will. Every once in a while, though, I get it out and take a sun sight. Most times, my calculations don't make sense, but occasionally they do, and when that happens I think of his—my—sextant guiding Thorney across the South Pacific.

And just last week, during a boring stakeout, I looked up and recognized a navigational star Thorney showed me.

He sure was an ornery old goat.

I miss him.

Keep reading for an excerpt from the next Rafferty P.I. mystery,

CANNON'S MOUTH

CHAPTER 1 - CANNON'S MOUTH

It was stinking hot in Dallas the week I followed a tobacco and candy delivery truck around town. The truck driver was a guy named Bartelles. He was either crooked or a born loser.

"Goddamnedest thing you ever saw," Shanahan had growled. "Three times so far, and he's due again, I'm telling you. Any day now that son of a bitch is gonna come in here with some song and dance about how he was mugged, or kids swiped product from the truck, or a pickpocket must have lifted the big wallet with the company cash. It'll be bull-shit, every word of it, but if I fire him, I'll be up to my ass in union troubles. Unless I can prove he's shitting me." Shanahan leered at me over his Manager—Transport desk sign. "Go prove Bartelles is shitting me."

I quoted Shanahan a flat price for a week-long tail, with a bonus for hard evidence. By three o'clock on the Tuesday afternoon I knew I'd screwed up. There should have been another zero on the end of that weekly rate.

We were downtown then, Bartelles and I, deep in the

broiling bowels of the inner city. The sun was still high. And hot. There was no breeze. Rush hour loomed large on the automotive horizon. The Mustang's air-conditioner was broken again. I had a soggy shirt-back, a knifing headache, and a helluva thirst, but nothing on Bartelles.

It was the kind of day they should videotape in living color and Sweat-O-Vision, and show it to anyone tempted to answer one of those BE A PRIVATE INVESTIGATOR! ads.

And what the day lacked in comfort, it more than made up for in boring. So far I'd watched Bartelles lug cartons of smokes and candy bars into maybe fifty grocery stores and newsstands and bars and bowling alleys and ... you name it, we stopped there. The damnedest thing was, Bartelles was doing all the work, not me, but the heat didn't seem to bother him. He was a short, jaunty guy who trotted everywhere.

Just one more day of this, I decided, or another three degrees. Either one, and I could learn to hate this guy.

On the fifty-first, or maybe it was the eighty-first, stop, I slipped into a loading zone half a block back from the parked tobacco truck. Up ahead bouncy little Bartelles rattled up the truck's roller door and grabbed another box. He walked toward a hotel service entrance, moving first through a shimmer of heat haze, then out of sight. *Abracadabra! And for my next trick ...*

I leaned forward slowly; my shirt came away from the vinyl seat-back with that slimy, cool pull that feels like it should make a loud noise. I creaked and grunted and levered myself out of the Mustang and trudged across the sidewalk to a postage stamp-size park wedged between two buildings.

Good move, Rafferty. A light breeze somehow meandered through the surrounding buildings and drifted through a shadow just my size. It was a good ten degrees cooler than the Mustang. Ahh, bliss.

I was not alone in the little oasis. There was also a man in a short-sleeved white shirt. He stayed out in the sun, the dummy, where he paced around in tight circles and glanced warily at me every five or six seconds. He had a rolled-up magazine in one hand. He alternated whacking the magazine against his leg and waving it around like he wanted me to notice it. Or notice him. He smiled at me. It was a nervous, hopeful smile.

I do not need this, I thought. Of all the things I definitely do not need, this is a biggie.

The man paced. I ignored him. I thought about cold beer and dinner that night with Hilda Gardner and how wonderful she looked whenever she—

"Great magazine, huh?" The man finally stopped pacing. He stood a careful six feet from me and held up his magazine like a talisman. Or a shield. It was one of those quasi-military magazines. They're aimed at ex-soldiers, I guess, but I've always wondered how many of their readers are wannabees, guys who think they, too, could be a gen-u-ine hairy-chested mercenary soldier if only they could figure out which end of the gun goes *bang*.

"What do you think?" the man said. "Good ads, right? I think so." He was forty-five, give or take, with a comfortable roll of fat around his middle and pale indoor-worker skin. He had thinning dark hair and a round chin. His hands shook; the magazine fluttered. He was sweating as much as I was, but I thought he had a different reason.

I glared at him. Okay, so it wasn't my very best glare. I was tired and hot; it had already been a long day.

"Look, I'm sorry I'm late," he said. His voice rose sharply at the end; he caught it, swallowed and started again. "I'm sorry. I was … detained. I'm not used to this."

"How are you on busted noses?" I said. Talking to him was a mistake, I knew that, but I figured if I came on strong, he'd get the idea and take a hike. Then it suddenly occurred to me that he might grin and offer me money to beat him up. Uh-oh.

Neither of those things happened.

"Good," he said. "You were right. In your ad, I mean. Aggressive. And look, never mind what I said; it's all right about the price. I'll pay it. I'm here, aren't I?" His face clouded briefly, and he said, "You're sure there won't be any problems? I mean, for that much money, there shouldn't be, but …"

Down the block the delivery truck wavered in the heat. There was no sign of Bartelles.

"No problems," I said to the nervous man. I reached across my chest to peel the clammy shirt away from my left side. He jumped back a half step, then seemed to realize I wasn't practicing my quick-draw technique. He sighed and came a little closer.

He dropped his voice to a hoarse whisper. "Okay, then. Thursday night. The day after tomorrow, if that's all right with you. Make it look like a robbery. He'll be alone. And for goodness sake, don't do it if there are customers in the—oh, yeah, you wouldn't want any witnesses, would you?"

I shook my head slowly and scowled. That felt good; the guy winced a little. Okay, the glare is out; the scowl is definitely in. I felt vaguely disassociated and tried to remember when I had last had anything to drink.

The man shuddered and turned his head away. "I just wish there was another way," he said. "But like I said on the phone, I can't think of anything. It's gone too far. We're about to go under. Without the cash from the keyman policy, I—" He braced himself and said harshly, "Just do it, all right? Do it."

Then he turned and slowly walked in a circle until he was back where he'd started, facing me. "Only, uh, can you do it without hurting him? Well, I know killing him is … but … do you know what I mean?"

I showed him another scowl.

He sighed. "All right," he said; then, "Oh, I almost forgot." He reached into his shirt pocket, tugged at something, couldn't get it free, dropped the magazine, picked up the magazine, and finally came up with a three-by-five index card. He handed it to me. His hand shook quite a bit now.

The card had an address written in pencil and a brief description of someone. *Five nine, balding, long ears, bushy eyebrows.*

"I wrote down what Max looks like," the man said. "So you wouldn't make a mistake." Then he seemed to think about that and blurted, "Not *mistake!* I didn't mean *mistake.* I just meant so … so you'd be … um, to help! I wrote it down to help you, that's all."

I scowled a third time. Hey, if something works, I stick with it. To go with the scowl, I tried for a voice somewhere between Jack Palance and Lee Marvin. "How do I reach you?" I said. My voice came out at least four tones too high; more like Jack Lemmon and Lee Remick.

"At the same number," he said. "At least until Thursday morning. Uh, should we go now? Before someone sees us together?"

Oh, damn. Down the block Bartelles had returned. He was closing the truck door.

"Well, yeah, but ..."

Bartelles sauntered around the truck and hopped into the cab. Why right now, for god's sake?

"I'll leave first," the nervous man said. He peered around the corner, then scurried away. He kept close to the buildings and darted rapid glances over his shoulder every five or six steps. He blended in with the other pedestrians about like Dolly Parton in the Cowboys' locker room.

But let's face it, I wasn't exactly Mr Cool myself. I followed the man for a few steps, then stood in the middle of the sidewalk with my head flopping back and forth. I didn't know whether to stick with the man who wanted Max murdered or continue my tail on Bartelles.

Down the block, the truck wheeled into traffic with a blurt of diesel smoke.

In the other direction the nervous man scuttled around the corner.

Make up your mind, Rafferty.

Well, hell, I didn't know who the nervous man was, but I knew where and when the hit was supposed to be. Whoever Max was, he'd be okay until Thursday night. The cops could take it from here.

Besides, I had a lot of sweat invested in the tobacco caper.

So I followed Bartelles.

When I screw up, I screw up big.

CHAPTER 2 - CANNON'S MOUTH

Two cigarette deliveries later, Bartelles began to work his way out of the central business district. Way to go! We were going to beat the rush hour. Bartelles might be crooked, I decided, but he was no dummy.

We went up McKinney toward Lemmon. When we went past Gardner's Antiques, I looked for Hilda. Too much sun glare; I couldn't see anything through the shop windows.

The air coming through the Mustang's lowered windows was warm and soupy, but it moved and that was a big improvement. So was a quart of orange juice I bought at a mom-and-pop grocery while my little buddy dropped off smokes at their competitor's across the street.

It was still hot, but the sun had begun to lose some of its bite. And I wasn't as dopey as I had been. The nervous man who wanted me to kill his employee or his boss or his business partner—whichever category Max fit into—seemed a trifle out of focus now. I decided I hadn't played that encounter as well as I might have. At the time I was more strung out than I'd realized.

Dehydration, probably. Maybe I should carry a water jug on these summer stakeouts. And a bucket of ice to keep the water—or, hey, juice—cool. Better yet, an ice chest in the backseat, with a couple of six-packs—

And then we were on the move again, trundling up Lemmon Avenue toward Love Field.

Two more stops on Lemmon, then Bartelles turned left into a sparse industrial area. We made a series of turns that didn't seem to be taking us anywhere logical. The truck slowed, sped up, then slowed again. I dropped way back now; this was no time to spook him.

Eventually the truck braked sharply and slewed to a sloppy stop, half-on and half-off the wrong side of the road. Bartelles got out, stood by the truck with his hands on his hips, and slowly looked around.

He had picked a good spot. A dozen scrub trees blocked the view from the north and west. The road ran south for fifty yards through open land, then turned east. The only structure with a view of Bartelles and the truck was a long, low, metal building eighty yards back.

That building faced away from Bartelles, and besides, it looked empty, possibly deserted. There were no windows in the back wall, only a stretch of corrugated iron with a single padlocked door. Empty asphalt, a loose jumble of rusty pipes, a stack of rotting pallets, and a big ABCO trash container.

The Mustang and I were hidden behind the trash container.

I had already taken two pictures of Bartelles by then, both of them reasonably tight and clear once the long lens of my dented old Minolta had dragged him up close to me. I snapped him again as he nodded his head twice and turned to stride briskly toward the stand of trees.

When I took the camera away from my eye, I couldn't see him. There was too much contrast between the bright sun and the dark tree shadows. But he was still visible through the Minolta, and I clicked away steadily as he used his pocketknife to saw through his belt and free the chain connected to the large leather wallet that held the company money.

Bartelles put the cash in a plastic bag he took from his pants pocket, then threw away the wallet with an artistic flip of his wrist. Then he took off his shoes, walked gingerly to the far end of the small forest, and buried the bag of cash under loose dirt at the base of a tree.

When he'd walked just as carefully back to where he'd dumped the wallet, he ripped the front of his shirt and threw himself down on the ground. He rolled around in the dirt for a minute, scrunching his back against the ground like a dog. *I fought 'em, boss. Like a tiger, I swear. But they were just too strong for me.*

Bartelles got up, looked around, and found something on the ground, probably a rock. Whatever it was, he dragged it sharply across his forehead three times. He winced noticeably each time.

Finally he stood still for a moment, apparently thinking; then he let his shoulders sag, and he staggered out into the sunlight again.

It was quite a performance, well worth the full roll of thirty-six exposures I'd run through the camera.

By the time I'd followed the road around to the parked truck, Bartelles was standing in the middle of the road.

When I stopped, he developed a bad limp and waved his arms feebly.

"Help," he cawed. "I've been robbed."

I leaned over and opened the passenger door. "Get in, Camille."

He threw himself in, babbling about his ordeal, saying take me to the cops and oh, my Gawd and things like that. During all that he mopped at his gashed forehead with a handkerchief and made sure I noticed his grievous wound.

After five minutes, though, when I hadn't said anything and had driven past two patrol cars, Bartelles pursed his lips and said calmly, "You wanna tell me what the fuck is going on here?"

"You've been a ba-a-a-d boy."

"What are you, pal, a cop or something?"

"Private," I said. "Shanahan will tell you all about it."

"Shanahan! That bastard. Hired you to catch me, huh?"

"Yup." Power repartee à la Gary Cooper.

Bartelles said, "You oughta know, pal, my brother-in-law is very big down at the local. Very big."

"Yup."

"You a union man, pal?"

"Federated Guild of Thugs and Leg-breakers," I said. "I'm on the committee negotiating our new contract."

"Get fucked," he said.

"Good idea for a contract provision. It beats the hell out of overtime and sick pay. You think your brother-in-law could give us a hand with that?"

Our relationship soured after that. He didn't call me pal again, for one thing. And he tried to kick me on the shin when I trotted him into Shanahan's office.

Grinning, Shanahan offered him a quick way out with a hastily typed letter of resignation and confidential confession. Bartelles spit on Shanahan's desk, so we did it the hard way.

It took several hours to recover the cash and the truck and help the cops assemble the small mountain of paperwork they needed to put one petty thief in the slammer. A sergeant named Worthington ramrodded the job; we'd been rookies together years ago. Worthington didn't like my wisecracks about terminal writer's cramp.

It was after nine-thirty that night, and the temperature was down to bearable, when I finally got away from all that heavy-duty crime busting. I had missed the planned candlelight Italian dinner with Hilda, which was bad. I phoned her a few hours back, though, and she'd suggested Whoppers and double onion rings whenever I could make it. Which was good.

Tomorrow, I wouldn't have to chase that stupid truck around town, which was also good. And Shanahan's check lay heavy in my wallet. Another good.

As the Mustang clattered along, I wondered whether the mysterious Max had enjoyed his day. I decided he could not have fully appreciated it, if only because he didn't know how close he had come to running out of days to enjoy.

GET YOUR FREE BOOK

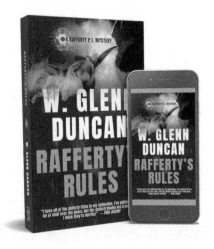

Score a FREE ebook of *Rafferty's Rules*, the book that started it all.

You'll also get all the scoop on the release of new books, special promotions and other behind-the-scenes stuff on Rafferty and the men who brought him to life.

**Fire up your favorite web browser and hightail it to www.RaffertyPI.com/RR
See you there!**

DID YOU ENJOY THIS BOOK?

Help the next reader to enjoy it, too.

Reviews are powerful tools in gaining attention for an author's books.

New York publishers spend huge bucks on newspaper ads, radio slots, and posters on the subway. We don't have pockets that deep, but we do have something those 'Big 5' would kill for.

A committed and loyal bunch of readers like you.

And no matter whether you loved this book or not, we'd be grateful if you'd leave a review wherever you purchased it. The review can be as short as you like.

Alternatively, feel free to drop us an email at **bill@raffertypi.com**.

Thanks.

W. Glenn Duncan, and

W. Glenn Duncan Jr.

ABOUT THE AUTHOR

W. Glenn Duncan, a former newsman, politician, and professional pilot, has lived in Iowa, Ohio, Oregon, Florida, Texas and California. He now lives with his wife in Australia. His novels in the Rafferty P.I. Series are: *Rafferty's Rules*, *Last Seen Alive*, *Poor Dead Cricket*, *Wrong Place Wrong Time*, *Cannon's Mouth* and *Fatal Sisters*.

Fatal Sisters won a Shamus Award for Best Paperback original.

The Rafferty P.I. Series is continued by his son, writing as W. Glenn Duncan Jr., with the release of *False Gods*.

Get in touch. We'd love to hear from you.
RaffertyPI.com
bill@raffertypi.com

facebook.com/billduncanwriter

twitter.com/bill_writes

bookbub.com/authors/w-glenn-duncan

amazon.com/author/wglennduncan

CPSIA information can be obtained
at www.ICGtesting.com
Printed in the USA
LVHW052346250820
664242LV00004B/1032